STAGE FRIGHT

A Jane Lawless Mystery

Ellen Hart

BALLANTINE BOOKS • NEW YORK

Library of Congress Catalog Card Number: 92–14966

ISBN 0–345–38142–4

This edition published by arrangement with Seal Press

Manufactured in the United States of America

First Ballantine Books Edition: June 1994

10 9 8 7 6 5 4 3 2

For Shawna Faith Kruger and
Bethany Joy Kruger;
two loving, bright, and very
beautiful young women—
(without whose teenage years I would
never have sat in a room and contemplated
murder!)

CAST OF CHARACTERS

TORALD WERNESS: Actor, Allen Grimby Repertory Theatre. Husband of Maureen, brother of Antonia and Lucy, son of Gaylord.

JANE LAWLESS: Owner, Lyme House Restaurant in Minneapolis.

CORDELIA THORN: Artistic Director, Allen Grimby Repertory Theatre. Old friend of Jane's.

BERYL CORNELIUS: Jane's aunt, recently moved to Minnesota from her home in England.

BILLY BREWSTER: Actor, Allen Grimby Repertory Theatre, staying at Jane's home.

ERIN BREWSTER: Billy's wife, staying at Jane's home.

MAUREEN WERNESS: Wife of Torald, mother of Erling.

ERLING WERNESS: Torald and Maureen's thirteen-year-old son.

ORVILLE TREVELYAN: Detective, Minneapolis Police Department.

ANTONIA WERNESS: Playwright, author of *Audience for a Bride Doll*. Sister of Torald and Lucy, daughter of Gaylord, life partner of Fleur.

IDA JOHN: Actress, Allen Grimby Repertory Theatre.

RAYMOND LAWLESS: Defense Attorney in St. Paul, Jane's father.

DORRIE HARRIS: Member of the Minneapolis City Council.

GAYLORD WERNESS: Playwright. Father of Torald, Lucy, and Antonia.

FLEUR O'NEIL: Professor of Economics, University of Minnesota. Life partner of Antonia.

LUCY WERNESS: Daughter of Gaylord, sister of Torald and Antonia.

VICTOR PAVIC: Broadway producer, old friend of Antonia's.

MALCOLM COOPERSMITH: Unitarian minister, friend of the Werness family.

GLORIA LINDY: Secretary for Gaylord Werness.

PART ONE

Masquerade

We're not at one. We've no instinctive knowledge
like migratory birds. Outstripped and late,
we force ourselves on winds and find no welcome
from ponds where we alight. We comprehend
flowering and fading simultaneously.
And somewhere lions still roam, all unaware
while yet their splendor lasts, of any weakness.

Rainer Marie Rilke

1

Torald Werness was annoyed. Everyone around him was quite obviously deaf and blind! Surely he couldn't be the only one who'd noticed. "Septimus, pour me another." He leaned heavily against the bar, running a well-tended hand through his thinning blond hair.

"You know Mr. Werness, I used to mind it when you called me that. But I got to thinking. I've always hated the name Sherman. I mean, nobody gets to pick their own name, do they? Lots of the customers call me Septimus now. I kind of like it." Sherman reached underneath the counter for the bottle of Chivas Regal.

"It suits you," said Torald, swirling the ice around in his empty glass. "You're this town's only legitimate Greek philosopher. Why, after two drinks, I can't tell you from Socrates." He smiled maliciously.

Sherman beamed his approval, not realizing he had just been insulted.

The bar at the Maxfield Plaza was a favorite haunt of the St. Paul theatre crowd. After rehearsals, Torald often walked the two blocks from the Allen Grimby Repertory Theatre in order to sit in the dark, understated elegance of the old hotel's first floor bar and restaurant. Once ensconced in the plush velvet and marble interior, he could drink himself into a state of grace—or oblivion, whichever came first. Anything was better than going home. Maureen, his wife of twenty-four years, would be the first to agree. What had once been a union of love had now disintegrated into a marriage of state. Torald's father, the famous American playwright Gaylord Werness, believed firmly in the sanctity of the home. One simply did not divorce—or, more to the point, one did not divorce if one wanted to stay in the good graces of the great Gaylord. Unfortunately, Torald fell into that latter category.

Angrily, Torald grabbed the fresh drink from Sherman's hand and took a hefty swallow. As he set the glass down on the counter, his eyes came to rest on a picture of himself hanging behind the bar. It had been taken many years ago when he'd played Brick in an award-winning production of *Cat on a Hot Tin Roof.* He smiled at the handsome face. Torald Werness was a celebrity in the Twin Cities. Sure, he knew he was a big fish in a small pond, but what the hell. He liked the attention—even the notoriety. At forty-five, he was fit for little other than the stage. Living in the shadow of his father had not been easy. A great many people thought he'd never really paid his dues. Cretins. They didn't understand that he'd been paying his dues since the day he was born. And anyway, nobody could deny his talent. For good or ill, on or off the stage, Torald was a consummate actor.

Pushing the glass to one side, he grabbed a handful of pretzels. "Listen, Septimus old boy, let me ask you one more time. Don't you see it? I mean, come on! My two sisters may be blind as bats, but surely you aren't."

Sherman scratched his chin. "I don't know. It's hard to tell. And, well . . . if you don't mind my saying so, Mr. Werness, isn't it kind of a personal matter? None of my business really." He picked up a soft cloth and began polishing the marble bar top. "Hey, by the way, I got tickets to your new play. The wife and I can't wait. We've seen just about everything your sister has ever written. If you ask me, Antonia's every bit as good a playwright as your father. Must run in the family." He winked.

The family, thought Torald sourly. He sipped his drink. "Yeah, we're a brilliant bunch of folks." He shook his head at the very idea. Just look at us. There was Dad, champion of the Sixties morality play. He'd instructed the entire nation about the evils of war, taking the exploration of human viciousness to new depths. And for that, *for that* he'd become the darling of the war resisters, the revered symbol of truth in a land that generally preferred bald, proudly stated lies. It was unfathomable. Torald laughed out loud at the irony.

"Something funny?" asked Sherman.

Torald looked up. "Funny?" He shook his head. "Actually,"—he lied—"I was just thinking about my older sister. Antonia the Great. Often referred to as simply Antonia Regina. You know, somehow in the last few years, she's become a rising star in the women's movement. One day that heavy crown will break her neck, mark my words." His smile again grew malicious. "Poor old girl. No one wants to wear a crown, not when they find out what it really means."

"You have a younger sister, too, don't you?" asked Sherman.

Torald stifled a burp. "I do. Lucy. She's the only sane member of the family." He raised a finger. "I didn't say normal, Septimus, merely sane. In our family it's the best one can hope for. Perhaps it's because she has no interest whatsoever in anything theatrical." He finished his drink and set the glass down with a crack.

"Another?" asked Sherman.

Torald looked at his watch. "Why not. I have a little time before my next appointment."

"Appointment? It's nearly eleven-thirty. I would think you'd be getting home to bed."

"In due time," said Torald, spreading his arms wide and stretching his back. "Since everyone around me seems to prefer blindness, I'm going to force a little light on the subject. So to speak." For a fleeting moment, his voice took on an ominous tone. "They all want proof? Well damn them, I'm going to get it."

2

Jane lugged the heavy suitcases up the front steps and deposited them next to the railing. As she opened the door, her two small dogs bounded down the central staircase and, wagging their tails wildly, began to sniff her hands and shoes. From the side of the house came a voice—"Ah, you still have your . . . darling little beasts." The dogs stopped sniffing.

Around the corner of the building came a plump, white-haired woman carrying an over-stuffed shopping bag and a heavy purse.

Both dogs pricked up their ears.

"I've got the door open, Aunt Beryl," said Jane. "Can Cordelia handle that trunk all by herself?"

"Yes, love. She said she'd been along in a moment."

Bean, the larger of the two animals, raced quickly back into the house and dove at a green tennis ball in the corner of the dining room, leaving Gulliver, always the optimist, to welcome Aunt Beryl to her new home.

"Nice doggy," said Beryl absently. She sailed past Jane into the front hall. "Your house is every bit as lovely as I remember it."

A soft light glowed from the living room archway. In the kitchen, Jane could see Bean lying on the rug in front of the refrigerator, the ball held firmly in his mouth. This did not bode well. She switched on the lights and walked back out to get the luggage.

"I do so love these large American houses," said Beryl. "To think that the little girl I knew so many years ago has made such a fine life for herself."

Jane watched her aunt as she moved about the house, touching a chair here, a photograph there. It was true. Jane was proud of her home. She and Christine, her partner of almost ten years, had worked hard to make a place of comfort as well as beauty. Christine had loved to work with stained glass. Before her death, five years ago, she'd completed two stunningly intricate windows to replace those on either side of the formal buffet in the dining room. She'd created a new pattern from an old window she'd admired once in a book on the historic houses of Salem, Massachusetts. Even now, as Jane looked up at them, she could see Christine bent over her table upstairs, piecing the colored glass together, a late-night talk show blaring from a radio in the corner. Carefully, Jane tucked the memory away. Every remembrance had become so precious.

"Give me a clue, Beryl," boomed a husky voice from the doorway. "You've got bowling balls in this thing, right?"

"Bricks," replied Beryl, using her best Cheshire cat smile.

Cordelia collapsed on the edge of the trunk, dramatically gasping for breath. The cold, misty night air swirled around her feet like the angel of death from *The Ten Commandments*.

"Want some help?" asked Jane.

Cordelia grunted. "What makes you think I need help? Just because my arms are several inches longer than they used to be—"

Jane hoisted her up. "Come on. Just a few more inches."

"Easy for you to say."

They dragged it into the foyer.

"What time is it?" asked Beryl with a tiny yawn.

Jane glanced at her watch. "Nearly twelve-thirty. Your train was half an hour early."

"Perfect!" announced Cordelia, flinging her red cape over a chair and sweeping into the kitchen. She returned a moment later carrying a Lady Baltimore cake and a bowl of fresh strawberries. Carefully, she set everything down on the dining room table next to a bottle of champagne. "Time for celebration! Beryl, remove your coat and that silly hat and come over here."

Beryl winked at Jane.

"I propose we drink a toast to your new home here with Janey. No more cold, dreary old England. No! Now you can proudly tell all the world that you live in cold, dreary old Minnesota." She uncorked the bubbly.

Jane and Beryl gathered around as Cordelia filled the glasses. "To Aunt Beryl," said Jane, slipping her arm around her aunt's shoulder. "Welcome to Minneapolis. Welcome home."

They all clinked their glasses and then took long sips.

Overcome by her fatigue and the emotion of a long journey now complete, Beryl wiped a tear from her eye. "I have a toast to make as well." She held her glass high. "To my dear nephew Peter and his lovely fiancé, Sigfried."

"Sigrid," said Jane.

"Yes. To their forthcoming marriage. And, to our family." Her voice turned wistful. "May we grow together in love—and understanding."

"Here here!" boomed Cordelia.

"Shhh!" said Jane, giving Cordelia a cautionary look. "You're going to wake Billy and Erin."

Beryl cocked her head and turned her face to her niece. "Who?"

"I'll cut the cake," suggested Cordelia, "while you do the explaining."

Jane and Beryl made themselves comfortable at the lace-covered table.

"Well," began Jane, "it's kind of a long story. Billy's an actor. Actually, he's in the new play Cordelia is directing at the Allen Grimby. He and his wife, Erin, are from out East. Billy is trying to convince the Grimby to hire him full-time as part of the repertory company. In the meantime, they needed a place to stay. Since they don't know whether they'll be making their home here for good or not, they wanted a place they could rent temporarily—and cheaply—until the decision is made. Cordelia suggested my third floor."

"This new play is really inspired," continued Cordelia, licking frosting off her fingers. "*Audience for a Bride Doll*. I read it last December and knew I simply had to stage it. When we all found out who wrote it, the Grimby was more than willing to make room on the spring schedule. It's not being done by the repertory company itself. I did a general call. But the Grimby did allow me to use two staff actors whose schedules weren't filled. We went into rehearsals last month. The opening is tomorrow night, and I'm counting on you two to come. There's going to be a cast party afterward at Antonia Werness's home in Kenwood. Next to my annual *Richard the Third* extravaganza, it will be *the* event of the season."

"Antonia Werness," repeated Beryl. "I met her once. Several of her plays were produced in Bristol. You know how active I was in the theatre guild there." She smiled delightedly at Jane. "I'd consider it an honor to attend the first performance of her newest play! I wonder—did I bring something suitable to wear?" She scrunched up her nose and stared at the bubbles in her glass.

Jane took a bite of the cake Cordelia had just plunked down in front of her. "So, getting back to Billy and Erin, they don't have much money. Living here seemed like a reasonable alternative to a hotel or some crummy apartment. Hopefully, the Allen Grimby will be making their decision about Billy's future soon. Otherwise, the play runs for six weeks."

Bean peeked his head out of the kitchen doorway, hungrily watching Cordelia eat her cake.

"You know," said Jane, "I think I'd better put the car in the garage. My battery's been kind of strange lately. And it's supposed to get cold tonight."

Cordelia groaned. "If you ask me—"

Jane held up her hand. "No comments about my car. It got us to and from the train station, didn't it?"

"It *is* rather . . . tattered," said Beryl.

Cordelia snickered into her champagne.

"And," continued Jane, her voice utterly serious, "I don't

want either of you to give the dogs any cake while I'm gone."

"No cake?" said Cordelia.

Jane narrowed one eye. "Absolutely no cake." She grabbed her keys and headed out through the kitchen.

"Meany," said Cordelia under her breath. She glanced down mischievously at Bean. "Look at him. He's forced through sheer starvation to chew on a tennis ball. You might as well be living on a prison barge. But don't worry, Auntie Beryl and Auntie Cordelia are here now. We'll take care of everything." She patted his little head.

Before Jane turned on the backyard light, she glanced at the dark garage that sat about twenty yards from the house. For some reason, she thought she'd seen a dim light coming from inside. She squinted to get a better look, but it was gone. It must have been a reflection from the alley light. She looked up at the third floor where Billy and Erin were no doubt fast asleep. Everything was quiet.

Finding the ignition key, she climbed into her car and pushed the garage door opener. A second later, the right door began to lift. Jane quickly eased the car down the long drive into its berth inside the cold, wood-frame building. She was positive that, by now, Cordelia had fed the entire cake to the dogs and was sitting, sipping her champagne, telling Beryl how Jane didn't truly understand the dietary needs of small animals.

After turning off the motor and the headlights, Jane slipped out of the front seat. As she was about to start for the house, she heard a faint noise near the front of the garage. It sounded vaguely like rustling papers.

"Hello?" she called.

The rustling stopped.

Everything was still. Most likely it was a cat or a squirrel that had managed to get inside, away from the chilly night air. It had happened before. Come to think of it, the neighbor's cat, Fur Face, had been missing for several days. Not that it was an unusual occurrence for him to take a little vacation, but Jane decided it was best to check.

She made her way carefully to the tool box to find a flashlight. As she rummaged through the bottom tray, she hesitated. Was it her imagination or was there now a faint creaking sound behind her? She felt a sharp intake of breath as recognition dawned. It was the squeak of a leather shoe! Her hand closed tightly around a screwdriver.

Before she turned, it was already too late. In vain her eyes searched for the source of the sound. A dim form was moving toward her out of the darkness. As she tried to dart out of the way, a canvas tarp was brought down roughly over her head. She struggled against powerful hands fumbling to twist her around.

"Stop!" she shouted. The word seemed lost in the heavy fabric. She could feel herself losing balance.

A sharp pain shot through her right knee as it hit the cement. Seconds later a strange explosion went off inside her head. Thousands of bright specks of light began to swirl and dance in front of her eyes. In an instant, the world lost focus. Her body slumped unconscious against a cast-iron stove.

3

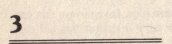

The soothing sound of Cordelia's voice woke her. Struggling against the dull, throbbing pain in her temple, Jane tried to sit up.

"Just lie still," said Cordelia, brushing several tangled chestnut strands away from Jane's face. Her shaky hand belied the calmness in her manner.

"What—" Jane tried to focus her eyes. For some reason, there seemed to be two Cordelias. A frightening thought.

"I found you like this a few minutes ago," said Cordelia,

her voice gentle. "You're going to be fine. I called 911 right away, and they said to keep you quiet. They'll be here any minute."

Jane winced at the pain in her knee. "What happened?"

"I don't know, dearheart. I was hoping you could tell me." Cordelia moved from her crouching position and sat down on the cold cement floor next to her friend. She took Jane's hand in hers and squeezed it softly. "You scared me to death, you know that?"

"Where's Aunt Beryl?"

"I'm right here," said a voice from behind them. "You be still now, love. Everything's going to be fine."

With all these glowing reassurances, Jane wondered just how bad she really looked. She raised her hand to her aunt in greeting. "I really think I can sit up now," she said, pulling herself back against the wood pile. Her head hurt like hell.

"Do you remember anything?" prodded Cordelia.

Jane closed her eyes to help focus her mind. "Well, I think I'd just gotten out of the car. I remember hearing this rustling sound. I thought maybe it was a cat. Then I heard . . . I don't know. Someone was coming toward me. I tried to get away. Next thing I knew, I was staring up at your face."

"Whoever was hiding in here must have thrown that canvas over your head and shoved you against this old cast-iron stove. Cast iron doesn't give. Your head, on the other hand, does."

Gingerly, Jane touched the bump just above her hair line.

"No one was here when I came out," said Cordelia.

"I wonder what they wanted?" asked Beryl. "Jane, can I get you anything? A glass of water?"

Carefully, Jane shook her head. "No thanks." In the distance, she could hear a siren.

"Must be the paramedics," said Cordelia with a wistful sigh. "You know, I dated a paramedic once. Amy Langbratten. We drove to Colorado together for a vacation one summer. On the way back, we were coming through southern Minnesota. It was really late at night. She was driving. I was sleeping. She must have been awfully tired because, when we stopped for coffee, she told me she'd seen a five-hundred-foot duck standing in a corn field. Needless to say, I drove the rest of the way. After that, the relationship just seemed to disintegrate."

"I shouldn't wonder," said Beryl seriously.

Jane smiled at both of them. Even the smile hurt.

Into the drive pulled the paramedics, the truck's lights flashing ominously. Jane was sure the commotion was going to wake the entire neighborhood. Two men hopped out. The shorter of the two carried a bag into the garage and knelt down next to her.

"How ya doin'?" he asked in a concerned voice.

"I hit my head," said Jane. "And I banged my knee pretty hard on the cement when I fell. Other than that, I think I'm okay."

The paramedic quickly checked her over. As he did so, he asked more specific questions about what had happened. The other paramedic listened from the doorway and after a few moments, walked back to the vehicle and called for the police. The squad car arrived a few minutes later.

Jane gave the policeman the same story.

"Is anything missing?" inquired the officer.

Jane asked the paramedic to help her stand. Slowly, she examined the garage's interior. Now that the overhead light was switched on, she could see more clearly.

Cordelia pointed to the empty corner near the side door.

"The snowblower," groaned Jane. "I just bought it last January."

The officer wrote it down, along with a description. "Anything else?"

"No," said Jane. "I don't see anything."

"What's all that stuff in the back?" asked the policeman.

Jane turned to look. "Oh, that. I have a couple of house-guests right now. They're storing their things in here until they can find a permanent place to live." For a moment, she thought again of the rustling sound.

"Is there some problem?" came a deep voice from the doorway.

Everyone turned to see a tall, lanky young man and an equally tall, attractive young woman approach the back of the car.

"Billy," said Jane, her tone a mixture of surprise and fatigue.

As the couple stood in the harsh garage light, both of them looked sleepy, their blond hair still tousled from lying in bed. Yet, strangely, as Jane looked closer, she saw that under their bathrobes, each was fully dressed.

Billy walked further into the garage. "What happened?" he asked, his voice full of concern.

In the past month Jane had grown to like these temporary renters a great deal. She found Billy Brewster to be a generally pleasant, apple-faced young man in his mid-twenties—still boyishly handsome. There was a crispness about his voice which, combined with his Eastern accent, made him sound almost British. Erin was quieter, rarely needing to be the center of attention like her boisterous actor husband. Yet, if anything, Jane found Erin much more willing than Billy to be friendly and to spend time just hanging out, talking. To be fair, Billy was often away at the theatre. Erin was currently without a job and therefore had much more time on her hands.

"Someone attacked me," she said, touching her forehead with her fingers. "I think I'll let Cordelia fill you in on the details."

Erin crossed quickly to the back of the garage and began to examine a box sitting on top of an old desk.

Jane couldn't help but notice the tense expression on her face.

"Is anything missing?" asked the police officer.

"No," came her too swift response. "Everything's fine." She glanced at her husband with a look Jane could only read as anger.

"We're going to have to ask you to take a drive with us," said the paramedic, helping Jane over to the door. "You need to be checked by a doctor. Most likely, they'll want to admit you to a hospital overnight for observation. You may have a concussion."

Realizing there was no use in arguing, Jane nodded her agreement. She would much rather have gone upstairs to bed but knew he was probably right. She hugged her aunt and told her she'd call first thing in the morning.

As the paramedic helped Jane get organized inside the back of the truck, she thought of her poor aunt and what a miserable beginning this was to her stay in Minnesota. Before he left, she asked if she could speak with Cordelia for a moment.

"Yes, dearheart?" said Cordelia, climbing in beside her.

"Listen, do me a big favor. Will you stay here tonight? Make sure Beryl gets settled in."

"No problem. I'd already decided I would." Cordelia patted Jane's hand.

"I planned a wonderful breakfast for tomorrow. There's fresh melon, eggs, mushrooms and cheese for an omelet, and her favorite tea. It's in the right hand cupboard over the stove. St. Gervais English Blend. I drove all over the city to find it. And under the cake stand on the counter I brought home an entire assortment of breakfast pastries from the restaurant." Jane could see Cordelia's face twitch at the word pastry.

"I'll take care of everything," Cordelia assured her.

Jane leaned her head back against the pillow. "This is not the warm welcome I'd envisioned. Peter and Sigrid are in San Francisco visiting Sigrid's parents. And now I'm headed for the hospital."

"You just go and be a good patient. We'll be fine."

"Cordelia?"

"Yes?"

"Tell me you didn't feed the dogs any of that cake."

"I didn't feed the dogs any of that cake."

"I'm serious!"

"Jane, it hurts me to think—"

"Promise you won't give them any of the breakfast pastries."

"Jane dear, I would never—"

"That's not a promise."

Cordelia slapped her knees in disgust. "You're such a martinet. What must the neighbors think?"

"Cordelia!"

"Have you ever tasted that dry dog food you feed them? Well I have. It's vile and disgusting. I wouldn't feed it to a hastily called session of the John Birch Society."

"They're dogs!"

"Which? Oh, you mean the dogs. Exactly. Your best friends! You must treat them with a certain culinary respect. No one wants to eat dry, tasteless little pellets. I will say the canned variety is usually a bit better. A little too salty for my taste perhaps, but a decided improvement."

Jane closed her eyes, feeling a vein throb brutally in her temple.

"Don't worry, Janey. I have everything under control."

"We need to get going," called one of the paramedics.

Cordelia leaned over and gave Jane a quick kiss on the forehead. "Rest easy, dear one. All is well."

4

Torald flopped over on his back and stretched his long body as his wife brought in the breakfast tray. The shades had already been opened, revealing a cloudy, drizzly day, full of damp March dreariness. The bedroom of his Lake Minnetonka home did little to cheer the early spring gloom. Torald hated neutral colors. As far as he was concerned, spending a night in this room was like spending a week in a motel. Except, had he been in a motel, the night might have held more promise.

Maureen lifted the tray over his legs and sat down beside him. She was a striking woman in her early forties, with a long, equine face, enormous brown eyes full of doglike ear-nestness, and large teeth. Normally, although not this early in the morning, she wore bright red lipstick that served to put a frame around her mouth, thus making the teeth seem even larger. Cosmetically, it was a mistake, though Maureen was not a stranger to cosmetic mistakes. Her light brown hair was clipped short in the back but hung to her jaw line in the front. This elongated her face even further. Viewed in the right light, Maureen Werness looked a bit like Captain Hook.

"Where's the morning paper?" asked Torald, propping himself up in bed.

Maureen picked up a buttered toast point and began to chew the end. "Maybe Erling took it. He was going to clean the hamster cage this morning."

Disgusted, Torald reached for his coffee.

"He's your son, too, you know. You could show him a little attention once in awhile."

"You know I've been in rehearsals for the last month." He straightened his pajama top and smoothed his thin, rum-pled blond hair. *Vanity, thy name is Torald.* What did he care what he looked like in front of her? "And anyway, Erling and I reached a mutual . . . détente of sorts. I don't bug him about his appearance and he doesn't bug me about—"

"Your broken promises," said Maureen, finishing his sen-tence.

Torald eyed her testily. "No. Besides, what kind of a son is he? He wants to be a cricket scientist, or some such use-less thing."

"Entomologist," said Maureen, correcting him.

"Whatever. If that's what he likes, I won't stand in his way. I even promised I wouldn't insist that he continue with his acting lessons. He's completely hopeless on stage. Even Gaylord's noticed."

Maureen sipped her orange juice, raising a thinly plucked eyebrow. "What did your father say? Specifically?"

"Oh, don't worry. Nothing to get worked up about. Just that Erling was a born philistine."

Maureen dabbed a napkin at the corner of her mouth. Her expression grew impatient. "You know what's happening next weekend, don't you? You haven't forgotten?"

"I assume you're referring to Gaylord's birthday." Torald yawned.

"Of course that's what I mean!" she erupted. "You take everything *so* lightly."

"Calm down."

"And for God's sake quit calling him *Gaylord*. He's your father. Some day you're going to slip and call him that to his face."

"He wouldn't notice. He never listens to me."

Maureen shook her head.

"Look," said Torald, "not everyone had a wonderful childhood. My two sisters haven't spoken to the old goat for over fifteen years. At least I *speak* to him. And anyway, he's used to being called Gaylord."

"But you call him *Father* when you talk to him, right?"

"No, I don't."

Maureen tapped her long red fingernails on the plastic tray. "What do you call him then?"

"Nothing. I call him *nothing*."

She laughed, a deep ugly laugh. "Listen, big shot. That man may be nothing to you, but to the rest of the world he's the great playwright, Gaylord Werness. And next weekend is his seventieth birthday. On that day, in case you've forgotten, he's promised to assign the rights to his plays to an heir. And you—God save us all—are the one he's promised them to. So, I strongly suggest that you be on your best behavior until it's all legalized. And while you're at it, buy him something glitzy and expensive. You know how he loves presents."

Torald played with the scrambled eggs. "One day this farce will end, Maureen."

"Which farce?"

"Take your pick."

She stiffened at his nasty tone but recovered quickly. Folding the napkin in her lap, she replied, "I don't suppose you'd believe me if I told you I still loved you?"

"No. I wouldn't."

Without the slightest indication that his words meant any more to her than a simple "pass the sugar," she nodded. "Well, I have some important things to do today. I'd better get going."

"Here," said Torald, handing her the tray. "I don't have to be at the theatre until four this afternoon. I think I'll try to sleep a little longer."

"You were awfully late getting home last night." Maureen tried to keep her voice carefully neutral. She was good at it—she'd had years of practice.

"A late appointment," he said, pulling the covers up over his head. "Close those shades, will you? And tell Erling to keep the music down to a dull roar. I need to look as fresh as a baby tonight." He patted away another yawn. "You know, the opening night of Antonia's new play may turn out to be an interesting evening after all."

5

Jane stood in front of the full-length mirror in her bedroom and adjusted the strap on her evening gown. She was more than a bit surprised at the way she looked. Not being one to dress up very often, she felt a little like she was gazing at a total stranger. Her long chestnut hair was pulled back into a perfect French braid. The black and silver gown she wore fit her tall, shapely body like a proverbial glove. Not so bad for someone approaching forty.

Aunt Beryl appeared in the doorway. "Don't you look wonderful! I thought, after last night's fright, you might not be up for this."

Jane turned around, steadying herself on the edge of the

dresser. She still felt a little dizzy from the knock on the head. The doctors had said she had a mild concussion and suggested rest for the next couple of days. This, unfortunately, was a difficult prescription for a woman who normally worked a good seventy hours a week. The Lyme House restaurant, located on the south shore of Lake Harriet in Minneapolis, had been entirely Jane's creation from its very inception. She'd worked extremely hard over the past eight years. The main dining room was now considered one of the finest gourmet experiences in the entire Twin Cities. And the downstairs bar and eatery was becoming known for a wide variety of carefully chosen domestic beers, fresh, reasonably priced English-style pub food, and a comfortable spot to sit with a friend and play a game of cribbage. Jane was pleased with what she'd accomplished. And even though she knew the restaurant could plug along without her constant attention, she still felt the need to be there most of the time. Taking it easy was not part of her usual agenda.

"I've never seen you so dressed up before," continued Beryl, who was herself wearing a long, emerald green evening gown. A single fire opal hung from a gold chain around her neck. Her fluffy white hair sat like a crown above her plump cheeks.

Jane smiled a bit self-consciously. "I don't think I've ever owned a dress like this before. You know me. Jeans, boots, and an old rag wool sweater suit every occasion. Cordelia insisted we go shopping last week. She said the party later tonight at Antonia Werness's house was going to be strictly formal. I wasn't given a choice."

"Well," smiled Beryl, "I think you should dress like this more often. It suits you."

Jane moved over to her bed and sat down. She opened the middle drawer of her night stand and took out Christine's ruby ring. Gulliver hopped up on the bed and snuggled next to her. As she stroked his curly white and brown fur, she slipped the ring on her left hand. Lately, it had become a ritual of sorts. A kind of talisman of protection. Jane wasn't absolutely sure what it was supposed to be protecting her from, but she found herself wearing it more and more. It wasn't so much that she was reaching back into her past for a memory. More for a continuity.

Beryl stepped in front of the mirror and adjusted her shawl. "Tell me a little more about this play. Cordelia mentioned that there are only five people in it."

"That's right." Jane thought for a moment. "Well, it revolves around the women in this one family. The grandmother, the mother, and the daughter. Billy plays the daughter's boyfriend, and Torald was cast as the father. Each woman has her own bride dolls whom she talks to at great length—and who in turn, talk to her. The staging is very exciting. The bride dolls are dressed appropriately for their particular era. Cordelia commissioned six figures in all. Two for each woman—and most of the time they remain behind this huge gauzy curtain."

"It's called a scrim," said Beryl, patting her cottony white hair into place. "I learned a bit of terminology during my years with the Bristol Theatre Guild."

Jane smiled. "Anyway, the difference in these women's ages—and therefore the difference in their life experiences and expectations—form the basis for the story. It explores not only how women are defined by society in this last decade of the twentieth century, but how they view and to an extent, form each other. I guarantee, you'll find it highly thought-provoking. It's dark, and yet also quite funny. Antonia is always entertaining."

Out in the hallway, the phone began to ring.

"I'll get it," said Beryl. She stepped back into the hall and picked up the receiver. "Lawless and Cornelius residence," she said, giving Jane a slight smirk. "Yes. One moment please." She put her hand over the mouthpiece. "It's for you. A Detective Trevelyan."

Jane got up and crossed into the hall, taking the receiver from Beryl's hand. "Hello?"

"Ms. Lawless," came the low, businesslike voice. "It's been awhile. I was informed this morning that you had some trouble again at your home."

Orville Trevelyan had never been one of Jane's favorite

people. Years ago he'd made a point to tell her that he had little tolerance for her *lifestyle*, as he put it. "Have you discovered anything?" she asked. Might as well get to the bottom line. Social niceties seemed a bit out of place.

"It depends." He cleared his throat.

Here we go, thought Jane. Trevelyan was rarely in a hurry to hand out information. He loved the power of knowing something the other person didn't.

"We have located your small snowblower. It was tossed in a dumpster about three blocks from your house. It would appear that the motive for the attack was not simple burglary. The item was obviously taken as a cover. The individual in question was admittedly pretty stupid to dump it so close to the scene of the crime. Definitely not a professional."

Was this supposed to make her feel better? "My aunt said several officers came out to look at the garage this afternoon. Unfortunately, I was still at the hospital."

"Forgive me," said Trevelyan. "I should have asked how you were."

She could hear him cracking his knuckles. "Fine. But what would make me feel even better is finding out who broke into my garage last night. And why."

Trevelyan was silent for a moment. "I can't promise we'll ever know that. You understand that a report has been filed. Your stolen property will be returned to you. However, a crime of this sort is not high on our list of priorities. The men we sent out this afternoon searched your garage thoroughly. It was their considered opinion that the attacker was interested solely in the storage boxes in the back. I believe they belong to a couple of houseguests."

"That's right," said Jane.

"We tried to contact them today, but they were out."

"Billy is an actor. He's in a play that's opening tonight. If you have a message, I'll be glad to pass it on. I'll be seeing him and his wife later this evening."

"Good. Ask him to call me at my office." He gave her the number. "I'd like to talk with one or both of them as soon as possible."

As Jane wrote the number on a notepad, she heard the grandfather clock in the downstairs living room strike seven. If she and Beryl didn't get a move on, they'd be late for the theatre. "Of course. I'll be sure to tell him."

"And Ms. Lawless, one more thing. I know in the past you've tried to lend the police a hand."

Before he could finish his admonition, Jane interrupted him with, "Why, Detective Trevelyan, I didn't think you'd remember how easily I cleared up that little business at the sorority two years ago. It's so nice to be appreciated. Now, I must go or I'll be late. I'm sure we'll talk again soon. Give my best to your schnauzer." She dropped the receiver back on the hook.

"What was all that about?" asked Beryl, a quizzical look on her face.

"Oh nothing. Just a little conversational parry and thrust with the police. Always such a delight."

6

Billy Brewster sat in front of the mirror in his dressing room and stared at the image of a man so unlike himself that, for a moment, he had the strange sensation of being separated from his body. This was one of the things he liked best about acting. Becoming someone else. Taking on another form. And yet, at the same time, knowing that this new creation was not possible except for the life his own body and mind brought to it. Strangely, this new person *was* him, or at least part of what he had never explored, or even conceived of in himself before. The possibilities were infinite. Billy knew he would never cease to be seduced by the magic.

He picked up a comb and brushed the black hair away from his forehead. Who did he look like tonight? A young Henry Fonda? He knew that idea was rank flattery. As he combed the hair back down on his forehead, he thought of Antonia. The whole Werness family looked so unalterably Scandinavian. Torald was the spitting image of the middle-aged Max Von Sydow. And Antonia. He knew instantly how he thought of her. She was the aging, regal, Kristin Lavransdatter. As a young boy he'd read the famous trilogy by Sigrid Undset at least five times. Something about it charmed and, at the same time, haunted him. The dark, Nordic coldness. The bleak yet exquisite settings. The grim human tragedy. This, too, was magic. Even though life rarely had the same kind of romantic symmetry as art, he knew his own life was about to unfold like a book. Here he was, twenty-five years old, with a major part in a play written by the daughter of one of his theatrical idols, Gaylord Werness. Antonia was every bit as incredible in her own right. The entire family was amazing. One day soon he would meet Gaylord. He was putting that off—waiting for just the right moment. He relished the nervous anticipation, knowing it was much like the stage fright he always felt before the first act began. And wasn't that exactly what this was? Finally, taking his own, personal stage!

Someone rapped softly on the dressing room door.

"Come in," he called.

Erin entered carrying a huge bouquet of red roses. She crossed to the dressing table and stood directly behind him, gazing down in amazement. "Remarkable," she said, touching his wig. "I haven't seen you in full makeup before."

He turned and took the flowers, cradling them appreciatively. "You didn't have to do that."

"I know."

He grinned his approval. "You look lovely. That silver locket I bought you makes your skin look like honey."

She smiled and sat down in a chair across from him, fidgeting with her gold wedding ring. "Well, tonight's the big night."

He turned to look at himself in the mirror again. "Yes."

"I'm not talking about the play."

"I know you're not."

"You're sure you want to go through with it?"

"Erin, I have to."

"Once it's done, you can't change it."

"I don't want to." He turned to face her, his expression thoughtful, his eyes bright. "We've talked about this for months. I know how you feel. And I respect it. You think what I'm doing is dangerous. But have you ever considered that you're too cautious? Life is simply a series of risks."

Her eyes opened very wide. "God save us from the truly innocent! What on earth do you know about risk?"

"Look," he sighed, "I don't want to turn this into another argument. You can always leave. Go back home."

"You're my home now."

He touched her hand. "And you're mine."

"This could ruin everything."

"You've got to trust me, Erin. It'll be fine."

"You know what you need, Billy Brewster? You need a protector. A ferocious dragon with a sword to stand outside your gate and breathe fire at your enemies."

"Are you applying for the job?"

Sadly, she shook her head. "What about last night? Who do you think was going through our things?"

His expression instantly turned cold. "I don't know. But I'm going to find out."

"How?"

"I'm not sure. Someone may have figured things out. Don't worry. I'll take care of it."

"If someone thinks they know something, why haven't they just come forward with their suspicions?"

"Good question. I don't have a good answer. But, come on, let's not dwell on that now. Tonight will be enough to handle, all by itself."

Erin got up and laid her hands on his shoulders. "Are you nervous?"

"About absolutely everything. But I love it. And you'll be with me tonight. After the party, that's when I'll make my move."

She noticed a strand of blond hair escaping from under his wig. Carefully, she tucked it back into place. "All right, but remember your promise."

He crossed his heart and held up his hand. "Don't worry. Everything will go just the way I want. I've thought of every possibility. Just you wait and see."

7

Antonia Werness and Fleur O'Neil lived in a stately, three-story wood-frame home in Kenwood, one of the oldest and most prestigious areas of south Minneapolis. Jane had been invited to the house once before. It had been a party for the retiring Nils Johanson, a well-known and very dearly loved theatre professor at the University of Minnesota. Then as well as now, she'd found the house to be a curious mixture of elegance and neglect. The sweet, overpowering smell of carnations seemed to cling to the central foyer like a heavy, dime-store perfume, adding a certain air of old-fashioned, almost Southern decadence to the slow decay. Indeed, Fleur O'Neil, Antonia's partner of almost twenty years, had lived most of her young life in the garden district of New Orleans. She was from a wealthy Catholic family that had been more than happy to see their daughter—the one with the unusual lifestyle—move to a different part of the country. However, their generosity had never been dampened by prejudice. Fleur shared in the family riches, just as every other sibling had. Without additional finances, houses like this were simply not affordable, even to a playwright such as Antonia, or a professor of economics like Fleur.

Jane and her Aunt Beryl stood under the delicate crystal

chandelier just outside the first floor parlor, sipping champagne and watching a steady stream of sartorially splendid guests arrive through the double front doors. The curtain had come down on the last act of the play less than an hour ago. Cordelia had been right. This after-the-theatre party was definitely a formal affair.

"It smells a bit like a funeral home in here," said Beryl. She sniffed the air.

Jane had to laugh. It was so true. Every vase on the first floor was filled with carnations, Fleur's favorites. The only thing missing was the coffin.

"It is a lovely home though, isn't it?" asked Beryl. Her eyes danced around the room, coming to rest on a couple who had just arrived. As the man took their coats into one of the side hallways, the woman, one of the actors in the play, strolled over in their direction.

"Haven't we met before?" asked the woman, extending her hand to Jane.

"I think we've run into each other a couple of times outside the theatre. I'm a good friend of Cordelia Thorn's. Jane Lawless."

"Of course. I remember now. And I'm Ida John." She smiled briefly at Beryl.

Ida appeared to be in her mid-twenties. She had a haunting, deeply sculpted face, a bone thin body and a rather remote personality. Her eyes slanted ever so slightly, giving her face a faintly exotic look. And her smooth, brown hair was cut to fit her head like a helmet.

"You were wonderful this evening," beamed Beryl.

"I was, wasn't I?" agreed Ida. The young man who had taken her coat now joined them.

"*Star Tribune* reporter to your right," he whispered in her ear.

She ignored the remark. "I understand Billy Brewster and his wife are staying at your house, Jane. I'm just curious. How do you put up with all the arguing?"

Jane cocked her head. "Excuse me?"

"I suppose it's none of my business, but my dressing

room is right across from his. I don't know how you stand it."

Jane wondered if they were talking about the same people.

"Well, I suppose it has gotten a bit better lately. But the first few weeks we were in rehearsal, I thought I'd lose my mind."

Jane had no idea what to make of this. In her experience, she'd never once heard either Billy or Erin so much as raise a voice to the other. "They must reserve their louder disagreements for the theatre basement," she said. For some reason, Ida's comment had annoyed her. Not that she believed what she was saying. Except, why would she bring something like that up if it wasn't true?

Ida's smile was sour. "Well, I guess it's lucky for me, then. It was nice meeting you, Beryl. Jane. I'm sure we'll run into each other again."

As she walked away, Beryl said softly, "She dyes her hair."

"What?" said Jane, arching an eyebrow.

"Didn't you see those blonde roots? You'd think she'd be more careful than to let something like that show."

Jane hadn't noticed. She rarely noticed things like that. As she was about to suggest that she and her aunt head upstairs to the third floor ballroom and check out the hors d'oeuvres situation, she saw a woman wave at her from the hallway just outside the library. It was Dorrie Harris, the new City Council representative from her district. Jane had worked on Dorrie's campaign last summer and fall. The night she'd won, Dorrie had thrown a victory party at the Lyme House. Jane waited for her to emerge from the crowd and come over.

"Dorrie, I'd like you to meet my aunt Beryl. She's just arrived from England."

Dorrie took her hand and shook it warmly.

Jane had really grown to like this highly energetic woman over the past year. She had a wonderfully wry sense of humor and a very quick kind of intelligence. Her attractiveness had not been lost on Jane, either. And yet, even though Dorrie had the ability to make *everyone* feel as though they were her best friend, Jane knew she was a very private person. Her face rarely betrayed any emotion she did not want to consciously project. It was no doubt an asset in politics, if not in life. Jane felt they had become close during the campaign, but still, for whatever reason, she'd never been completely confident she ever understood what Dorrie was thinking. Jane judged that Dorrie Harris was in her early forties. She had a prominent, rather elegant nose, a high forehead, pleasantly full features and lovely, deep-set blue eyes. Her dark-gold, naturally curly hair was worn short. The over-all impression was one of bookishness mixed with a certain sensuality.

"I spent several years in England after college," smiled Dorrie. "I absolutely loved it. You must be related to Jane's mother. I knew she was English."

Beryl was obviously delighted by her interest. "I was married to Jane's mother's only brother. And even before that, Helen and I were best friends."

"Is that right? How wonderful for you both. Sounds like a close family."

Jane cleared her throat. "Dorrie is the new city council representative from our district. And, if we get lucky, our next governor."

"Stop!" she laughed. "You're going to turn my head. And besides, why think so small. There's always that senatorial race in four years." Dorrie whispered in Beryl's ear, "Better watch this one. She may have some political aspirations of her own."

Jane shook her head vehemently. "No thank you! Helping *you* is about as close as I ever want to get to elected politics."

Dorrie's smile was sly. "Don't you believe it," she whispered, giving Beryl a knowing nod. "By the way, not to change the subject too abruptly, but have you two been in to see Fleur's famous art collection?" She nodded to the door directly across from the library. Then, hesitating, she added, "It's—how can I put this delicately? Unique? About what one would expect from a professor of economics."

This was as close as Jane had ever heard Dorrie come to making a snide remark about an acquaintance. For some reason it made her feel included in a way she'd never been before. Perhaps Dorrie was finally feeling comfortable enough in her presence to drop some of the glad-handing political persona. If that was the case, Jane was happy about it.

"We'll be sure to take a look," said Jane, turning just in time to see a tall, elegant gray-haired man in the company of an equally elegant gray-haired woman. They had just entered the foyer together and were handing their coats to a young man. Oh no, she groaned, swallowing hard. This was all wrong. It wasn't supposed to happen like this. Taking a deep breath, Jane turned to greet her father.

Sensing Jane's sudden nervousness, Dorrie discreetly excused herself and continued on up the stairs, leaving Beryl standing alone, clutching her shawl closely around her shoulders.

"Dad," said Jane, casting a sideways glance at her aunt. "Hi!" She grinned stupidly. "Yes . . . well. What a surprise! I mean, I didn't know you'd been invited this evening."

Raymond Lawless escorted Marilyn, his partner of some twelve years, to the center of the room. He brushed a hand casually through his thick, shaggy mane as he positioned himself next to his daughter.

Jane recognized a certain tenseness in the gesture.

"I *am* a patron of the Allen Grimby," he said, his deep voice rumbling like distant thunder. "It's standard operating procedure to invite patrons."

Jane nodded. She began to stumble around in her mind for the right thing to say.

Raymond obviated the need by continuing, "Beryl. You look well. Did you have a good trip?"

Inwardly, Jane breathed a sigh of relief. However briefly, her father was going to be civil. Then again, Jane could see the stiffness in his posture, hear how he clipped each word. Perhaps she shouldn't leap to any happy conclusions just yet.

Beryl smiled graciously. "Thank you, Raymond. Yes. It

was a wonderful trip. You know how much I hate to fly. An ocean voyage is one of life's rare pleasures. It gives one time to think."

Jane's plastered-on smile faltered for a moment. Surely *Beryl* wasn't going to start something.

"And what did you have to think about?" asked Raymond, pleasantly.

Jane could see Marilyn give her father's arm a small tug. Such a minimal effort was never going to be enough to sidetrack him onto another subject. And my God, why should it? They'd barely begun to speak.

"I thought about my life," answered Beryl. "Our family. The mistakes I've made."

Jane watched her father as he slipped his arm around Marilyn's waist. Under normal circumstances, he would have introduced her immediately. In this situation, Marilyn's presence barely registered. "Then I'm sure you had plenty to think about," he scowled.

Beryl stiffened.

There it was. The first shot. As much as she wanted to think she could have prevented it by orchestrating their first meeting differently, Jane knew it was hopeless.

"If you'll excuse us?" said Raymond, his eyes flashing at his daughter. "I'd like to congratulate Antonia. Jane, I'll talk to you later."

I'm sure you will, she thought glumly. Something to look forward to. Before her father swept Marilyn away, Jane noticed an amused smile creep across her face. Some weeks ago, she and her father's housemate had had lunch together. Marilyn was of the decided opinion that Beryl's and Raymond's problems did not merit the melodrama both of them brought to it. And besides, even if they did have reason to hate each other, Marilyn found their inability to keep a lid on it, in a word, pathetic. She was of the school of thought that said, if you can't change something, you damn well better learn to live with it. She'd obviously had no success changing Raymond's hard line against his sister-in-law. So, she told Jane that she, for one, was simply going to ignore their little skirmishes. The problem was, for the last three months Jane had come to see herself as the one person who might be able to bring the warring parties to the peace table. Living with this animosity was not part of her plan. Yet, Marilyn had been quite clear in telling Jane that Raymond had no intention of reevaluating his antipathy toward Beryl. Given that set of circumstances, Jane's peace efforts might be totally useless.

With an apologetic grin, Jane glanced at her aunt, who also seemed to have noticed Marilyn's smile. "Perhaps she has the right idea," she said, nodding in Marilyn's direction.

Beryl frowned. She made no reply.

"Would you like to see the art collection?" She desperately hoped the evening hadn't been ruined.

For a moment Beryl seemed to be considering something. Then, her face brightening, she said, "Why not? I'm not going to let him get to me. If I do, I might as well leave right now."

"That's the spirit!"

Arm in arm, they waded through the crowd and down the hallway to the room that housed Fleur's now infamous collection.

"There you are," called Cordelia, bustling into the gallery. Before she could reach Jane, she was surrounded by a group of appreciative and highly excited theatre patrons. They clapped boisterously, all the while shouting their congratulations on her inspired direction.

Jane watched Cordelia, swathed in magenta taffeta, a gold lamé turban wound around her auburn curls, as she gracefully accepted the flow of compliments. It was something Cordelia had become quite good at. She took a small bow, exchanged a few brief words, and then headed for Jane with the intensity of a water buffalo charging a field mouse.

"That's the second time someone has noticed the genius it took to cast the angel-faced Billy Brewster as the malicious, conniving, darkly evil young man in Antonia's play." Cordelia looked momentarily smug. "What they don't realize is that casting against type is my specialty."

Jane decided to bite. "Why's that?"

"But my dear," she sighed voluptuously, "I understand its potential force with great intimacy. After all, I've been cast against type all my life." She winked and then paused, giving her head a small twist and closing her eyes. "Now, on to more important matters." She put her arm around Jane and drew her close. "You may need an armed guard tonight, dearheart. Your father's here."

"I know." Jane looked over at her aunt who stood at the other end of the room, intently examining a particularly awful watercolor. "We've already run into him."

Cordelia's voice grew low and thrilling. "And?" she said, her eyes growing wide.

"It's all right. No blood."

"No no, that's not enough! I want the *details*!"

"Cordelia, this is no time to indulge in voyeurism." She looked around the room. People were beginning to stare.

Cordelia pretended a hurt look. "Jane, dearheart, I'm merely . . . concerned."

"Right."

"You wound me when you say things like that." She moved in closer, whispering, "Just give me a clue. Were any threats made?"

"Cordelia!"

Raising a finger to her lips, Cordelia stood up very straight, looking down at Jane from her nearly six foot height. "I understand," she said, conspiratorially. "This is not the place. We shall talk later." She nodded her complete understanding.

Jane rolled her eyes.

"Are you and Beryl coming over to the Maxfield Plaza after this is over? We're going to celebrate well into the wee hours of the morning. Come on, Janey. You're going to miss the party of the century if you poop out. Why, I may even be forced to climb up on the bar and do my famous impersonation of Richard Burton doing an impression of Kermit the Frog singing, 'It's Not Easy Being Green.'" She leaned closer. "I've even been working on a new one. You'll never guess." She looked around, making sure they weren't being overheard. Dropping her voice a full octave she said, "I plan on doing Ronald Reagan on the witness stand singing, 'If I Only Had A Brain.' " She began to giggle. "Get it?"

"I think the entire nation got it," said Jane.

"Right." She stood up straight. "Well. It was wonderful tonight, wasn't it?" She lowered her head majestically at a group of people who were obviously trying to overhear their conversation. "Well, wasn't it?" She tapped her foot.

"Absolutely some of the finest theatre I've ever seen," said Jane gravely. And she meant it. "The play was wonderfully written, and the way you handled it turned it into magic."

Not immune to flattery—even of the sincerest kind—Cordelia visibly expanded under Jane's words. "Thank you, Janey. We all have a very limited audience who we really want to please. Coming from you, those words mean a great deal." She gave Jane a big hug. "Now," she said, lifting her chin at the hall just outside the room, "my public awaits." She caught Beryl's eye and gave a cheerful wave before moving her Reubenesque form through the room and out into the crowd. Jane heard a burst of applause as Cordelia, a high-priestess at the peak of her professional powers, entered the front foyer. In her mind's eye, Jane could see Cordelia walking up to accept the Tony Award from a terribly impressed, virtually tongue-tied Dustin Hoffman. No, that wasn't right. Cordelia would have insisted on Bette Midler.

8

Antonia Werness paused on the wide balcony outside the ballroom, breathing in the cold, misty night air. After many hours of celebration, the guests had finally left. For the first time since the craziness of the evening had begun, she felt she could spend a few moments savoring the full intensity of triumph at the first successful production of her new play. It was a rare moment. Something to be deeply relished. All these years, working quietly on the script, telling no one about it except Fleur and Lucy, yet never losing hope that this might be the best work of her life. The characters had lived so vividly in her mind that it was almost as if they had moved into her house, walking the halls with her at night as she struggled to understand how their lives fit together and the reasons which motivated them to become the people they were. It had been an exhausting process. And now, the dream had finally come true. She would let nothing spoil her feeling of exhilaration.

Yet, there it was again. That small uneasiness that crept disturbingly around the edges of her mind. What if her brother was right about Billy? The resemblance was uncanny. No, it was impossible. Nothing but an alcoholic's aberrant fantasy.

"Brooding already?" asked a voice from behind her. "Afraid your women friends won't think your new play is politically correct enough?"

Antonia turned to find her brother, Torald, leaning against the French doors, taking a final drag off a cigarette before pitching it into an empty flowerpot.

"Do I look like I'm brooding?" She turned to face him,

her powerful presence an eloquent denial that anything could possibly be wrong. "Just zip it, Torald." As usual, he had no idea what was on her mind.

Torald raised his glass to her in mock salute and took several swallows. "To my eminent sister. Long may she reign." Then, grunting porcinely, he pushed himself away from the doorway and settled his long frame on a marble bench.

"You're going to have difficulty convincing people that you're a perfect study in ironic detachment while you're swilling down so much gin," she said, studying him with little interest.

"You fail to understand," said Torald, emptying the glass. "Tonight I'm doing a rather splendid imitation of our grand and glorious daddy."

Disgusted by his sloppiness, Antonia brushed past him and reentered the now empty ballroom. Slowly, she lowered her tired body onto a well-padded chair and kicked off her shoes. Her feet hurt like hell.

"There is nothing more fundamentally stupid than a mob," said Torald, following her into the room. He threw himself into the chair next to her. "Any mob."

"Is that how you refer to theatre-goers these days? No wonder your popularity is slipping."

He leaned over and patted her knee. "All these Sapphic women in my life. You're hard. Cruel." He smiled with perfect insincerity.

"And you're full of shit."

Antonia caught a glimpse of herself in one of the long side mirrors. My God! *Stout*—that's what it was. The word that had escaped her all evening. Amazingly, over the past two years she had grown not quite fat, but unmistakably stout. Even the wild blond hair of her youth was beginning to show signs of age. She laughed when she thought of an old high school friend's comment so many years ago now. After choir practice one afternoon, she'd invited him to her family's home for dinner. Sometime later he'd admitted to feeling as if he'd been invited to a meeting of the Hitler Youth. *Everyone*, he insisted, had such terribly blond hair and blue eyes. The funny thing was, it was the first time Antonia ever realized there was any family resemblance at all. As she looked in the mirror now, it was hard not to recognize how closely she had come to look like her father. The image was so dispiriting, she turned away.

"Ah, and who have we here?" asked Torald.

Antonia turned to find Billy and Erin Brewster entering the room. Billy looked very nervous, his eyes jumping from one object to the next as he made his way to the spot where Antonia was sitting. Erin followed a few paces behind.

"I thought everyone had gone," said Antonia, leaning back and stretching as she lifted her sore feet onto a small table. "Cordelia and company were all headed over to the Maxfield Plaza."

Billy shook his head. "I was hoping I might have a few minutes to talk to you."

Sensing his seriousness, she sat up a bit. "Sure, why not. Do you want Torald to leave?"

Torald's body stiffened at the suggestion, betraying an interest he might have preferred to keep to himself.

"No," said Billy quickly. "I think . . . perhaps Torald should hear this, too. I don't know." He looked at Erin. She nodded her agreement.

Torald leaned back and drew out another cigarette. "Do you mind?" His voice was composed, his manner carefully subdued.

"Would you like to sit down?" asked Antonia. She nodded to a love seat.

"Thanks," said Billy. He let Erin get comfortable before sitting down next to her. As he reached for his wife's hand, he cleared his throat several times, his anxiety all too visible. "This is . . . difficult," he smiled. "I guess there's no easy way to do this except to begin." Looking down, he continued, "You see, all my life I've known I was . . . different. My friends had parents, and so did I, but from the time I was a little boy I've known that I was adopted."

Antonia felt her mouth twitch. Her hand moved reflexively to her throat.

"When I turned twenty-four, I asked my parents if they

knew anything about my biological mother and father. They responded by giving me a letter that had been included in the adoption papers. They'd never read it but decided if I ever expressed an interest, they would pass it on to me along with this." Billy lifted a thin gold chain out from under his shirt. Attached to it was a small ebony carving of a cat sitting on top of a six-pointed star. "I haven't taken this off since the day it was given to me."

Antonia's eyes fixed on the tiny object. The rest of the room became a blur.

Billy drew a yellowed piece of paper from his pocket and opened it. "I'd like to read this to you," he said, his voice very gentle. "I must have read it to myself a thousand times. It starts out,

Dear Son. One day you'll read this—I hope early enough in your life so that you will understand some important things about who you are. The most necessary is, you are a very deeply loved, precious little boy. Perhaps my love is the kind you can't understand right now, but one day, when you have children of your own, you will. The hardest thing I've ever done is to give you up. Yet, I know if you are to have a chance in life, a chance I can't give you, it's the only way. I have so many hopes and dreams for you, little one. And you must know something else about yourself. You are good. You are strong, and you will be prayed for every night of your life by a mother who wishes you only happiness and joy. Please forgive me, and try to understand that there are reasons for what I've done. I love you, my dearest. You will be in my thoughts forever.

Your Mother
1967

Billy folded the paper carefully and slipped it back into his pocket. He took a moment before looking up.

Antonia was shaken to the core. She couldn't seem to find any words. Instead, she just stared at him helplessly, her eyes filling with tears.

"My parents said they'd adopted me privately through a lawyer in New Orleans. It was a simple matter for me to locate the man. He still had the papers on file. I may be wrong, but I had a feeling he wasn't a particularly reputable attorney. The day I came to see him—it was last winter, just before Christmas—he was terribly busy. The police were breathing down his neck about something, and his wife kept calling. I think he gave me the file just to get rid of me. I took it outside and sat down on a bench. There it all was. My birth certificate. Mother, Antonia Werness. Father, E. Hatch."

Antonia grasped the sides of her chair. "Paul," she whispered.

"Is that my name?" he asked eagerly. "Is that what you called me?"

She nodded, glancing at Torald. "I'm sorry," she rasped. "This is . . ."

"I know," said Billy. "Believe me, I've thought about little else for months. After I traced you here I was in shock to find out who you were! The daughter of Gaylord Werness, one of the idols of my youth. You have to understand. All my life, ever since I can remember, I've been drawn to the theatre like there was a magnet inside my gut. It was so right. So incredibly right! That's when I saw the general call for your play in the Minneapolis paper. I'd already made quite a name for myself out East. My credentials were impeccable. Studied at Juilliard. Spent three years at the Central School of Speech and Drama in London. My stage credits were growing. And then, the miracle happened. I was cast in your play. That gave me the one thing I wanted most. Time. I knew I couldn't just walk in and introduce myself. This way, I had a chance to get to know you. And I've grown to respect you so much. This entire family . . ." He stopped, sensing the effect his words were having on her. "Just listen to me. I'm blathering on like an idiot. Only—you have to know how happy I am to finally find you." Massaging his forehead, he looked away. "I know it's tough to spring something this way. Erin thought I should send you a letter. But I couldn't!" He could barely keep his growing exuberance in check. "I had to be *with* you when you found out. I had to see your face. It means everything to me, don't you see?"

Antonia blinked as she took in his words. After a moment, she realized he was waiting for her to respond. "Yes," she whispered.

"I'm not blaming you for anything. I'm not even asking for explanations. My own childhood was wonderful! I've never suffered, not really. Except—I simply never got to know you—or the rest of my family. But I understand. Really I do. You made the only decision you could. But now, it's different. I'm older. I've come to know you as a friend. There's nothing to be afraid of any longer. Please, won't you *say* something?" he pleaded. "I need to know that you'll at least acknowledge me!"

Quickly, Antonia rose and went to him "You don't understand," she said, kneeling down and touching him gently on his cheek. "You can't. My darling," she said softly, taking him in her arms. "Of course I acknowledge you." She held him fast as he cried, his entire body shaking. "Dear boy," she whispered, closing her eyes, feeling his need, "If this is what you really want."

9

Jane peeked into Beryl's room. Her aunt appeared to be asleep. Since the Werness home was only a ten-minute drive from Jane's, Beryl had been able to turn in shortly after one-thirty. Now, nearly two, Jane padded downstairs in her flannel robe and slippers and sat down on the couch in the living room, watching the moonlight stream in through the double front windows. After a hot shower, the throbbing in her head felt considerably better. Still, the bump just above her hairline was an unwelcome reminder of what had happened last night. She'd never expected the feeling of anxiety that now swept over her every time she thought about it. Yet, simply brooding wasn't going to help. The problem was, she didn't know *what* to do.

Taking a deep breath, she closed her eyes and tried to put everything out of her mind. That was better. The house was so silent, so peaceful. What an evening it had been. She could still see her father's expression as he stood glowering at her aunt, barely controlling his frustration at finding her *back once again*, as he'd put it so succinctly last week, *on THIS SIDE of the Atlantic*. She and Beryl would have to talk soon. If her dad didn't want to discuss the problems that existed between them, perhaps Beryl would choose to shed some light on the subject. It was worth a try.

Wearily, Jane opened her eyes, realizing she had simply exchanged one set of worries for another. This wasn't working. She pulled a small quilt off the back of the sofa and tossed it over her legs. At least she had to try to relax, even though she knew she was too wound up to sleep.

An hour later, she blinked open her eyes at the sound of someone moving around in the kitchen. Sleepily, she got up, following the wonderful aroma of frying bacon. As she crossed into the front hall, she heard a loud rap on the door. Who on earth? She looked out through the peephole. But of course. Who else? "Cordelia," she said, swinging open the door. "What a surprise." Cordelia breezed into the room, looking a bit worse for wear. Her turban had tipped precariously to one side.

"It's a long, pathetic, *ugly* story," she said, removing her cape and throwing herself dramatically into a chair.

"Am I going to hear it, or is it a secret?" Jane stood with her hands on her hips, waiting.

Cordelia sniffed the air. "Bacon?"

"Possibly."

"What are we waiting for?" She jumped up and headed for the kitchen.

"Cordelia?" Exasperated, Jane followed.

There, in front of the stove, still dressed in his tuxedo pants and dress shirt, stood Billy Brewster. He was humming softly above the sizzling sounds. Cordelia swept into the room and, with great flourish, grabbed the spatula out of his hand. "Where are the eggs?" she demanded.

"Hi!" said Billy, surprised to see her. "The eggs? They're over there." He pointed to a bowl next to the sink.

"Have you added the cream cheese yet?"

"Cream cheese?" He looked confused.

Behind them, Jane leaned against the doorway, her arms folded over her chest.

"You do have cream cheese, don't you Janey?" Cordelia glared.

"In the refrigerator." She gave Billy a resigned shrug.

"Ah," said Cordelia, finding it quickly. "Now, both of you just sit down quietly at that table. Let Cordelia show you how to prepare a real three A.M. meal." She paused, staring at Billy for a moment. "William, since you're the one who's dressed like a butler, you set the table."

Billy grinned at Jane. "Yes ma'am."

"And while you're at it, find that strawberry rhubarb jam in the fridge. It's a little too smarmy-sweet for my taste, but I suppose *some* people here," she raised a skeptical eyebrow at Jane, "may find it to their liking." With great skill, Cordelia set about chopping and sautéing vegetables, scrambling eggs, and toasting English muffins. "Where's that salsa I saw in here last night?" She poked her head into the refrigerator. "Ah, and the Monterey Jack. And here's the sour cream."

"Murder by Cholesterol," said Jane softly.

"What?" Cordelia turned around.

"A new book I'm reading," smiled Jane. "I'm giving it to Billy when I die—I mean, when I'm done."

"Humph," she said, getting down three plates from the cupboard. Quickly, she finished the last touches at the stove. "William, time to pour the milk. That's part of the secret, dearhearts. To avoid total digestive disintegration, meals during the wee hours of the morning require great quantities of milk." She lifted the filled plates over to the table. "Now, as my dear, departed father used to say, *over the teeth, over the gums, look out stomach, here she comes*! Dig in." With great relish, she took the first taste. "Five star. Definitely a culinary disaster—just what one hopes for after the theatre, don't you agree? We couldn't do better if we'd gone to White Castle."

Jane looked warily at Billy, offered up a quick prayer, and took a bite. "Really, Cordelia," she said taking another taste, "this is quite good."

"Oh ye of little faith." Cordelia buttered her English muffin.

"So," said Jane, "Give. To what do we owe your unannounced visit?"

Cordelia flapped her napkin and stuffed it haphazardly into her rather remarkable décolletage. "You remember I told you my car was in the shop for repairs? Well, the party was breaking up over at the Maxfield Plaza, so I asked Arty Bernson if he'd give me a ride home. He lives only a couple blocks from me. When I got up to my door, I realized I'd left my keys and my pocketbook over at the bar. I could tell Arty wasn't in the mood to drive all the way back to St. Paul, so we stopped at a gas station and I called over to the Maxfield to make sure Sherman would put them away for me. Then, he brought me here. You don't mind if I spend the night, do you Janey? I promise I shall be as quiet as a church mouse."

"And do all these dishes in the morning."

"And do all these . . ." She stopped, raising her head imperially. "We'll see." She took a bite of her muffin.

"And you're up kind of late yourself," said Jane, turning to Billy.

"Not to rely on cliché," said Cordelia, adding a little more salsa to her eggs, "but you look like the proverbial cat who just ate the proverbial canary. Must be your huge theatrical success tonight. By the way, you were brilliant. Everyone was."

"Thanks." Billy beamed. "But that's not why I'm on cloud nine." He sat back and took a sip of his milk. "You're both going to find out about this soon enough, so

I might as well tell you. To make a long story short," he paused, "Antonia Werness is my mother."

Cordelia stopped chewing. "What did you say?"

"It's the truth. I've always known I was adopted. Both my parents are great. Dad's an architect and Mom's a teacher. They never lied to me about it. Last year I made the decision to see if I could find my birth parents. The search led me here."

Cordelia fixed him with a hard stare. "Did you know she was your mother before you took the part in the play?"

He smiled his delight. "Sure did. That's what was so perfect. It gave me a chance to get to know her. Erin was always telling me I should take it easy, be very careful. She was concerned I might be getting into something that wasn't as marvelously rosy as I had it pictured."

Cordelia swallowed hard. "Truly amazing, William. Finding your mother and ruining my career all in one night."

Billy ate his eggs hungrily. "Oh, don't worry. Antonia knows you had nothing to do with it. It's just so right, don't you see? I can't wait to meet my grandfather. I saw him once—from a distance. I suppose you've both met him."

Grimly, Cordelia nodded.

"That's incredible," said Jane, shaking her head in surprise. "And yes, I've meet Gaylord. Once. I was pretty young. It was shortly after Antonia and Fleur bought the house in Kenwood. I remember because she came and talked to a theatre class I was taking over at the U. They'd just moved up here from New Orleans."

"That's where I was born," said Billy eagerly.

Jane smiled at his enthusiasm.

"So? What did you think of him?"

"Well, I don't know. My father introduced us. He represented Gaylord in some legal matter years ago." She paused. "He was quite a big man. I'd say at least six-five. And he had very blond hair and a long blond beard. I thought he looked like Father Time. He seemed nice enough. A rather striking voice. Very deep and *very* calm. I guess I liked him. I don't think we said much to each other. I've always been heavily into sitting quietly in corners, observing people."

"She tells everyone she's an *introvert*." Cordelia sniffed. "It's a sad, psychological malady. Comes from reading way too much Kafka." She bugged her eyes out at Billy. "In case you don't remember, he spent a good part of his life wondering what it would feel like to *be* an insect. Ah, the creative life."

Billy laughed. "Yeah, I was a shy kid, too. Still am. I wonder why my grandfather and Antonia don't speak to each other anymore?"

"Father Time, huh?" mused Cordelia. "And Mother Earth. Perhaps they can't agree on who gets top billing."

Jane thought of her own family. "Maybe you can get one of them to talk about it."

"Maybe," said Billy. "Antonia, I mean *Mother*—I guess I'm going to have to decide what to call her—anyway, she said she would invite Erin and me over to the house early next week. She wants us to meet her sister, my aunt Lucy. I'd also like to get to know Fleur a little better."

"Did you talk to her at the party tonight?" asked Jane.

"Some. She has kind of a . . ."

"Prickly personality?" said Cordelia, finishing his sentence.

He shook his head. "I was going to say 'serious outlook,' but your description is better. The thing is . . ." He stopped. "I'd like to find out more about my father. It just said 'E. Hatch' on the birth certificate. Antonia didn't say anything about him when we talked. I didn't want to bring it up— not yet. I want her to get used to me first before I start asking questions. It's just—I hope she doesn't stonewall me on this. I really need to know."

"Billy," said Cordelia, giving him a cautionary glance, "your wife might be right. What's that old saying? Be careful what you wish for. You might get it."

Jane could tell the late hour was beginning to take its toll. She rubbed the back of her neck, feeling a tight soreness that wasn't usually there.

"Just listen to me," said Billy. "Rambling on about myself. I haven't even asked how you're feeling after that crack on the head you took last night."

"I'm fine," said Jane. "Really. The doctors just said to take it easy for the next few days."

Billy's expression turned a bit sheepish. "What happened to you may be partially my fault."

Jane looked up from her plate of food. "Why do you say that?"

"Well, see, I'm almost positive whoever was in the garage last night was going through Erin's and my things. Lots of our papers were messed up." He drew in his breath and let it out slowly, pushing himself away from the table. "I think I might even know who's responsible."

"Who? Billy, come on! If you know something . . ."

"I'm not absolutely positive about this, so you can't quote me."

"There are no reporters here," said Cordelia, adjusting her turban. "You may speak freely."

"Well," he hesitated, "to be honest, I think it may have been Torald."

"Torald!" shrieked Cordelia.

"Lately, I don't know. He's been kind of suspicious— always watching me when he thought I wasn't looking. I think he might have seen a family resemblance. At the very least, he probably thought I was talking to Antonia way too much."

"I believe the term you're looking for is *sucking up*." Cordelia smiled.

"Yeah, well . . . whatever. I'm sure he must have known about her pregnancy all those years ago. Since he couldn't prove anything, I think he took a chance that I might have some records or something that would link me to the family. He knew we'd stored all our things in your garage, Jane. I remember his asking about it. To be honest, I don't think he was trying to hurt you last night, he merely wanted to get out of the garage without being seen."

"Very un-Torald-like," interjected Cordelia. "The object of an actor's life is to *be* seen."

"Where does that leave me?" asked Jane. "Do I tell the police?"

"And ruin my play! Not on your life." Cordelia was aghast.

"At least I have to talk to him," said Jane.

"Fine. Do it tomorrow. The stage manager has called a meeting at four. Everyone in the play will be at the theatre. It should only take an hour. When we're all done, then you can accost him with your suspicions."

"The thing is," said Billy, "you have no way to prove it. But I suppose you could make some trouble for him if you want. I don't mean to speak ill of my uncle, but I think he's kind of a turkey—if you know what I mean. He's basically an ignorant man. Lazy. Still, he's one hell of an actor."

"Don't be so lyrical in your praise," smirked Cordelia.

Jane had seen Billy and Torald together only once. At the time, she'd felt that Billy was totally unaware of Torald's malice toward him. If Torald perceived him as a threat of some kind, then his sarcasm was more understandable. But what was the threat? "I think I'd better sleep on all this," said Jane.

"Finish your milk," ordered Cordelia. She turned to Billy. "You, too."

Dutifully, they both emptied their glasses.

"Good. Now. I'm off to find my jammies, crawl under the covers, and finish Barbara Wilson's latest mystery." She tossed her turban at Jane. "See you both anon."

10

Torald inched carefully down the wide, carpeted stairs and crossed into the living room. As long as nothing moved suddenly, as long as there were no loud noises, his head might just possibly remain attached to his body. His hangover was immense.

"What are you doing?" asked Maureen, stepping briskly into the room carrying a newly framed photograph of their son.

Torald covered his ears. "Shhh!" he hissed.

"Why?" asked Maureen, looking around. She whispered, "Is something wrong?"

"Yes. My head is about to implode."

"Oh." Her demeanor resumed its normal indifference. She held the photo above the mantel. "What do you think?"

"I think you should paint a bull's-eye on it and take it to the basement. We can use it for darts."

"Torald, he's your *son*."

He glanced at the photo. "I know."

"He's simply at that awkward age right now, but he adores you, surely you know that? He's just trying to separate—to establish who he is apart from us."

"Spare me the pop psychology."

Ignoring his tone, she moved two figurines and placed the photo on the mantelpiece.

Still holding his head, Torald eased his lanky frame into a chair. He eyed the room morosely. God, he hated the way Maureen decorated things. Nothing aged more quickly than what was once considered modern. They might as well be living in a theatre lobby, for all the warmth the room evoked. From upstairs came a blast of rock music.

"Make him stop!" whined Torald. He covered his head with his arms.

"It's nearly noon," said Maureen, standing back to admire her somewhat-less-than-handsome son. Unfortunately for Erling, he had inherited the worst features of both sides of the family. A long, narrow head. Tiny gray eyes. A large, permanently worried mouth. Extremely fine, wispy blond hair. And skin so pallidly white, his teachers constantly insisted his blood be checked for anemia. Still, Maureen beamed her approval.

Torald pulled his sweater up over his ears. "There's

something I haven't told you." The words, said almost sweetly, produced the desired effect.

"Oh?" She glanced at him out of the corner of her eye.

"Yes. I'm sorry to say, I may have some competition for Gaylord's undying devotion."

She turned around. "What are you babbling about? Pull that sweater down and talk to me like a normal human being."

Watching her, he let it drop partway. "Antonia has a son." There it was. What delicious fun. Just like chucking a log into a stagnant pond and watching the scum ripple.

"What? You're crazy! Antonia? My God, Torald. Your sister is a *lesbian*! She's been in a sporadically monogamous relationship with *the same tedious woman* for over twenty years!" It took a moment for the full intent of his words to sink in. "You mean, your father . . . the plays?"

Torald chewed the fingernail on his right thumb. "Yup, 'fraid so. There's another potential heir. In case you're interested, it's Billy Brewster. He plays the boyfriend in the new play."

"But . . . how . . . what are you saying?"

"I suppose it's possible Daddy might now leave the farm to someone other than Prince Torald. And you know, I don't even care anymore." He paused and then added, *"Almost."*

"How can you say that? It's unthinkable!"

Torald's headache couldn't stand the pitch to which her voice had risen. He had to put a stop to her near hysteria before his head cracked open. "Don't worry. I'll take care of it."

"How can you tell me not to worry?"

"Listen to me, Maureen. I know what I'm talking about. The last person on earth Gaylord will want to see is . . . Billy Brewster."

Maureen sank into a chair. "I don't understand."

"You don't need to."

"But . . ."

"We have nothing to fear, I guarantee it. Gaylord

Werness will do everything in his power to avoid ever setting eyes on that kid. I'll make damn sure of that."

"I don't understand how you can be so positive."

He gave a sullen, self-absorbed little smile and picked up the morning newspaper. End of discussion.

11

Beryl leaned over the kitchen sink, finishing up the dishes the kids had made last night. As she moved through the spacious room, she savored the feeling of luxury. She'd been living in that cold, drafty cottage on the southwestern coast of England far too long. Of course, Jane's kitchen was much better equipped than most American homes. Beryl knew her niece often tested new recipes for her restaurant here. Copper pots and pans hung from a wrought-iron bar high above a large chopping-block table. Besides the restaurant-sized gas stove, Jane had installed a commercial mixer on one end of the counter. Compared to Beryl's small kitchen in Lyme Regis, this was a cook's dream.

On her first Sunday in her new home, she'd decided to celebrate by preparing a lovely chicken she'd found in the refrigerator. She'd even taken a minute to whip up some of her favorite homemade bread stuffing. The bird was now in the oven, roasting slowly with wine and vegetables. It was going to be a wonderful surprise when everyone finally got up. The clock next to the refrigerator said it was nearly noon.

Hearing a car door slam, Beryl walked to the bay windows in the dining room and looked outside. In the drive she could see a large brown car. She was crooking her neck to get a better view when the doorbell sounded.

She opened the front door and there stood a very tall, elderly gentleman in a three-piece navy blue suit. His longish white hair and beard made her think of an Old Testament patriarch.

"Excuse me," he said in a kindly voice. "I'm looking for Billy Brewster. My name is Gaylord Werness." He nodded pleasantly, waiting for a response.

Only then did Beryl realize she was wearing an old Elton John T-shirt and faded bib overalls. She'd been going to scout out the backyard, see what she could do about planting a garden as soon as the weather turned a little warmer. But her surprise got the better of her self-consciousness. "Mr. Werness," she smiled. "How nice to meet you. I'm Beryl Cornelius." She extended her hand. "Jane's aunt. I had the honor of being at the opening of your daughter's play last night. Perfectly splendid! Won't you come in?"

At the mention of Antonia, some of the warmth faded from Gaylord's face.

"Of course." He entered, taking a moment to glance around the rooms.

Beryl noticed that he'd put on a good deal of weight since the documentary she'd seen about him many years ago. It was a BBC production. Very enlightening, if one was interested in the theatre, as she was. His fair complexion now looked reddish and waxen, his skin deeply lined. And the eyes. She remembered them now. They didn't fit with the rest of his kindly persona. They were too distant. Too constantly clever for the simplicity of his speech.

He turned to her, speaking softly. "I understand Billy Brewster and his wife are living here."

"Of course," said Beryl. "You understand correctly. My niece invited them to stay upstairs, on the third floor. Since it used to be an office, it has a separate phone number. Why don't I just give them a ring and tell them you're here?"

Gaylord nodded his thanks.

"Please," said Beryl, motioning to the living room. "Make yourself comfortable. Would you like some tea?"

"No. You're very kind. But I've just come from a late breakfast with friends."

Beryl excused herself and walked back into the kitchen. She picked up the phone and called upstairs. Billy answered. She could hear the surprised excitement in his voice as he held his hand over the receiver to talk to Erin. After a moment he returned and said they'd be right down.

Beryl thought it best to give them some privacy. So, giving Gaylord the message, she took a tray of tea, jam, and buttered buns with her and climbed the stairs to her room.

Erin entered the living room first, followed quickly by Billy. Everyone seemed terribly nervous as Gaylord stood, his eyes fixed on the tall young man in front of him. He hesitated for only a second before opening his arms and closing them tightly around his grandson. "Billy," he whispered, his voice cracking with emotion. "I didn't believe you really existed."

"Did you *know*?" asked Billy, taking a step back. He still held Gaylord's arms.

"I'd heard something once. But I was told it was none of my business. You have to understand, in the past, I'm afraid my family has found my opinions rather ... harsh. My children stopped confiding in me at a very early age." He hugged Billy again. "It's the present we have to be concerned with now, son, not the past." He turned to Erin. "And this must be your lovely wife. I'm so delighted to meet you." His smile lit up his face.

Erin let him put his arms around her, too, yet, she knew she couldn't be like Billy. She felt tense and awkward. She couldn't give herself so completely without knowing more. Sometimes she hated that part of herself. But one of them had to keep their heads. This entire family was so incredibly seductive.

"Can you stay for a few minutes?" asked Billy, sitting down on a wing chair by the fireplace.

"Just for a bit," smiled Gaylord. "I'm already late for another appointment." He waited until Erin was seated before resuming his position on the couch. "I simply had to see you."

"How did you know?" asked Billy.

He grinned. "I have my spies. Dear God, look at you! A grown man. And an *actor*! From what I hear, a good one."

Billy blushed furiously. It was the curse of many fair-skinned people.

"I'm coming to see you in that play, my boy. Next Friday night. And on Sunday . . ." He cleared his throat. "I was wondering if you two might accompany me to church. In my younger years I scoffed at things like that. But now, I've found a great solace in the Bible."

Erin knew Billy loathed organized religion. It was an opinion they both shared. Surely he would say something. If nothing else, he would at least politely decline the invitation.

"Of course," said Billy, glancing at her briefly. "We'd love to come."

"Wonderful," said Gaylord. "And then afterward, I'm giving a little party. It's my seventieth birthday. It would mean the world to me if you'd both be there."

Billy shook his head. "I can hardly believe this is happening! Do you know how often I've dreamed of this day? Of finally meeting you? Of course we'll be there!" His smile was expansive.

The grandfather clock ticked in the corner. Erin stared straight ahead.

"And one more thing." Gaylord's voice sank to its most serious register. "You probably know Antonia and Lucy haven't spoken to me in many years. I felt I should say something about the matter. First, you must understand that it's entirely their decision. I'm here any time they want me. But, you know how people sometimes hurt each other, even when they don't mean to. I may have said things years ago that upset them. My standards have always been high—my children think *too* high. All I'm asking is that we give each other a chance." He laughed a bit ruefully. "I suppose it's my age. Perhaps my daughters won't believe this, but I've mellowed. We're a family, after all. We've got to at least try to love each other." He stood. "That's why I've come. With you, maybe I can start fresh."

Billy jumped up and shook his hand. "You don't know how much this means to me. To us."

Erin noticed that this time, he didn't even look at her.

"Fine. Just fine. Well, I'll be off then. I'll call you next Saturday. Let you know what I think of the play." He winked. "And then we can settle our plans for Sunday."

Billy walked him to the front hall, giving him a brief hug before opening the door. "Thanks," he called after him. "We'll talk Saturday."

As soon as they were alone, he whirled around, clenching his fists and socking the air. "Do you believe it? That was Gaylord Werness! This is the greatest day of my life! I can't believe this really happened ... he actually came to see *me*!"

Quietly, Erin remained seated and stared at her hands.

12

"Meeting behind the main stage in ten minutes!" shouted Cordelia. She strolled down the wide, brightly lit hallway in the basement of the Allen Grimby, humming her favorite contralto air from Handel's Messiah. Most all of the dressing rooms were downstairs. "Listen up. No excuses, golden ones. Four o'clock sharp!" It was clear that no one appreciated the potential operatic quality of her voice.

As she was about to launch into a particularly brilliant one-woman version of the "Amen Chorus," she paused in front of Torald's door. He damn well better have made it, she grumbled to herself, remembering how plastered he'd been last night at the party.

She knocked. "Torald, are you in there?"

No answer.

She waited a moment before pushing it open. To her surprise, instead of Torald, Ida John knelt in front of his desk, one of the bottom drawers pulled all the way out.

"I will assume because of your young age that senility has not yet set in and you know where you are." Cordelia walked further into the room and tossed a script on top of the desk.

Ida looked only slightly stricken at being caught.

"What are you doing here?"

"I'm waiting," she replied, smoothing back her sleek brown hair.

Cordelia put her hand on her hip. "For a bus? For Godot? Can you be a little more specific?"

"I'm waiting to talk to Torald."

"You think perhaps he's going to emerge from the desk drawer?"

Ida got up. "I was looking for a cigarette."

"Sure, sweety."

"I was. You can believe it or not. It's no skin off my nose." She sat down behind Torald's dressing table and picked up an eyebrow pencil.

Cordelia wasn't convinced. Mostly she was annoyed that anyone would feel so unabashedly comfortable invading another colleague's space. No, to be honest, that wasn't it at all. Actors invaded each other's space all the time. More to the point, she was annoyed with Ida *in general*. Recently, Ida had begun to grow increasingly aloof. At the same time, her concentration was beginning to suffer. She was starting to caricature her part in the play. It was always the easy option, but not one Cordelia would ever allow an actor to take. One had to look for the truth behind the part, no matter how extravagantly drawn that character might be. Theatre was always attempting to walk a fine line between the desire to be real at the risk of losing clarity, and the effect of being beautifully shaped but disappointingly superficial. As a director, Cordelia knew she was forever searching for that one perfect form that would create absolute balance. When she saw an actor caving in to the easiest route to solve a problem, she became incensed. They *had* to take their hopelessly narcissistic little eyes off themselves and *focus*. This is what Ida John seemed unable to do.

"Time to get upstairs," said Cordelia. "Torald's probably already up there."

Ida didn't move.

"I need to make a phone call," said Cordelia, bristling. "I don't have time to go all the way back up to my office." She shoved the drawer closed with her knee and sat down behind the desk. "If you don't mind, I'd like a little privacy."

"Of course." Ida's tone was cool. "I'll just talk to Torald later." She picked up her purse and left the room.

Nervy, thought Cordelia. Not that she had anything against nervy people. She grabbed the phone and dialed Jane's number. "Here's the scoop," she said when Jane answered. "I'm just heading upstairs for the meeting. It shouldn't take more than an hour. Then, I thought, since you want to speak with Torald, why don't you drive over. When you're done, if Torald hasn't called in the authorities to have you arrested for libel, I thought you and Beryl and I might go out for dinner. What do you say?"

Jane quickly agreed. "Where will I meet you?"

"Come up to my office when you're done. I have some paperwork I need to do, so I'll wait until I hear the pitter patter of little feet." She wished Jane a safe drive and hung up. On the desk next to the phone, she noticed a piece of paper with the time "five-fifteen" circled in red ink. That was interesting. Jane just might have to wait in line for an appointment. She got up and switched off the lights before leaving the room.

Jane arrived at the theatre shortly after five-thirty. There had been an accident on I-94 that had put her a good half hour late. Since she knew the stage manager was apt to be long-winded, she assumed everyone might still be assembled in the main theatre. Besides, she'd called and left a message on the answering machine in Torald's dressing room before she'd left. She was pretty sure what she'd said would pique his interest. She doubted he would take off before she got there.

Jane parked her car next to a red Triumph in the rear lot and entered through the back door, pressing the correct numbers into a small security box to the left of the entrance. She took the elevator to the first floor and stepped out into the main lobby.

The Allen Grimby, built in 1919, was a huge rectangular edifice with a neon marquee spanning the entire front of the building. Inside was a strikingly lovely Byzantine interior. A relic of earlier times, it still embodied the glamorous aura of Hollywood in the twenties. Two Italian crystal chandeliers were suspended from a coffered ceiling in the foyer. Between statuary set into niches along the walls, original oil paintings depicted scenes from Minnesota's history. The building was a landmark, part of the historic register. Jane had always been fascinated by the roped columns and Moorish arches. She had seen several musicals here as a teenager.

As she walked across the deep, wine-colored carpet, she waved at Bliss Curry, the woman who played the mother in Antonia's new play. Bliss was talking softly to another actress who Jane recognized as the grandmother in the production. Both were wearing their coats and standing near the ticket counter.

Leaving them to their private conversation, Jane thought she'd check out the main stage area first. If Torald wasn't there, she could take the elevator down to the dressing rooms in the basement. She paused for a moment in front of a life-sized stand-up poster of a woman in a business suit, one hand holding a ten-pound sack of potatoes, the other an ax. It advertised a new play being produced by the Allen Grimby, coming this summer. Jane studied the picture briefly, taking out her wire-rimmed glasses so that she could get a better look at the fine print. As she bent down to read something near the bottom, she heard a strange thud come from inside the theatre. Glancing over her shoulder, she saw that Bliss and her friend were gone.

Jane listened for a moment. Except for the faint hum of

the outside traffic, the lobby was quiet. All the doors lead-ing into the main stage area were closed. She moved slowly to one of the side entrances and walked into the dark, silent auditorium. The stage was lit with a single, yellow spot-light. The largest wooden bride doll—at least seven feet high and holding a long-tined metal fork—stood with its back to her. As Jane's eyes moved over the scene, taking in the fifteen hundred seats, the ornate underside of the bal-cony and the three immense chandeliers, a slight flutter near the front caught her attention. She took a few steps further into the hushed theatre, her eyes searching the stage for the source of the movement.

"Hello?" she called.

No answer.

As she neared the wrought-iron railing in front of the or-chestra pit, she thought she heard something. Was it her imagination? The stage was empty, yet a slight rasping sound was coming from somewhere. She made her way up the side steps and approached the back of the doll. It was amazing to see the detail on the bridal gown up so close. Tiny pearls had been sewn onto the back of the bodice. She reached out her hand to touch the silken folds around the bustle. As she did so, the wooden figure seemed to twitch. Instantly, Jane pulled her hand away. Almost at the same moment she realized that it was the *bride doll* that was making the rasping sound! Summoning all her courage, she took a step to the side.

An arm fell limply in her path.

Jane froze. She felt a scream well up inside her until it broke the fragile silence.

As if in a dream, she moved around to the front. Torald's body lay motionless, impaled backward on the five foot metal dinner fork held firmly in the bride doll's hands. From the position of his body, he looked as if he might have fallen off the bleachers just above where the doll stood.

Jane felt disoriented. She closed her eyes and tried to get her bearings. She knew she had to see if he was still alive, yet the entire scene repelled her to her very core. The tines of the fork had gone straight through the center of his body. One tine looked very close to his heart. Blood was leaking from the side of his mouth. His eyes were open unnaturally wide yet he was not looking at her. Before she touched him, she knew. The rasping had stopped.

Torald was dead.

Carefully, she felt for a pulse. Nothing.

Out of the corner of her eye Jane thought she saw another movement. This time it was behind the thin, gauzy curtains. She watched for a moment but everything was still. She could make out the form of six dolls, all different sizes and costumes.

Glancing back at Torald, Jane began to shout for help. She knew it would be easier to simply go find a phone herself and call the police, but her legs felt rooted to the stage floor. Her mind was swimming in a kind of confused reverie. The single spotlight that illuminated the stage gave the unavoidable impression that Torald's death was a scene from a play. He was merely waiting for the curtain to fall, for the thunderous applause to fill his ears. Wasn't it every stage actor's finest moment? The death scene.

"What's wrong?" called a female voice from the back doors.

Jane turned. "There's been an accident." The instant she said the words, she wondered if they were true. "I think Torald is dead! Call the police. Call 911 right away!"

Immediately, the woman left. Jane didn't remember ever seeing her before. She doubted any of the regular staff would be around today. As she returned her eyes to the stage, she knew something wasn't right. A cold shiver ran through her body as she looked again at the dolls behind the curtain.

This time there were only five.

She reached a hand to steady her body against the edge of the bleachers, giving herself a moment to think. Five bride dolls. And the one Torald was . . . That made six. There couldn't have been six behind the curtain before. She must have miscounted.

Keeping her back to Torald's lifeless body, she glanced

around the empty stage. Such absolute quiet in the very same theatre that had been so packed with people just last night. It gave her an eerie feeling. As she continued to look around, something on the floor next to her boot caught her eye. She leaned down to get a better look. Attached to a thin gold chain was the image of a tiny cat sitting on top of a six-pointed star. It appeared to be carved from a single piece of mother-of-pearl. Jane had never seen anything quite like it before.

"In here," said a voice Jane recognized at once. It was Cordelia's. She led four men down the center aisle. Two of them were policemen. The other two were probably paramedics.

Jane stood by watching as Torald's body was hastily examined. The conclusion they reached seemed to be the same as hers.

"Don't touch anything," ordered the sergeant. He turned abruptly and ran back to the front of the building.

"Did you find the body?" asked the patrolman. He walked over to Jane.

She nodded.

"You haven't moved anything, have you?"

"I tried to get a pulse. That's all."

The policeman glanced around. "When did you find him?"

"Just a few minutes ago. I was out in the lobby and I heard this thud."

He turned to look at the body. *"Jesus."*

Cordelia inched over to where Jane was standing and whispered, "Did you get a chance to talk to him?" Her eyes darted furtively to Torald.

Jane shook her head.

Erin Brewster appeared at the edge of the stage. "What's going on?" She held her car keys. "I thought I saw a police car." She stopped as her eyes took in the sight. "My God," she cried, her hand flying to her mouth.

"And who are you?" asked the officer.

Erin seemed unable to speak.

"Her name is Erin Brewster," said Cordelia. "She's married to . . . the deceased's . . . nephew."

In the back of the theatre, Jane could see three people being herded down the center aisle by the sergeant. Ida John and Billy Brewster appeared to be arguing. The other person was the woman Jane had sent to call 911.

"We're going to have to ask you to stay for a few minutes," said the sergeant. "Someone will be here shortly to ask you all some questions. It shouldn't take long."

Jane sat down on the bleachers. Cordelia sat down next to her, putting her arm around her shoulder. It was only then that Jane realized how badly she was shaking.

13

"Oh, great," said Cordelia out of the side of her mouth. "It's Inspector Clouseau."

A tall, burly man in a dark wool topcoat entered through the back doors of the theatre and made his way slowly to the front. A police photographer had already come and gone, taking pictures of the death scene from every conceivable angle. The body itself had been examined in great detail by a woman from the Ramsey County Medical Examiner's office. Shortly after she'd finished, both the body and the large wooden doll had been removed to a waiting van.

"Ms. Lawless," said Detective Trevelyan, giving her a suitably glacial look. "What a surprise to find you here." He leaned against the wrought-iron railing in front of the orchestra pit and glanced up at the stage.

"A little out of your jurisdiction, aren't you?" asked Cordelia, pleasantly.

Trevelyan turned around and smiled at her. "Ah, and Ms. Thorn. This must be my lucky day. Actually, you're right. But there's a good reason I'm here this afternoon. You see, it appears we have an eyewitness to the burglary of Ms. Lawless's garage on Friday night." He turned to Jane. "One of your neighbors, a Mr. Arnold Dimitch. It seems your aunt was out in your backyard this afternoon and introduced herself to Mr. Dimitch's wife. During their conversation, she mentioned something about the garage break-in. Mrs. Dimitch repeated the story to her husband, and he, in turn, called us. He'd been out walking the dog late that night. He's also an avid theatre-goer so he immediately recognized Torald Werness running down the alley carrying a small snowblower. He said he thought it was strange, but didn't think anything more of the incident until his wife said your garage had been burgled." He motioned for one of the policemen still on stage to come down. "Sergeant, will you escort these people out into the lobby. I'll want to talk to each of them briefly. I'll start with Ms. Lawless here."

"Good luck," whispered Cordelia, giving Jane's hand a squeeze. "And be careful. The good detective looks to me like he's in an unusually rotten mood. Don't let him take it out on you."

"Ms. Thorn? If you'll be kind enough to accompany the sergeant?" Trevelyan glared at her. As he watched her scuttle to catch up, he slipped a stick of gum out of its wrapper and folded it into his mouth. After everyone was gone he drew out a small notebook and settled himself several seats away. "I was told you found the body at approximately five-forty P.M. Is that correct?"

"That's right. I was out in the lobby when I heard this strange thud. I went in and found him—" The end of the sentence was quickly abandoned.

"Did anyone else hear this thud, Ms. Lawless?"

Jane shook her head. "I don't think so. Two of the other actresses were standing by the ticket counter when I arrived, but they left before anything happened."

"Did you see anyone in the theatre when you came in?"

Jane thought of the image behind the curtain. "I'm not sure. This may sound kind of odd, but when I first looked around I thought I counted six bride dolls behind the curtain. A few minutes later there were only five. I suppose I could have miscounted."

Trevelyan stopped chewing his gum. "Yes. That's possible."

"The thing is, I'm almost certain there was a figure on the far right." She pointed.

"What did it look like?"

Jane shook her head. "I don't remember. All the bride dolls are different—represent different things. I've only seen the play once so I don't know them all that well. Most of the time they stay behind that curtain. They're all life-size—except for the one with the fork. It's bigger than life."

Trevelyan wrote quickly in his notes. "Why were you here tonight, Ms. Lawless?" In the silence of the dark theatre, his voice sounded angry.

"I'd come to talk to Torald. The truth is, I'd been given some information that led me to believe he might have been the person who attacked me in my garage the other night. I thought we should talk."

"What information?" Trevelyan watched her very closely.

"Well, Billy Brewster—he's Torald's nephew—said he felt his uncle might have been in the garage looking through some of his papers. He said they were all messed up."

"Did Mr. Brewster say *why* Mr. Werness would be interested in his things?"

Jane sighed. "It's kind of a long story."

"Indulge me."

"Well, you see, Billy was adopted as a baby. A few months ago, he found out his biological mother was Antonia Werness, Torald's sister. Billy thought Torald might have noticed a family resemblance and wanted to check it out. Perhaps he thought he might find proof, one way or the other."

"And did he?"

Jane shook her head. "I don't know."

Again, Trevelyan bent over his notebook.

"Do you think Torald's death was an accident?"

Trevelyan continued to write. "Do you?"

She glanced up at the stage. "I'm not sure. I suppose he could have accidentally fallen off the bleachers."

"Possibly. But unlikely."

Jane watched him write. "You think it was murder then?"

"At this point, Ms. Lawless, I don't officially think anything."

"Unofficially then?"

"Let's not kid each other. We both know what it was."

What on earth did he mean by that?

At Jane's startled look he added, "We've already searched the building. Only six people were here when the death occurred. You, Ms. Thorn, Mr. Brewster and his wife, a Ms. Ida John, and then the young woman who called the police. I believe her name is . . ." He checked his notes. "Gloria Lindy."

"Someone could have been in the theatre and slipped out before the police arrived."

"True, but it wouldn't have been an easy proposition. The security here is tight. Nevertheless, we'll be checking everything over thoroughly."

Jane had been wondering who this Gloria Lindy was. While waiting for the police, she'd seen her sitting alone on the other side of the aisle. She hadn't spoken to anyone. "I'm curious, Detective Trevelyan. Do you know anything about this Gloria Lindy? I'm familiar with a lot of the people who work here. I've never seen her before."

Trevelyan cracked his knuckles. "From what I've been told, she'd come to drop off some papers from Gaylord Werness."

"Really. Papers?"

"That's all I know."

In other words, thought Jane, back off. "Do you think Torald's death had anything to do with the burglary of my garage?"

"I don't know. But it's something we're going to look at. The fact that you found the body . . ." He let his voice trail off ominously.

"What are you saying? You can't possibly think I had anything to do with this!" She sat up very straight in her chair.

"That's something else I don't know, Ms. Lawless. But once again it seems you're mixed up in a murder investigation. Why do you suppose that is?"

Under her breath Jane whispered, "Rotten karma."

"What?"

"Is that all?" she asked.

"No. It's not. I have one last question. When you arrived at the theatre, where did you first go?"

"I took the elevator directly to the lobby."

"You didn't stop by Torald's dressing room first?"

She shook her head.

"You haven't been down there at any time since you arrived?"

"No. Why?"

He ignored the question and continued to write. After a moment, he looked up. "Before you go, I want to finish what I was about to say to you on the phone the other day. Don't get involved in this any more than you already are. You're not qualified to help us. I should think that experience at the sorority several years ago would have taught you a lesson."

His demeanor was calculated to make her feel like a naughty child. It was an approach she despised. "Are we finished?"

"Yes. For now. On your way out my sergeant will take an official statement from you. We'll need you to come down to the station to sign it later. Please ask Mr. Brewster to come in next. And Ms. Lawless?" He snapped his gum. "Have a pleasant evening."

PART TWO

A Child of Spleen

Create her child of spleen, that it may live
And be a thwart disnatured torment to her.

King Lear
William Shakespeare

14

"But, why didn't you tell me?" demanded Fleur, following Antonia down the wide central stairs of their house. Both women were dressed in black; Fleur in a long wool dress, Antonia in a silk pants suit. "How could you keep something like that from *me*?"

Antonia adjusted a vase of carnations on the table near the arch into the hallway. "It's nearly four, Fleur. We've been talking about this long enough. I need some time to calm down before people start arriving for the reviewal." She glanced into the quiet parlor. Torald's body was laid out in a casket just under the front windows, two magnificent pink gladiola arrangements—his favorites—standing guard on either side. Several dozen thick white tapers were scattered about the room, creating a soft, faintly reverent light. Torald would have approved. The drama of the setting would not have been lost on him. "If you don't understand, I'm truly sorry. I did the best I could. I don't have all the answers. I'm not God."

"But it's . . . it's . . ."

"I know," said Antonia, taking her in her arms. "Believe me, I know."

"What are you going to do?"

"I'm not sure. But something isn't right."

"You don't believe him?"

She lowered her head. "My gut tells me he's telling the truth."

"But your head?"

She frowned. "Let's just drop it for now, okay?"

"He could be an imposter, you know. He has a great deal to gain, especially if your father . . ."

Antonia cut her off with a withering stare.

"But, if they were adopted together, why didn't he mention his sister?"

She shook her head. "You keep asking me the same wretched questions over and over! I don't *know*, Fleur. I didn't bring it up the other night. He and Erin are coming for dinner tomorrow after the funeral. We can give him the third degree then."

Fleur sank into a comfortably lumpy chair by the front door. "I'm not sure that's the best way to handle this." She removed a carnation from a vase on the table next to her and sniffed it thoughtfully. "Where's Lucy?"

"She's upstairs. Dressing. To be honest, I'm not even sure she's planning to come down. This has all hit her pretty hard."

"Is Malcolm still here?"

Antonia nodded. "He spent the night. He's going to conduct the funeral service tomorrow."

"Having a minister in the family—well, almost in the family—does have its points. Why doesn't she just marry the poor guy and put him out of his misery."

Antonia looked away.

"I'm sorry. I didn't mean . . ." Fleur touched the back of her tightly curled, black hair, trying to regain her composure. "What we really need is a good lawyer."

"No!" roared Antonia. "No more! You have to let me handle this. I won't have you going behind my back."

Helplessly, Fleur shook her head. "All right, but something should have been done a long time ago."

"Don't second guess me on this, Fleur. I know what I'm doing."

The front bell sounded.

Antonia glanced at her watch. "This is too early for people to begin arriving."

"Perhaps it's Maureen and Erling." Fleur got up and opened the door. "My God," she said, her shock registering in a sudden intake of breath. "Gaylord." Her voice had risen a full octave.

Antonia moved directly behind her. Silently, she stared at her father. The last time she'd seen him was a little more than five years ago. She knew his health hadn't been good. Yet, how very strange that in such a short time he could have become an old man.

"You don't need to talk to me," he said softly. He was carrying a large spray of wild flowers, a cane over one arm. "I just want to see my son. I thought I'd come early. That way, you won't have to explain my absence."

His heavily lined face was deep in shadow. Antonia wondered if he'd been crying. It was hard to tell.

With an almost ecclesiastical air, he passed them, cane in hand, and walked uncertainly into the parlor. He seemed even more hesitant as he approached the casket and laid the flowers over the top. Antonia watched from the edge of the archway. An old man, she kept thinking to herself. She had never thought of her father that way. Mortal. Dying?

He leaned down and kissed Torald on the forehead. As he straightened up, he took a quick look at the room and then turned around.

Antonia held his eyes, a flush climbing her cheeks. Upstairs she could hear the sound of Gershwin coming from the stereo in Lucy's bedroom. *Rhapsody in Blue.* It was as if she were suspended in time, eighteen years old and ready once again to defy this man's wishes for as long as it took. It was all her fault, and she knew it. She'd always been too selfish. Too much like him.

"Nothing has changed, has it?" said Gaylord. It was less a question than a statement of fact.

She shook her head.

He crossed to where she was standing. "I loved him." He said the words with great vehemence.

"You should have told *him* that."

Gaylord touched his beard and glanced upstairs. "He called me, you know. On Sunday. Said we had to talk. We made a date for after his meeting at the theatre. Even though he made it sound like nothing out of the ordinary, I knew better."

Antonia gave him a blank look.

"I'm going to demand that the police get to the bottom of his death—no matter *where* it leads."

"Good."

He hesitated for a moment and then said, "He was my only son, goddammit!"

"I'm not going to listen to this. Do your mourning—if that's what this parade is meant to suggest—some place else."

His face grew stoney. "You're hard. What they say about you is true."

Antonia stood up very straight. "And what do they say about me?"

Gaylord looked momentarily at Fleur. "That you keep Lucy a prisoner in this house."

Antonia tightened her grip on Fleur's arm. "Get out."

Gaylord began to walk toward the door. As he opened it, he wiped a shaky hand across his mouth. "I'll be seventy next Sunday. There's going to be a gathering." His voice was low, almost a whisper. "I thought perhaps you and Lucy—"

Antonia's mouth tightened.

"Billy and Erin will be there," he added quickly.

God, he'd already found out about Billy. She could feel the triumph in his voice. That must be what all this was really about. "Lucy and I won't be."

"No," he mumbled. "Good night then."

15

"What have you got there?" asked Jane. She leaned against the chopping-block table in her kitchen, sipping a cup of coffee and watching Billy carry an armful of bricks into the back porch.

"They're Beryl's," he said, kneeling down and stacking them neatly under the window.

"What? You mean she really *did* have bricks in that trunk?" Jane couldn't believe her eyes. Poor Cordelia. She'd been right all along.

"I told the truth," said Beryl, following him into the room. "Can I help it if no one took me seriously?"

"But why on earth?"

"For my raku kiln," she said, palms held up in total innocence. "I thought it would be good luck to bring some from my kiln at home. You know? A cosmic link. That sort of thing."

"A cosmic link," repeated Jane.

Billy stood, slapping brick dust off his jeans. His chambray shirt was unbuttoned in the front. As he threw his arms back carelessly and stretched, Jane noticed a small piece of jewelry dangling from a tiny gold chain around his neck. She stepped closer. "Interesting," she said, adjusting her glasses to get a better look. "A cat sitting on a six-pointed star. What's it carved from?"

"Ebony. My parents kept it for me until I turned twenty-one. Antonia apparently gave it to me when I was a baby, before I was adopted. Since the day I received it, I've never taken it off." He touched it with the tips of his fingers.

"It's certainly unusual," said Jane. "I doubt there are many others like it."

"Nope," he grinned. "One of a kind."

Except that Jane knew she'd seen an exact duplicate three nights ago, the same night Torald died. She remembered finding it on the floor of the stage near the bleachers. The only difference was that, instead of ebony, that one had been carved from mother-of-pearl.

She forced a smile.

"We better get changed if we're going to make it to poor Torald's reviewal," said Beryl, brushing a smudge off Billy's shirt.

"Yeah," he said, his cheerfulness fading. "Erin should be back any minute." At their questioning looks he added, "She wanted to pick up some flowers."

"Of course," said Beryl. "We had some delivered."

Just what the Werness house needed, thought Jane. More carnations.

Cordelia stood under the harsh fluorescent lights just outside the emergency room of Hennepin County General and fed a quarter into the pay phone. She waited, examining with growing horror the sallow color of her hand, until the phone began to ring on the other end.

"Hello?"

"Janey. Thank goodness I caught you."

"Where are you?"

"The emergency room."

"A hospital? Are you all right?"

Cordelia could hear the surprise and concern. "I think so. My skin looks a little strange. I suppose one could be philosophical about it. I doubt I'd need much makeup to star in a horror flick."

Silence. "You're at the emergency room because your skin looks strange?"

"No, *no*. It's these lights. Boris Karloff would have loved them."

"What lights? What are we talking about?"

"If you'll just *listen*." She gave an exasperated snort.

"I'm here because of Celeste's mother. It's her gall bladder."

"Celeste's mother's gall bladder."

"Exactly." She paused to push up the sleeve of her sweater. Even the skin on her arm looked faintly jaundiced. Perhaps she should have a blood test.

Nah.

"And dearheart, you know Celeste. Laura, her new lover, is out of town right now, and Celeste has never been very good at handling emergencies. She called me and told me I simply *had* to come down. They're going to operate."

"On Celeste's mother's gall bladder."

"The very one." She chewed off the tip of a fingernail. "Anyway, I won't be able to make it to the reviewal."

"Okay, I understand. I'll pass along your regrets."

"Actually, if it hadn't been for this, I might not have gone anyway. My back is killing me."

"Poor baby. Any particular reason?"

"Yes, since you're kind enough to ask. I spent the morning trying to figure out what to salvage from the mess in Torald's dressing room."

Jane hesitated. "What mess?"

"Didn't Trevelyan tell you? Someone trashed it. I mean trashed it good and proper!"

"Why?"

"Your guess is as good as mine. It must have happened either shortly before or shortly after he died. All his framed posters—the ones of him in his father's plays— were ripped to shreds. The entire room was torn apart." Cordelia noticed Celeste waving to her from a doorway further down the hall. "Uh oh, I gotta go. Celeste is having a spasm of some sort."

"Give her my best."

"Will do. I'll call you later." As she hung up, she took one last look at her horrifying skin.

Vitamins! That's what she needed. She'd buy a bottle of children's chewables as soon as she got to a drugstore.

* * *

Less than an hour later, Jane pulled her aging green Saab up in front of 1811 Irving. It was just after sunset. In the gentle evening light, the Werness house looked somewhat less neglected, the barren vines along the steep gables not quite so twisted and dark. She waited as her aunt unwedged herself from the car seat. Glancing around, she noticed the same red Triumph she'd seen the other night at the theatre. This time, it was the first car parked in the drive. She made a mental note to find out who owned it.

"A lot of people are already here," whispered Beryl as they walked up the cobbled front walk. Piles of dirty snow sat melting against the north end of the yard. The frozen ground was already beginning to thaw, giving off the un-mistakable smell of raw earth.

As they moved into the front foyer, Jane noticed Billy and Erin standing next to Antonia in the main parlor. The open coffin rested on a stand behind them. Candles burned brightly in every corner.

"Erin looks so tired," said Beryl, taking off her coat and handing it to an older man who seemed to be in charge of coat detail. Jane did the same. "I'd better get in there. She looks like she could use the support."

"I'll be in in a minute," said Jane. "I want to get some cider." She'd noticed a small scene taking place just outside the library. Ida John had come out of the room and nearly bumped into Maureen Werness.

"Excuse me," said Ida, drawing away from Torald's widow as if she were made of hot coals.

Maureen simply glared.

"I . . . I'm sorry about Torald."

"Stuff it." Maureen glanced around to see who might be watching. Moving closer to Ida she whispered, *"Get out of here."* Her eyes were almost wild. "I won't have you in this house!"

"Maureen," called Antonia from the doorway. "Could you come into the parlor for a minute? There's someone I'd like you to meet."

Holding Ida's eyes a moment longer, Maureen turned on her heel and left.

Interesting, thought Jane. She wondered what it all meant. Having heard a little about Torald's reputation with women, Jane felt she could make an educated guess.

Seeing Jane standing next to the cider table, Ida sauntered over, the expression on her face suggesting she damn well wasn't going to let the likes of Maureen Werness chase her off.

"I'm sorry you had to see that," she said, taking a sip of cider. "It's not what you think."

"And what do I think?" asked Jane.

Ida smiled. "You can cut the crap. People like you love to spy on other people at parties. I doubt you miss a trick."

"I'd hardly call this a party."

Ida looked away. As an afterthought, she shrugged.

"By the way," continued Jane, "I don't suppose you own a red Triumph."

"Hardly. Why do you want to know?"

"Well, I guess you could say I'm in the market for a new car. I thought I'd ask whoever owns the one outside how they liked it."

Ida openly stared at Jane's clothes. She shook her head. "Since you obviously don't spend a dime on what you wear, maybe you do have the bucks for decent wheels. Ask Maureen. It's hers."

"Is that right?" Maureen. Jane hadn't seen her at the theatre that night. But if her car was parked outside, that meant she must have been inside. Somewhere. And for some reason. She'd probably slipped out before the police arrived.

Searching the crowd for a new conversational target, Ida set her empty glass of cider down on the table and mumbled, "See you around." Then, her eyes finding a suitable subject, she walked off in the direction of the parlor.

Half an hour later, Jane found herself still standing in the same spot in the foyer. She knew she'd have to eventually go into the sanctum and pay her last respects, but she hadn't quite gotten up the nerve. She wondered idly how Celeste's mother's gall bladder was doing.

Glancing into the parlor, she could see Antonia standing

next to the casket, a balding man with round, rimless glasses and a very full mustache standing next to her. Jane remembered meeting him once, several years ago. His name was Malcolm Coopersmith, and he was, if she remembered correctly, a Unitarian minister. She was pretty sure Malcolm and Lucy Werness were a couple, but tonight, in Lucy's all-too-apparent absence, Malcolm seemed particularly, even overly, attentive to Antonia.

As Jane took a deep breath and was about to head into the room, a tall, barrel-chested man burst through the front door carrying a suitcase, his eyes searching the candle-lit interior until he found his target.

"Antonia!" he called, his rich, booming voice cutting through the respectful, hushed quiet like a bullhorn. He rushed to her and held her fast in his arms. "I'm so *sorry*." His turbulent silver hair was as thick and uncombed as a lion's mane.

Jane could see that he was expensively dressed, yet there was a kind of defiant untidiness about him. His face was square and solid, the nose more of a snout. But, no mistaking it, his presence was electric. Like Antonia, he was the kind of person who commanded attention as soon as he entered a room.

"Victor," she said, pulling away from his embrace and holding him at arm's length. "I didn't think you were coming until the end of the week."

"After our talk last night, how could I wait?" Gently, he touched her face. "Ah," he said, turning to the coffin. "Poor brother Torald." He glanced at the macabre scene for only a moment before refocusing his entire attention on Antonia. With a barely concealed thrill in his voice he asked, "And Billy? Where is Billy!"

Malcolm moved closer to Antonia's side and held out his hand. "Malcolm Coopersmith," he said softly. "I'm a friend of the family."

Victor's face froze. For a bizarre instant, Jane thought he was going to strike the middle-aged minister. Then, regaining his composure, he shook the proffered hand. With an impatient snap of his head, he waited for a response to his question.

Antonia, realizing everyone in the crowded room was watching, backed up a step and held out her hand to Billy. "Son," she said very slowly, "I'd like you to meet a dear old friend—"

Instantly, Victor's eyes lit up. "My God," he said, his voice dropping to its lowest register. "You're a wonder!" He grabbed Billy's hand and pumped it heartily.

Jane could almost feel the younger man's discomfort.

"You are?" asked Billy, glancing at Antonia for some explanation.

"This is Victor Pavic. He's . . ."

Billy's eyes grew wide. "I know who he is," he said, cutting her off. His face was full of astonishment. "You're a producer. Broadway."

Victor beamed. "I'd originally planned to arrive at the end of the week. I wanted to see Antonia's new play. If it's what I think it is, we have to get it to New York right away! But then when I heard about—"

"Torald," said Antonia, quickly finishing his sentence.

Jane was pretty sure that wasn't the name he was going to use.

"Yes," he said sadly. "Exactly. I had to come right away."

Fleur moved quietly out of the corner and walked over and stood next to Antonia. "Pavic," she said, her voice impassive, "Good to see you again."

"Fleur," he grinned, lifting her hand to his lips.

"Still trying to annoy me after all these years."

Jane could see the affection in her eyes. They must have known each other a long time.

"Some things never change." She squeezed his hand.

"I wonder?" he said, looking down at her.

She gave a small shake of her head. It was enough to silence him.

"How do you know my mother?" asked Billy.

Victor turned around. The room was now completely silent. "Well, we first met in college. At Columbia. We were both poor and terribly enamored of the theatre. I think we must have seen literally hundreds of plays together. It was one of the richest and most memorable times of my life." His eyes glowed as he looked at the young man standing before him. "Youth is magic, Billy. Remember that."

"Enough of this," said Antonia, taking his arm. "We'll have time to talk later. Victor, you're exhausted. Fleur and I will show you to your room. You'll want to get settled."

It was all too apparent Antonia didn't want an audience for this little scene. Jane moved out of their way as they passed slowly through the crowd and up the stairs. After they were gone and conversations had been resumed, she couldn't help but wonder what she'd just witnessed. All the interactions had seemed so suffused with intensity, and yet, she felt everything had been said in a kind of shorthand. Thinking of the funeral tomorrow afternoon at Pinewood cemetery, she made a decision. She knew she had to talk to someone who'd known the family for years. There was an important question she needed to ask. For some reason, her eyes kept coming back to Malcolm Coopersmith. Yes, he was the best choice. It might lead nowhere, but she had to at least make a stab at finding out the truth. Wincing at her choice of metaphors, Jane squared her shoulders and walked resolutely into the parlor. It was time to pay her last respects to a man who had, just a few nights ago, given her the worst headache of her life.

16

"I'm ready," shouted Gaylord. He pulled up the sleeve of his red flannel shirt and rested his arm on the table next to him.

Gloria Lindy stepped out of the kitchen tapping an air bubble out of a small syringe. "A beautiful morning," she smiled, holding the needle up to the light of the window. She squeezed a little liquid out of the tip.

"I'm feeling *so* much better since you've been giving me these vitamin shots." He closed his eyes and turned his head away as she carefully eased the needle into a muscle. In a moment it was over.

"What you need more than vitamins," said Gloria, her tone taking on a motherly quality, "is to stop smoking so much—and *drinking*. Your blood pressure is way too high. And you've got to start remembering to take your blood pressure medication."

Gaylord lifted his arm off the table and examined the small mark the needle had made. "It makes me tired all the time, dammit. And my mouth gets dry. Who knows how long I've got left? I'm going to spend the rest of my days feeling like a piece of dead meat."

Gloria stood over him, a plump squirrel of a young woman. With a receding chin and a thick pair of glasses that magnified her eyes unpleasantly, she'd always known she wasn't one of the beautiful people. No loss, as far as she was concerned. Gloria was a pragmatist. And, more to the point, she was smart. Brushing a strand of newly dyed red hair away from her eyes, she smiled at Gaylord and said, "Are you going to the funeral today? I'd be happy to drive you."

He reached for her hand. "Do you know how indispensable you've made yourself to me in the last month? I never thought when I asked that secretarial agency to send someone over—well, let's just say you're several cuts above their usual employee."

"Thank you, Mr. Werness."

"Someone asked me the other day who you were. I told them you were my 'gal Friday.' He cocked his head. "Does that term upset you?"

"No. Should it?"

He laughed. "All these women's libbers today. If you ask me, they're ruining the English language. As far as I'm concerned, 'gal Friday' is a perfectly good title. Push that thing over here." He lifted his legs as Gloria slid a softly padded footstool underneath.

"What about the funeral?" she asked, dropping the syringe in a wastebasket on the other side of his chair.

"No. There's no point in going. I paid Torald my last visit yesterday evening. By the way, I wanted to tell you again how sorry I was that I picked that evening to send you over to the theatre with my proposal—the night he was . . . the night he died." He cleared his throat.

Gloria walked over to his desk and straightened a pile of papers on the top. "If you don't mind my saying so, Mr. Werness, you don't seem like you're on very good terms with your daughters. That's too bad."

Gaylord stroked his beard. "Yes, Gloria, I agree with you. The family isn't close anymore. The worst thing is, I really don't understand how it happened or what I can do to change it. I invited Antonia and Lucy to my birthday party next weekend."

"Are they coming?"

He shook his head, closing his eyes and leaning his head back.

Gloria knew it meant he was in the mood to talk. It was fine with her. The more she learned about him, the more power she would eventually have. She sat down behind his desk and waited.

"You know," he continued, "I'm really worried about my younger daughter, Lucy."

"Why? Is she in some kind of trouble?"

He sighed. "To be honest, she's been in trouble of one kind or another all her life. As a teenager, she was a wild one. Bad grades. Even stole a car once. But nothing was as awful as the drugs. I did everything I could to show her I loved her. Well, I mean, I got pretty upset at what was happening, but who wouldn't? I've never been one to hide what I thought. She knew I didn't approve of the way she was living her life. Still, no matter what she did, I was there. My family is terribly important to me, Gloria. Always has been. I thought my children felt the same way.

But as soon as Lucy turned sixteen, she left. I suppose they all felt I'd driven her away. She couldn't stand my . . . opinions, so to speak. My inflexibility. I suppose, in retrospect, I could have been a bit more tactful." He scratched his ear. "But right is right, Gloria. And wrong is wrong. Anyway, she went to live with her sister Antonia down in New Orleans. After that, I never saw her much. It's almost . . ."

"Go on," said Gloria, prompting him. She knew he liked that.

"Well, it was as if Antonia wanted to turn her against me. That Antonia," he grumbled. "I know for a fact that she's always been jealous of my professional accomplishments. She may be a decent playwright, but she'll never achieve the success I have. I'm not trying to blow my own horn, Gloria, it's just a simple statement of fact. I don't know. Maybe she wanted to control Lucy. Still does. I never really felt that my eldest daughter was part of the family. Not in the same way Lucy and Torald were. After my wife was institutionalized . . ."

"I didn't know that," said Gloria. "I'm sorry."

He held up his hand. "It's so long ago now, it doesn't hurt the way it used to. She was a loving woman, and very beautiful. But she wasn't strong. I knew when I married her that she had emotional problems. It got to the point where she couldn't even leave the house, not even when I was with her. The doctors thought they could help, but after several years I could see I was going to spend the rest of my days alone. I've never wanted to remarry. She was the one true love of my life." He continued to stroke his beard thoughtfully. "The thing is, after she was institutionalized, I thought I could count on Antonia to help me with Torald and Lucy. She was the eldest but, unfortunately, also the most willful."

There was a soft knock on the front door. Gloria got up and crossed quickly into the living room. "Must be your breakfast," she said over her shoulder. For the last six years, Gaylord Werness had lived in a suite on the twenty-third floor of the Maxfield Plaza. Gloria couldn't imagine what he must be paying for the privilege of having his meals sent up from the hotel kitchen, morning, noon, and night. Yet from the opulence that surrounded him, she doubted his bank account felt much of a strain. "Good morning, Jerry," she said, taking the tray and setting it on a low table just inside the door. She pulled some cash out of her pocket and handed it to him.

"Bring it in here," called Gaylord. "I'll eat in the study."

"Do you want to sit at your desk?" she asked, returning to the room.

Stiffly, he got up, rubbing his lower back. "Why not. Didn't you want anything?"

"I had some coffee earlier," she said, helping him get settled.

He lifted up the metal cover over the plate. "Good. The hollandaise looks lovely. Why don't you stay while I eat? Keep my company."

"Of course." She curled herself into a leather chair on the other side of the desk. "You were saying about Antonia?"

He nodded as he sipped his prune juice. "Yes. I hadn't finished that, had I? Antonia had made plans to attend college out East. She'd been accepted at Columbia. After my wife left, I begged her to stay at home and attend the University of Minnesota, but she wouldn't hear of it. She defied me at every turn. Eventually, I just gave up. What else could I do?"

"But a little while ago you said you were really worried about Lucy. Why is that?"

He chewed his eggs Benedict hungrily. "Well, see, I've heard people say that Antonia almost keeps Lucy a prisoner in that house. It's terribly upsetting to a father to think one sibling is abusing another. I mean, what's she afraid of?"

"Perhaps that Lucy would come here to talk to you?"

He grunted. "My God, the worst thing I could do to her—I'm speaking from Antonia's standpoint now—is to convince her she should go to church." He stabbed a piece of melon.

Gloria looked at her watch. It was nearly ten. She hadn't yet made a decision whether she would attend the funeral or not. In the end, curiosity would probably get the better of her and she'd go. "Your son was an interesting man," she said, changing the subject. "We talked several times. I'm sorry about his death."

"When he was young," said Gaylord, wiping a bit of egg off his mouth, "he was a good boy. Smart. Thoughtful. A real go-getter. Oh, we had our run-ins, but that's to be expected. But in the past few years, I don't mind telling you he's gone to pot. That's hard for a father to say, but it's the truth."

"When he was here last week he mentioned something about you leaving all the rights to your plays to him."

"Did he now?" Gaylord glanced up at a wall of books. "All those volumes bound in red are my works. *Deadfall. War Front. A Message for Mary.* And my most famous play—written just as we were really getting involved in Vietnam—*Circus.* As you might guess, they're worth a great deal of money. The papers you dropped off at the Allen Grimby on Sunday night were a response to a proposal their board made me several months ago. They want to produce six of my plays in the next two years. People are doing retrospectives of my work all over the country. We're a violent nation. My plays will always be relevant. Whoever inherits the rights will be a rich man."

"Or woman." Gloria smiled.

Gaylord nodded. "Yes. Now, I wouldn't consider leaving them to my daughters. Why should I? Neither will even speak to me. And long ago I decided that Torald was not the man. No sir. Not by a long shot. That left Torald's son, Erling. Unfortunately, he's hopeless. No interest in the theatre whatsoever. Nevertheless, he was my only choice. That is, up until a few days ago."

"Really?" said Gloria. She watched him shovel the food into his mouth. Eggs and long beards simply did not mix. It was a disgusting sight.

"That's right. I found out I have another grandson. You may have heard of him. Billy Brewster?"

Gloria's eyes widened. "That actor? He's . . . your grandson?" She strained to recall his image. She was sure he'd been at the theatre the night Torald died. God, she had no idea. "That's amazing."

"I agree. Just between you and me, on my birthday next weekend, I'm going to announce that he's to be my heir." He almost giggled.

"What about Maureen?" asked Gloria.

"Oh, I've already talked to her. She understands that I want to go ahead with the party. I know it's a sad time for us all, but . . ."

"No, I mean, won't this come as quite a blow to her? I'm sure she's counting on Erling inheriting your plays now that Torald is gone."

"We don't always get everything we want in life, my dear. Maureen will simply have to cope. Besides, Torald left her well taken care of. I don't have to worry." He wiped his mouth, completely ignoring the congealed egg yolk that had dribbled down his white beard. He leaned back in his chair. "You know, Gloria, you've never told me very much about your family."

"Not much to tell," she said.

"Where are you from?"

"South Dakota. A little town called Lemon."

"Any brothers or sisters?"

"Nope, just me." She got up. "Mr. Werness, I've go to make some phone calls if I'm going to finalize the menu with that caterer for your party on Sunday."

"Of course." He lifted a book off a stack of papers. "It's nice we can talk. Get to know each other better. I always find other people's lives so interesting."

She smiled. "Me, too."

17

Several hours before the funeral was due to start, Jane found herself at Pinewood Cemetery, walking up the winding graveled path to the Werness family plot. Just before she'd left her restaurant, she'd called the Unitarian church in Minneapolis where Malcolm Coopersmith was a pastor. The woman who answered explained that he'd already left for the afternoon. He wanted to get over to the cemetery early to make sure everything was running smoothly. The memorial service was going to be held at the Prairie Gothic chapel at the edge of the lake. Jane hoped he would have a few moments to speak to her before the crowds began to arrive.

As she moved quickly up the deserted path, she pulled her navy blue peacoat more snugly around her body. Since early morning, a stiff March wind had been blowing. Occasionally, the sun would peek through the gloom only to be swallowed a moment later by the low, swiftly moving clouds.

Jane spied him standing about a hundred yards away, talking quietly to one of the grave workers. As she approached, she could see that he hadn't changed yet into his dress clothes. Malcolm Coopersmith looked much more like an aging hippie than a minister. What was left of his light brown hair was pulled back tightly into a ponytail. He wore jeans, a tie-dyed cotton shirt, a short corduroy jacket, and a cap pulled low over his eyes. His mustache was so thick, it covered part of his upper lip. Jane knew he was well into his forties, yet he had the look of a much younger man.

She waved to him as he turned around. "Hi!" she shouted. At the reviewal last night they'd gotten reacquainted.

"Jane," he called back, adjusting his round, rimless glasses. "What a nice surprise. You're a little early."

She crossed to where he was standing and gazed down into the newly dug hole. The cement vault had already been lowered into it. "Actually, I came to see you. I'd hoped we might have a few minutes to talk before the service."

"Of course." He glanced at her curiously. "You want to sit or walk?"

"Walk," she said.

"Walk it is." He turned back to the workman and finished with his instructions. Then zipping up his jacket, he nodded to the path. "This is good. I wanted to get a little exercise before I have to speak this afternoon. The fresh air clears my head."

"Do you have something prepared?" she asked.

"I'm going to talk about Buddha's Fire Sermon." His voice was low, his manner gentle and intelligent. "Do you know it? All things are on fire, full of passion. The passion of birth, the passion of death. The passion of love . . . and of hate." His voice trailed off.

They strode together toward the small lake that bordered the west end of the cemetery.

"What can I do for you?" he asked restlessly. He seemed somewhat distant today. Preoccupied.

"Well, I was wondering. You've known the Werness family a long time, haven't you?"

"Since I was in high school. Torald and I were in the same class."

Jane took a moment to decide how best to phrase her next question. Awkwardly, she rubbed her palms against her jeans. "I know this may sound like I'm prying, but there's something I need to find out, and I think you might be able to help me."

Malcolm said nothing. He simply nodded.

"Did you know about Billy Brewster? I mean, did you know Antonia had given birth to a son years ago?"

He continued to nod. "I knew about him, yes."

Jane could tell he was being very careful. This might be more difficult than she'd first imagined. She had to give him a reason to confide in her. "Look, I'm not sure if you know this, but I'm the one who found Torald's body the other night at the theatre."

He looked up. "I didn't know that. I'm so sorry."

She could hear the genuine empathy in his voice. He seemed like such a decent person. He simply *had* to help her. "The thing is," she continued, "before the police arrived, I noticed a thin gold chain on the stage floor. When I bent down to take a look, I saw that it was attached to a small pendant—a cat sitting on top of a six-pointed star. It was carved from mother-of-pearl."

His eyes wandered away, studying the landscape.

"Yesterday, I saw one almost exactly like it. The only difference was, it was carved from ebony. It belongs to Billy Brewster."

"I see."

"I've formed kind of a theory about it."

"And what would that be?"

"Well, I think the one I saw at the theatre might have belonged to another child of Antonia's. Perhaps Billy has a brother or sister." She paused. "Am I right, Malcolm? Was there another child?"

Malcolm kicked a dead branch out of their path. He adjusted his glasses and cleared his throat, yet curiously, he continued to say nothing.

"I have to be honest with you," said Jane. "If Billy does have a sibling and he or she was at the theatre that night, this person may have had something to do with Torald's death."

Malcolm stopped. As he turned to her, she could see his face was deeply troubled. "Yes. Of course you're right."

"Will you help me then?" she asked. "It could be terribly important."

After a long minute he said, "All right. I know you well enough to trust that you won't use the information for anything prurient. If the local papers were to pick up on any of this, well, you can see the problem. The Werness family is very prominent in the Twin Cities. It could be a nightmare."

Jane nodded.

"Okay, to answer your question. Yes, there was another child. A girl. Billy's fraternal twin. It's unlikely she'd look very much like him, but then she's a Werness. There'd be some family resemblance." He watched Jane for a moment. "What are you going to do with this information?"

Jane shook her head. "I don't know. Try to find her, I guess. Did you know that Torald broke into my garage the other night?"

Again Malcolm seemed to be taken by surprise. "No. I had no idea. Why?"

"Billy and his wife have been staying with me since the beginning of rehearsals for Antonia's play. They had all their belongings stored in my garage. When I got home last Friday night, unknown to me, Torald was going through their papers. After I'd put the car away, he tossed an old canvas over my head and pushed me to the floor. I'm sure he didn't want to be seen. In the meantime, I ended up with a slight concussion."

"That's awful!" said Malcolm. He touched her gently on the arm. "Are you all right?"

"Yes, I'm okay. The thing is, Billy felt Torald had been rather suspicious of him lately. He thought he'd probably broken into the garage to snoop through his things, see if he could find some proof, one way or the other."

"Uhm," said Malcolm. "I did know of his suspicions. He'd mentioned them to both Lucy and Antonia. They thought he was crazy. Turns out, he wasn't."

"I'm curious," said Jane. "Did he know Billy had a sister?"

Malcolm nodded. "Yes. He knew."

"Well then, since the lost pendant points to this sister being somewhere around, did he ever mention having any suspicions about her?"

Malcolm jammed his hands deep into the pockets of his jeans. "Actually, he did."

"I don't suppose you'd tell me who he suspected?" Jane

could feel a twinge of excitement growing in the pit of her stomach.

Uneasily, Malcolm crossed to a gravestone. He stood silently watching the wind toss dry leaves around the barren grass. "I don't think he was sure. He thought perhaps the resemblance wasn't as strong as with Billy. Unfortunately—or fortunately, however you want to look at it—Billy is almost the spitting image of Torald as a young man."

"Is that right?" said Jane. "But whom did he suspect of being Billy's sister?"

"Well, three people actually. Have you met Ida John?"

"Sure. *Her?*" Jane's tone betrayed her feelings about the woman.

Malcolm smiled. "You don't like her?"

"No. I mean, well—"

"That's all right. She didn't impress me much either. The problem is, she seemed unusually interested in the Werness family. Asked Torald a lot of questions."

"Maybe she was coming on to him."

"Maybe. I'm sure that occurred to him. She had blond hair when she auditioned. It was dyed brown for the part."

"Who else?" asked Jane.

"Well, do you know Gloria Lindy? She's Gaylord's new secretary. She apparently bears a striking resemblance to Gaylord's mother."

Jane whistled. "You know, she was at the theatre the night Torald died. Come to think of it, so was Ida. Interesting. Who's the third?"

"This may come as a shock, but Torald thought Erin Brewster—Billy's wife—could really be his sister. Of all the people he suspected, she looks the most like a member of the family."

"Unreal," said Jane, shaking her head. "But if Billy came forward and told Antonia who *he* was, why hasn't the sister done the same—that is, *if* she's really here in the first place."

"I don't know," said Malcolm. His body seemed to sag under the weight of the question.

"Unless—what if?"

"What?"

"Well, I mean, Billy's so proud of being a Werness. What if the sister isn't? Maybe she's angry that she was given up for adoption. Or worse, maybe there's some specific reason she's upset. Perhaps she knows something. . . ." Jane could see the look on Malcolm's face change completely. She knew she'd hit a nerve. "What is it? What might she know?"

Malcolm gnawed nervously on his lower lip. "Well, she might have guessed at many things, none of which would make her happy. But as far as what she could know for certain, very little."

This was supposed to be an answer? "I don't understand."

"No, I didn't expect you would."

"All right. You obviously don't want to go into it. But what if this sister found out something which upset her. Say, something about Torald."

"In other words, perhaps she was so angry she murdered him." He shivered and looked away.

"We have to at least consider it," said Jane. "The police don't believe for a minute that Torald's death was an accident. Someone was on that stage with him last Sunday night."

"But we have no proof of anything. Just your statement that you saw a pendant that matches the one Billy wears."

Jane knew he was right. "The police must have found it," she said. "They went over everything thoroughly."

"Then I suggest you talk to them. Look, we're building a house of cards here with very little to go on."

"I know." Reluctantly, she had to agree. "And when you think about it, how could Billy's wife really be his sister. They'd never pull something like that off."

"But of course they could," said Malcolm. "Don't misunderstand. You see, if Billy's sister is here, whoever she is, she's part Werness. Innately, I believe she'd know how to play a part. I'm not saying Erin is Billy's sister, I'm merely saying it's possible. Torald saw something in these three women and who's to say he wasn't right about one of them? He was right about Billy. On the other hand, after talking to Billy and Erin the other day, it did seem to me that they were very happily married. To be perfectly honest, I don't see much of a resemblance in any of them. As far as I'm concerned, it's all one huge muddle." His eyes slipped away. After a moment he said, "You know, don't you, that I've loved Lucy since I was a very young man? I'd never do anything to hurt her."

She nodded.

He continued, even more defensively, "Contrary to some church doctrine, marriage is not the only way to express that love."

Jane felt momentarily uncomfortable. She didn't entirely understand why he'd brought up his love for Lucy but didn't feel this was the time to press the point. It seemed too personal. "I talked to her on the phone for a few moments yesterday afternoon. I'd called to find out what time the review was set for."

"Did you? That's nice." His voice was bland.

"I mentioned that her father had been over to my house to meet Billy."

Malcolm blinked several times and then took off his glasses, rubbing his eyes wearily. "Jane, listen to me for a minute. We don't know each other all that well, but you're obviously trying to pursue some of this on your own. There are things I simply can't tell you, but if you have problems, come to me. If nothing else, perhaps I can point you in the right direction."

It was a small promise, thought Jane, but right now, it was all she had.

18

"A little more sherry?" asked Victor. He stood smiling down at Erin, his bearlike paw gripping a heavy, cut-crystal decanter.

"Thank you," she said somewhat self-consciously. She held up the glass for a refill.

"A drop of sherry before dinner," sighed Victor. "It's a nicety long forgotten in today's stressful world. Anyone else?" He spun around, holding the decanter high.

Fleur lifted her glass and turned it upside down in a gesture that suggested she had been horribly abused and forgotten.

"Of course," said Victor, moving swiftly across the oriental carpet. "I forgot that you generally drink the rest of us under the table."

Fleur gave him a half-amused little nod. "When the need arises."

"So," said Antonia, who sat draped across a slightly threadbare, green brocade love seat in the parlor of her house and stared uncomfortably at Billy and Erin. "I'm so glad you could join us for dinner."

"Thanks for inviting us." Billy smiled. He knew he was positively grim with awkwardness. He'd hoped the first social get together after "The Grand Announcement" wouldn't be so stiff and formal. Yet, with the house the way it was, the uncomfortable antique furnishings, the excess of carnations, he felt like he was trapped inside some nightmarish Noel Coward play. And what was even worse, he hadn't a clue what his lines were.

"Where's Lucy?" asked Victor, resuming his position on

the tufted leather bench in front of the piano. "I haven't seen her since the funeral this afternoon."

"She's out in the annex," said Fleur, looking for all the world like a grizzled prospector standing at the bar in a wild west saloon. She polished off her sherry in one gulp.

"Annex?" repeated Billy.

"It's a small building out back," explained Antonia. "It's attached to the garage. Lucy takes care of injured animals for the University of Minnesota Wildlife Center. She's had a lot of training over the years. She's become a real expert."

"She insists she likes animals better than people," added Fleur. "A rather antisocial position, although not one without a certain merit."

Antonia was irritated by the characterization. "I don't think that's entirely fair, Fleur. Lucy has always lived in a family of extreme extroverts. She's simply—"

Everyone turned as the missing Lucy entered the room. She had a dark smudge on one side of her face.

"I'm simply worn out by all of you." She smiled pleasantly. "Good evening, Billy. Erin." She took a seat next to Victor, patting him on the hand. He pointed at the smudge, and she took out a tissue, wiping it off. "I'm afraid I was born into the wrong family. The theatre has never interested me even in the slightest. I find it all terribly embarrassing."

Billy noticed that Erin was, for the first time this evening, smiling. It was a good sign.

"That's true," said Antonia. "I doubt you've gone to see a play in years."

Lucy sighed. "To me it's always seemed like the actors are having a much better time than the audience. The magic, as everyone calls it, doesn't exist for me." She noticed Erin's amused agreement and gave her a small wink.

This was only the second time Billy had ever heard her speak. At the funeral today, he had found her agreeably shy, with a more pragmatic nature than her sister. Lucy wore her corn silk hair straight, bluntly cut about her shoulders. She had none of the Werness height or girth. She was simply average. Round-faced, pleasant. By no means conventionally pretty. All her clothing was practical. Billy was sure Lucy's understated presence was meant to allow her to blend into the crowd. She wasn't someone who sought attention. Yet, strangely, it had the opposite effect. Studying her was much like discovering a lovely agate on a beach filled with dull gray stones. He wondered if she knew that. For some reason, he doubted Lucy cared much what other people thought.

He cleared his throat. "Antonia said you take care of sick animals."

Lucy gave him an amused nod.

Billy knew she could read his discomfort. For some reason, it made him even more uncomfortable.

"Someone just brought over an injured raccoon. A jogger found him down by the Minnehaha Creek. From the looks of him, I'd say he was in a car accident, but not to worry. He'll survive. He's strong and healthy and his appetite is good."

Everyone stared at her with rapt attention. No one asked any more questions.

"Would you like a glass of sherry?" asked Victor, touching Lucy on her knee.

"Make it a ginger ale, and it's a deal." She shivered. "Even when I was drinking anything I could get my hands on, sherry always gagged me." She smiled congenially.

Again, Billy stole a glance at Erin. Well, at least there seemed to be one member of the Werness family she liked. He was also glad Victor had finally left the room. The old guy hadn't taken his eyes off him since he'd arrived. It was starting to drive him a little nuts. He couldn't help but wonder about Victor's relationship with Antonia all those years ago.

Fleur leaned forward in her chair. "Billy, when you were in New Orleans talking to that lawyer—"

"Fleur," said Antonia, giving her a disapproving stare.

"I have to know this," said Fleur somewhat coldly. "Did that lawyer happen to mention anything about—"

"Fleur!" said Antonia. This time her tone carried more weight.

"It's all right," said Billy. "Do you mean about my sister?"

Everyone appeared shocked by the casual way he answered the question.

Fleur nodded.

Billy could see that Antonia was in great distress. He hadn't meant for this to happen. "Sure, I knew about her. It's okay, really. It was something I was going to bring up when the moment seemed right. The truth is, when I talked to that lawyer in New Orleans, he said that, in a way, I'd just missed her. She'd contacted him by phone several weeks before. Said she'd be willing to send him quite a sum of money if he'd mail her birth records to a P.O. box in some small town in northern Nebraska. After receiving the money, that's just what he did. I assumed he was telling me the story to make it perfectly clear he expected money from *me* as well. Anyway, he gave me the address and I tried to track her down, but it turns out the box rental had elapsed by the time I called, and they wouldn't give me any forwarding address."

"Interesting," said Lucy. She picked up the glass of ginger ale Victor had just set on the table next to her.

"And convenient," said Fleur sotto voce.

"I'd love to meet her," continued Billy eagerly. "Maybe some day I will."

Antonia tried to look hopeful.

"Since we're on the subject," said Billy, turning to Victor. He couldn't wait any longer. He had to ask. "You said you knew my mother many years ago. Did you also know my father?"

The repressed emotion in the room was now so thick, Billy felt certain that if someone struck a match, the house would explode.

Victor finished his drink before answering. "No, I never knew him. At least I don't think I did." He watched Antonia's face. "Did I know him, Antonia?"

"No."

"How did you meet him?" asked Billy.

Antonia took a deep breath and attempted a smile.

"Well," she began lightly, "Victor and I had been living together for two years. We broke up just after we both graduated. I'd been offered a position at a community theatre in New Orleans. Victor wanted to stay in New York. In our younger years, we both thought we wanted to act. Only later did we realize our talents lay in other directions." She stopped and took a sip of sherry. "So I left. A year later I met Fleur. It wasn't something I was looking for, it just happened. But it was the most satisfying relationship I'd ever experienced. And it's lasted over twenty years."

"But, about my father," said Billy. He wanted everyone to get back to the subject.

"Yes, I was coming to that." Antonia played with a frayed corner of the couch as she looked out the window. It was already beginning to get dark. The wind was even stronger now than it had been earlier in the day at the cemetery. She could hear windows rattling in different parts of the house. "I'm afraid it's not a very interesting story. I met a man—an actor—when I was still living in New York. His name was Eric Hatch. This was shortly before I left to go south. Anyway, we had a short affair. No more than a week. When I found out he was engaged to a friend of mine I broke it off. After I'd gotten settled in New Orleans, I realized I was pregnant." She looked hard at Billy.

The silence in the room seemed to intensify everyone's discomfort. Victor cleared his throat. Erin stared at her hands.

There was nothing left but for her to plunge ahead with the story. Still, after all these years, none of this was any easier. "I thought about my options, Billy. I decided to give birth and offer the child up for adoption. I felt I had nothing to give a child. In the end, I had twins."

"Where is he now?" asked Billy, unable to keep his curiosity in check. "My father, I mean."

"He died four years ago in a car accident." She gazed at him tenderly. "I have pictures of him, if that's any consolation. I wish it could have been different. I truly do."

Billy took hold of Erin's hand as he asked, "You never told this man you were pregnant?"

Antonia shook her head. "No, he never knew." Barely looking at Victor, she said, "I'm sorry. I never told you any of this."

"Dinner is served," said a young male voice from the living room archway.

"Wonderful timing," said Lucy, rising and taking Victor's arm. "Just when everyone's completely lost their appetite."

19

"What's this next to the mayonnaise?" With only a brief acknowledgment, Cordelia had breezed into Jane's house, headed straight for the kitchen, and stuck her head inside the refrigerator.

"It's a cold crab and avocado salad," said Jane. She was sitting at the kitchen table having a cup of tea. A copy of *Ms.* lay open in front of her.

"Splendid!" Cordelia removed the bowl, grabbed a spoon and dumped herself into a chair. "I'm famished."

"I thought you looked a bit wan. Didn't you get any dinner?"

Since her mouth was already full of food, Cordelia merely fluttered her eyes.

"Did you go to the funeral this afternoon?"

Between bites, Cordelia said, "Sure did." She kicked off her shoes and propped her feet up on one of the two remaining chairs. "Who made this? It's delicious."

"That new chef," said Jane. "I can never remember her name."

"Tell her," said Cordelia, "that it needs a tad more Tabasco. Perhaps just a hint more lime."

She rolled her eyes.

"And where were you this afternoon? I thought I'd see you at Pinewood, dressed in your finest, whitest high-tops, reveling in morbidity like the rest of us."

Jane shook her head. "I had to work. I've missed so much because of this concussion, I simply couldn't. I had meetings all afternoon."

"Poor dear," said Cordelia, stabbing a large chunk of avocado. "Is there more tea?"

"On the counter."

"I had quite the conversation this afternoon." She got up and grabbed the blue and white china teapot.

"With whom?"

"Have you met Gloria Lindy?" She got down a cup.

"I know who she is."

"Well, did *she* corner *me*. She was trying not to be obvious, but my dear, she let fly with a veritable barrage of questions about Billy Brewster. At one point, I thought she was going to hyperventilate."

"What did she ask?"

"Oh, stuff like, how did Billy find out about Antonia? What does he think of his grandfather? What's his wife like? Did I think he was interested more in the family's reputation or their money? Of course, since she was getting so chummy, she thought she'd better dish a bit to me as well. Did you know Lucy was heavily into booze and drugs as a young woman?"

Jane shook her head. "No. That's awful. What else?"

"Gaylord's wife was institutionalized way back in the early Sixties. And get this. Torald tried to commit suicide shortly after Lucy left to go live with Antonia. That was 1967. He was eighteen. Lucy had just turned sixteen."

"How did she find all this out?"

"Here and there." Cordelia returned to the table with her tea. "Gaylord's told her some of it. She also knew Torald— talked to him quite a bit before he died."

"How long has she worked for Gaylord Werness?"

"A month or so. I'd say she's a quick study. And also incredibly nosy. After talking to her I had a bad taste in my mouth for the rest of the day. Sort of like—" She held her spoon in the air, "a delicate spring roll deep fried in three-month-old canola oil."

Jane turned her cup around in the saucer. "You know this Gaylord Werness much better than I do. How would you describe him?"

Cordelia put a finger to her cheek. "How about—a degenerate Santa Claus."

The image was so accurate. "No, I don't mean physically. What do you think of him personally?"

Cordelia shrugged. "I don't know. I've never actually worked with him, although I may get the chance next winter. The Allen Grimby is thinking of doing several of his plays. But let me think. Well, he likes to talk, I know that much. Sees himself as a great storyteller."

"What kind of stories?"

"About himself, mainly. His life."

"Did he and Torald get along?"

"You have to understand," said Cordelia, exaggerating her patient expression, "Gaylord doesn't confide in me. It's his loss, of course. He also doesn't mix with the theatre community much anymore. His health hasn't been very good."

"Well then, what can you tell me about Torald? Did anyone hate him enough to want him dead?"

"His understudy, perhaps."

"Cordelia!"

"All right, calm down." She cocked a world-weary eyebrow. "Jane, half the husbands in this town probably had contracts out on him. How should I know?"

"Was he stuck-up? Full of himself?"

Cordelia considered the question. "Actually, sometimes he was the exact opposite. You may think this is cheap pop psychology, but I don't believe I've ever met a man who indulged in more self-loathing than Torald Werness. I think that's what a lot of the drinking was about. Actually, he was kind of a sweet guy—if you could get past the womanizing. He never tried any of that shit with me."

"And Lucy Werness? What do you know about her?"

"Very little. She's the loner of the family. Loves animals.

I think she works with the rehab clinic at the U of M. Takes care of baby birds until they're ready to go to college."

This was all interesting, thought Jane, but not particularly helpful. She took her last sip of tea.

"Where's Beryl this evening?" Cordelia burped as she pushed the bowl away.

"Upstairs in her room. She had a TV program she wanted to watch until eight. Then we thought we might play a game of Scrabble."

"How utterly charming. Such inveterate homebodies." Cordelia pushed herself away from the table. "And Billy and Erin?"

"At the Werness house having dinner. And where are you off to in such a hurry?"

"I have a dinner date."

Jane stared at the empty bowl.

"Merely an appetizer. Celeste has been at the hospital every minute since her mother's operation. I told her tonight she needed a decent meal. We're going to Andy's Rib Joint."

Jane restrained herself from comment. "How *is* Celeste's mother?"

"When the pain medication kicks in, she's back to sputtering about Congress. I think she's on the mend."

"I see."

A ringing phone silenced them.

"I'll find my way out," said Cordelia, grabbing her coat. "Regards to Beryl."

Jane waved as she picked up the receiver. "Hello?"

"Jane?" said a female voice.

"Yes?"

"This is Dorrie Harris."

"Hi! How are you?" Jane hadn't seen her since the night of the cast party.

"I'm fine. But I hear you're having some problems."

"I am?"

"The scuttlebutt around City Hall has it that Orville Trevelyan thinks you might have had something to do with Torald Werness's death."

Jane was so stunned she couldn't speak.

"Are you still there?"

She cleared her throat. "He alluded to something like that when I was first being interrogated at the theatre, but I thought it was just frustration on his part. This is ridiculous, Dorrie. I can't believe he really thinks that."

"I know. But he can make trouble for you all the same." She paused. "How about we get together. Who knows, I might be able to help you."

"Sure, I'd like that." Jane thought it was a good idea even if Dorrie couldn't help. "Although I don't know what you could do."

"You never know. How about tomorrow night. I could come over to your restaurant. I'm afraid it would have to be kind of late."

"The main dining room closes at ten," said Jane. "But the pub downstairs serves food until midnight."

"Great. Okay, let's see. I have a meeting with a citizens group at seven. They're all up in arms about a proposed liquor store that wants to open in the neighborhood. I should think I'll be done by nine. Could be a bit later—depending on how long-winded some of the people get."

"No problem," said Jane. "Just come in and have somebody find me. I'll reserve a table in the pub back by the hearth. Owner's privilege."

"Great. See you tomorrow night then," said Dorrie.

As Jane hung up, she wondered just what Dorrie was up to. A city council representative had certain clout, but not in a murder investigation. Still, Dorrie seemed to think they had something to talk about. And anyway, a pleasant evening spent talking with an attractive friend, well, it was certainly worth a pint of ale. Maybe even two.

"*Zarf* is not a word," insisted Jane, raising an eyebrow at her aunt.

"Yes it is, love." Beryl began gleefully counting up her points.

"Define it."

"Well, it's a cuplike holder, usually made of ornamental metal. And it has no handles."

Jane threw up her hands in disgust. "That's twice you've beaten me and you've been here less than a week."

Beryl's smile was positively cherubic. She patted her white hair triumphantly.

"I can see I'm going to have to spend more time reading the dictionary."

"You'll get the hang of it one day, dear. Your uncle Jimmy and I played every night for years." She picked up her teacup and walked into the living room. Jane followed and together they sat down on the couch in front of the fire.

"Do you miss the cottage?" asked Jane. She could see a faint wistfulness grow in her aunt's eyes.

"A bit. But I love being here. I spent the entire morning out in the backyard. You know, it's such a lovely place. With a little work, it would make a splendid garden. Perfect for Peter and Sigrid's wedding."

Jane knew her brother was undecided about where the wedding should be held. Sigrid didn't want a huge production. Perhaps Beryl was right. "I'd forgotten how much you loved to garden. With the restaurant and all, I've simply let it go. But, you know, it's probably good for you. A little fresh air will help you get your full strength back."

Beryl turned to her niece. "Do I look ill, Janey?"

"No, I didn't mean it that way. You look fine."

The truth of the matter lay less in the way Beryl appeared physically than in her attitude in general. Beryl didn't look much different from the last time Jane had seen her. A little older perhaps, but that was to be expected. No, the difference had more to do with her energy. Hepatitis had taken a great deal out of her, and now the medication she was on was making her a bit shaky. She was much more tenuous about life, about what she did and where she would go. Jane remembered her aunt as an incredibly robust woman who took great pride in doing things for herself. For years she'd fixed her own plumbing, cared for the house and garden, repaired anything and everything that needed it—including an old car she insisted was much easier to keep running than these newer, fancier models. During the days and sometimes late into the evening, her husband Jimmy was away at their restaurant in Poole. But Beryl had never let any grass grow under her feet. Not only was she involved in a theatre group some miles from her home, but she worked periodically as an aide at the local hospital. She'd had some nurse's training after the war, and she'd never wanted to let her skills slip away.

"Oh, but the lilacs are wonderful," said Beryl, continuing her discussion of Jane's backyard. "And the crab apple tree will be flowering by May. All I'd have to do is add the finishing touches. One of your neighbors was telling me about this place called the farmer's market. It won't be long before the spring bedding plants are in." Her voice grew more and more excited. "Jane, if you'd let me, I would make your backyard a paradise by the time the wedding date rolls around. It would be my present to Peter and Sigrid."

Jane didn't even have to think about it. This was the first real enthusiasm Beryl had shown since she'd come. "It's a great idea. We'll have to run it by the two of them, of course, but I have a feeling they'll be delighted." She wondered if her father was going to be as impressed.

"Wonderful!" Gulliver had jumped up into Beryl's lap, and she patted his head lovingly.

This was a good sign, thought Jane. Beryl's normal antipathy to her dogs was even beginning to mellow. Now, if only her aunt and her father could reach some sort of similar détente. They'd simply *have* to before the wedding. "Beryl," said Jane, her voice tentative, "I'd really like to know more about why you and my father don't get along."

Beryl's lips drew together into a thin line. For a moment she gazed into the fire and was silent. "Oh, Janey dear, it's such old water under such an ancient bridge." She turned her head away. "I wouldn't even know where to begin."

"Well, for instance," said Jane. She wasn't going to let the subject drop. She'd done that too many times in her life. "I know that you and my mother were good friends before she met my father."

"Best friends," nodded Beryl. "Helen and I had known

each other since we were children. Our families were close. And of course, I married her brother, Jimmy. It just seemed so perfect to me. And then, your father arrived from America. He literally swept Helen off her feet. Did you know she was engaged to another man at the time?"

"No," said Jane. "I'd never heard that."

"She broke it off with him almost immediately. Raymond was a handsome devil, I'll give him that. And smart. No matter what their looks, Helen gravitated to that kind. I think after awhile, Ray was a little jealous of how close she and I were. To be honest, I don't think he understood it. He'd never had such a close friend himself. It irritated him to no end when Helen would tell me things. Especially about their relationship. But, by the time they were to be married, I thought he'd mellowed a great deal. He'd accepted the family, warts and all. I, unfortunately, was one of the most annoying warts. But he had a sense of humor, and so did I, and we all wanted Helen to be happy so we sailed through the wedding without a problem." Beryl looked down at her hands, giving herself a moment. "I guess you could say the real problem came in that I saw right from the beginning that if Helen did marry your father, he'd take her away from us. I know that was a selfish way to look at it, but there it was. It upset your grandparents a great deal, too, Jane. It wasn't just me. Your uncle was in an awful state when they were away on their honeymoon."

"And I guess that happened, didn't it?" said Jane.

"It did. As soon as they were back she was off to America. After you were born, I think Helen was terribly homesick. I received quite a few letters that said as much. So, I got to thinking. Why didn't they come back over for a visit. I suggested it to her, and a few months later she said Ray had agreed. That's when I got busy. I found a company in Southampton that was looking for a barrister with a background in American corporate law. I knew that Ray was a criminal lawyer, as you call it, but I also knew he'd studied the other as well. It was perfect. When they got to England, I suggested he might want to check it out. One thing led to another and he was offered the job. I suppose the entire family put pressure on him, but we so much wanted to get to know you, Janey, and we missed your mother so badly. Thankfully, he accepted the position."

"We stayed for almost nine years," said Jane softly.

"You did. You didn't return to the United States until both your grandparents had died." Her voice became sad. "After Helen's parents were gone, Ray saw his chance. He quit his job and insisted that you and your brother and your mother all return to St. Paul. It was the worst day of my life. I know Helen didn't want to leave. Peter had never known anything other than his home in Southampton, and you were more English than you were American. I pleaded with Ray to reconsider, but he wouldn't have any of it. He'd wasted enough of his life doing what other people wanted."

"So we came to Minnesota," said Jane, remembering the time vividly. "It was hard on everyone."

"But mostly on your mother. I'm afraid I broke down at Heathrow. I had the feeling that I was never going to see Helen again. I hated Ray for what he was doing. Putting his wishes above everyone else's." She wiped an angry tear away from her eye. "But Raymond Lawless was the head of his family. So full of himself, he was. He was finally going to make the decisions. Dear God, ripping everyone away from the only home they'd ever known. It was pure, hateful selfishness." She glanced hesitantly at Jane. "I'm sorry. I have no right to talk about your father that way."

"But you did come visit us the following year," said Jane, "so your premonition wasn't right."

Beryl shook her head. "We stayed for one week. But that feeling never left me. When I said goodbye to Helen in August, I knew for certain it was the last time I'd ever look into those dear eyes. Less than a year later she developed that blood infection. She died a week later."

Jane touched the bridge of her nose. "That's when I asked to come back to England to stay with you and Uncle Jimmy."

"You did that, love, and I wanted you to come." Beryl

took out her handkerchief and wiped her eyes. "That's when Ray and I finally had it out. He told me in no uncertain terms what he thought of me. It had been years in coming, and I don't mind telling you it was horrible. And then, to suggest I was pressuring you to stay with us . . ."

Jane shook her head. "I know he thinks that. But it was my decision. I felt closer to my mother when I was with you. I needed that desperately."

"I understood completely. I don't think your father ever did. You mustn't blame yourself, Jane, you were only thirteen. Just a little girl. Your father was the adult—he was the one who needed to do the understanding. I know you love him, and that's as it should be. But he's a jealous man. I finally saw him for what he really was. He was always jealous of Helen's family. I'm sure it was because his own was so cold and uncaring. In the end, he made all of us pay. And I'm sorry love, but as far as I'm concerned, what he did was unforgivable." Her body was still shaking as she got up and quietly left the room.

20

The thick window blinds in Orville Trevelyan's office cast deep, angular shadows against the far wall of the room. Jane watched a tiny spider crawl purposefully across the linoleum as Trevelyan sat behind his desk, making an arch of his fingers. "I appreciate your coming down this morning, Ms. Lawless. This shouldn't take long."

Jane was trying hard to relax. No use letting him know how anxious she felt about being summoned from her own office, less than an hour ago. Wednesday mornings she usually had a meeting with her staff. Today, it would have to wait. "Anything I can do to help," she said, trying to keep the curtness out of her voice.

"Good." He leaned back and crossed his arms over his ample stomach. "I didn't see you at Torald Werness's funeral yesterday. For some reason, I thought you'd be there."

"I had to work." She didn't feel she needed to offer any further explanation.

"Of course. But, then again, you were seen talking with a Reverend Malcolm Coopersmith shortly before the service. He's a close friend of the Werness family, I understand. I was just curious about what you would have to speak to him about."

Jane crossed her legs. "I've been concerned about the entire family since Torald's death. I just wanted to make sure everything was all right."

"Concerned?" He let the word hang in the air.

"That surprises you?"

"Nothing surprises me, Ms. Lawless. I know you're one of our more *concerned* citizens. I understand Billy Brewster and his wife are still staying with you."

"They are."

"How are they taking Torald's death?"

Jane decided this was probably just a fishing expedition. Drag her downtown and see what shakes loose. Yet, especially after Dorrie Harris's comment last night, she wondered if there wasn't some larger point to the harassment. Trevelyan liked to play with his mouse before he pounced. "Why don't you ask them?"

"I will." He sat forward. "And what about you?"

"What about me?"

"I know you want me to buy that business in your original statement about Torald being in your garage that night going through Billy Brewster's things."

"It's the truth."

"Is it? How well did you know Torald Werness?"

"We'd met. Talked a few times."

"You knew of his reputation with women?"

"I'd heard."

"Did you find him attractive?"

"Excuse me?"

He repeated the question.

"Are you—"

"He was artistic. Intellectual. The type of person who would appeal to a woman like you."

"Have you forgotten—"

"I've forgotten nothing, Ms. Lawless. You're going to insist you're a lesbian, right? Immune to a man's charms."

"This is crazy!"

"Is it? You and I both know lots of people swing both ways. Did you sleep with him?"

Jane was beginning to feel nauseous. And this time it wasn't because of the concussion. "Why are you doing this?"

He erupted. "Because, goddammit, I've got to find a plausible motive for a murder!" He got up and moved to the window, looking down at the busy street below.

"You think I murdered him because he made a pass at me in my garage?" She didn't move. Perhaps he was simply going to use her as a punching bag and toss her out.

"That Werness family's as strange as hell. Cut the crap, Lawless. You know a damn sight more than you're letting on. Now, either you cooperate, or I start building my case against you. Who's to say you didn't push him off those bleachers? Jesus, you found him. You had plenty of opportunity. All we have to figure out is a motive. Maybe he knew something about you—or maybe he thought he knew something but needed proof. That's why he was in your garage. Or—" His eyes narrowed in thought. "Maybe he forced himself on you, and you wanted revenge. Sure. We've been warned to watch for things like that. What with the Willy Smith rape trial in Florida and that Anita Hill thing, women don't trust the system anymore. I can tie you to this, *I know I can*."

"But why would you try?" Jane couldn't believe what she was hearing. He wasn't just playing. There was venom in his voice. "You've got to know I'm not guilty. None of that ever happened."

Trevelyan was on a roll. "And don't think you can rely

on that father of yours. He's not God. I'll beat him this time, mark my words. Even if I can't prove anything beyond a reasonable doubt, I can make life miserable for you. Do you want that?"

"I didn't kill Torald Werness, and I don't know who did!"

"No? Then what *do* you know?" He sat down on the edge of the desk and glared at her.

Jane had to think fast. Quickly, she ran through her conversation yesterday with Malcolm. If she gave Trevelyan any information about a possible twin sister being at the theatre that night, the press would find out almost immediately. Yet, if she didn't give him something, she'd be the one in deep trouble. Then, she remembered Maureen Werness's car. "When I got to the theatre that night, I parked in the back next to a red Triumph."

"So?"

"It belongs to Maureen Werness. She must have been inside the theatre, although I never saw her."

"Good. That's a start. We'll check it out. What else?"

God, what did he want? The murderer's name engraved on a lucky key ring? She knew she had to tell him more. Perhaps she could mention the pendant, but not say anything else. On the other hand, if this unnamed sister was on the stage that night, she might have had something to do with Torald's death. This was a real quandary. "Okay, about the pendant you found."

Trevelyan scowled. "What pendant?"

"The one on the stage floor near the bleachers."

"We found nothing on the floor."

Jane stared at him. "Where are the photographs that your guys took? It must be there."

Trevelyan reached behind the desk and pulled out a manilla envelope. "Here," he said, dropping it in her lap. "Show me."

Jane drew them out and flipped through the shots quickly. She found the exact spot where she'd seen it the other night, but the floor was bare. "I don't believe this."

"Perhaps you'd care to enlighten me," said Trevelyan.

Jane slipped the photos back into the envelope. "Well, when I came up on stage, I saw a small mother-of-pearl pendant. It was a cat sitting on top of a six-pointed star. Everything was happening so fast, I simply forgot about it. When I remembered it later, I assumed you'd found it."

Trevelyan raised his chin and looked down at her through narrowed eyes. "No. We'll need an exact description. In the meantime, what, if anything, do you know about it?"

Jane's mind was racing. Someone had to have picked it up before the police got there. But who? Everyone that night had been up on stage at one point or another.

"Well?" Trevelyan tapped his foot against the side of the desk.

"I don't know who it belonged to. I wish I did."

"But you know something about it, don't you?"

Was that a stab in the dark, or did her body language give her away? "Yes, actually I do. Billy Brewster has one just like it—only it's carved from ebony."

"Is that right?" Trevelyan scratched his ear. "Perhaps he and his wife have matching jewelry."

"I don't think so," said Jane.

"Why not?"

"The one Billy wears was given to him by his birth mother when he was just a baby."

"Antonia Werness."

"Exactly."

"And now you're saying you saw another one just like it, only carved from something different. What conclusion did you draw from that, Ms. Lawless? I'm sure your fertile mind has been chewing on that at the speed of light."

Idly, Jane wondered if he'd mixed a metaphor. "I don't know. Perhaps there was another child."

Trevelyan stood. "Without the pendant, it's going to be hell to prove."

"Maybe someone else saw it? You could ask."

"Oh, we will. We will. In the meantime, I suggest you think this all through again very carefully. If you come up with anything else that could help this investigation, I want to hear about it. Is that clear?"

Jane nodded.

He checked his watch. "I have an appointment. But remember Lawless, you're not off the hook. You're still as likely a suspect as anyone I can think of." He strode to the door and opened it.

As Jane moved past him she saw his lip curl into a smile.

"And give that eminent father of yours my humblest regards. He's a brilliant man, you know. Everyone agrees. One day I hope his brilliance will get him locked up with the same scum he defends."

Jane stopped and looked him square in the eye. "Is that what all this was about? You're pissed at my father?"

"Good day, Ms. Lawless."

21

"Slow down," said Cordelia, tapping a pencil against the side of her coffee mug. "I don't remember anything about a video camera." She sat at the huge mahogany desk in her office, the phone receiver propped between her chin and her shoulder, still annoyed that she had to be up at the crack of dawn. It was almost eleven A.M. All *civilized* people were still in bed.

"But your name is on the slip," said the voice on the other end. "Cordelia Thron, Artistic Director, Room 306, Allen Grimby Repertory Theatre, 121 East Basilica Avenue, St. Paul, Minnesota, 55106."

"That's *Thorn*."

"Of course."

"God, you've got everything down there but my bra size."

"Huh?"

"Go on."

"Well, anyway, we do have an account with your theatre there. I didn't think anything of it when the guy signed your name. He said he needed to tape part of some dress rehearsal. Something like that."

"Mmm," said Cordelia, straightening the sign on her desk which read, FEMINIST HELLHOLE. She stroked it lovingly. "All right. Send me the bill. I'll take a look at it."

"But what do I do with the tape?"

"Tape?" repeated Cordelia. "What tape?"

"The one in the camera. When it was brought back, there was a tape left in it. It happens a lot more than you'd realize. People forget. We try to make an effort to get it back to the owner."

"That's good of you," said Cordelia absently. "Just put it in a mailer and send it over. I'll take care of it. By the way, what did you say the guy looked like—the one who signed my name?"

"Oh, sort of average. Brown hair. Thin brown beard."

"Fat? Thin? Short? Tall?"

"I don't really remember. But youngish. Twenties probably."

"Okay," said Cordelia. "With such a detailed description, I'm sure I'll have no trouble getting it back to its owner." Screw this, she thought to herself.

"Thanks," said the man. "I'll have a courier bring it by today. We've got some other stuff being delivered in your neighborhood." He hung up.

Cordelia glanced up as she heard a knock on her door. "Abandon hope all ye who enter here," she shouted. "Cordelia isn't in, but *Ms. Thron* would be delighted to help you."

Jane stuck her head into the room. "Are you busy?"

"Do I look busy?" She rested her chin on a stack of scripts. "Come in. I insist." She swept her hand toward the only chair that wasn't full of books and assorted junk. "Sit thee doon."

"Late night?" asked Jane.

"Early morning."

"Nice," said Jane, nodding to Cordelia's new red and white striped dress.

"Oh, do you like it? I think it makes me look like a large barber pole." She picked up her coffee and took a sip. "Ugh. Awful. What brings you all the way over to St. Paul?"

"I was summoned to Trevelyan's office around ten this morning. We had a fun talk. Very friendly."

"I'll bet." She unwrapped a chocolate bar and took a bite. "Breakfast," she smiled.

"He thinks I have several good motives for murdering Torald."

Cordelia nearly choked.

"Don't you want to hear one of them?"

She grabbed the desk with one hand and covered her eyes with the other. "I'm ready."

"He thinks we were having an affair."

"*HA!!*" she shrieked, flinging her arms in the air and kicking her feet. "The man's brain dead!"

"He said some people swing both ways."

"He knows this from personal experience does he?"

"I didn't ask."

"Your first mistake. God, you and Torald. What a hoot. That would be like me and Jesse Helms."

"Cordelia?"

"I've got it. Let's start a rumor. Oh, don't give me that *goody-two-shoes* look. You suffer from terminal niceness sometimes, sweetie. Didn't you ever do this in college? I remember a professor I had once. God, he was a dork. He was a health-food fanatic, among other things." She wiggled an eyebrow. "Ate fresh shelled peas at his desk every noon. Well, we started this juicy little rumor that every night he stopped at LaDones—a notorious donut shop in Dinkytown—for coffee and a cherry filled. My lord, you would have thought someone had kidnapped his firstborn. It was *such* humor."

"Cordelia!"

"You're right. It would take just the right rumor about Orville. Let me give it some thought."

"Will you listen to me?"

"Why, dearheart, I have given you my *full* attention ever since you walked into this office."

"I need to talk to Maureen Werness."

"So? Go talk to her."

"No, you don't understand. I called her house this morning, and another woman answered. A neighbor. She asked me what it was about. You remember I told you I'd seen her car outside the theatre the night Torald died? I need to ask her about it. But how could I explain that over the phone?"

"Make up an excuse. Be creative."

Jane shook her head. "The woman said to call back later. I suppose I could just drive out to Minnetonka and take my chances."

"Good idea. If they won't let you in, there's a sturdy trellis on the west side of the house. I believe it leads directly into one of the second-floor bedrooms."

"This is not helping."

"No?"

"Aren't you interested why Maureen Werness was at the theatre that night?"

"Not particularly. I know she and Torald haven't gotten along for years."

"See! She has motive! Even more reason why you should call Maureen."

"Me?"

"Well, of course. You have a perfect excuse to see her. You can say you want to bring over some of her husband's things."

"*Pullease!* I do not carry heavy loads."

"I'll carry it."

"I have an appointment at two."

"We'll be back by two."

"Her son has a thing for insects. The house smells of formaldehyde."

"Make the call, Cordelia. Say you want to come over *now*." Jane handed her the phone.

"All right," she sniffed, giving a resigned sigh. "The sacrifices I make." She dialed the number. "Hello Maureen?" Her voice turned creamy. "This is Cordelia Thron—Thorn. Have you got a minute?"

"You've met my son, Erling, haven't you?" asked Maureen, showing them into the living room. Erling stood next to a tall, turquois lava lamp, a water pistol dangling ominously from one hand.

"Of course," smiled Cordelia. "Erling? It's good to see you again."

He snapped his gum.

"And you know Jane Lawless?" asked Cordelia.

"Of course." Maureen extended her hand. "You own that charmingly rustic restaurant on Lake Harriet." She waved them to a seat. "Erling, why don't you go out by the pool and play."

"It's filthy." He took his gum out of his mouth and examined it.

"That's because it's March, darling. We'll have it cleaned before summer. Besides, you might be able to find some nice bugs in it."

"They're not bugs," he said belligerently.

Maureen smiled.

"You have a lovely home," said Jane, eyeing a particularly hideous tie-dyed wall hanging.

"Yes," said Maureen wistfully. "Torald loved the Sixties. I've tried to surround him with what I knew he cared about. Are those his things?" She nodded to the box next to Jane's feet.

"Some of them," said Cordelia, with just the right touch of sadness in her voice. "I thought you'd want these particular things handled with care. The rest we'll send over with one of the storage men."

"You're very kind." Maureen pulled a tissue out of a

bright red plastic holder. It matched her nail polish. "This has been an awful time for me."

Jane nodded. "The police are doing everything they can to find out who was responsible. As a matter of fact, I was in Detective Trevelyan's office just this morning."

"Were you?"

Erling pointed his water pistol at a framed, velvet painting of Elvis Presley and let fly with a stream of water. Sadly, the King began to look as if he had an extremely runny nose.

Jane and Cordelia exchanged glances.

"I've told you not to do that," said Maureen, her voice peevish.

Erling lowered the offending weapon to his side but kept his eyes alert.

"I mentioned to the detective," continued Jane, "that I happened to park next to your car the night Torald died. A red Triumph. That's yours, isn't it?"

Maureen straightened her back. "Why, yes it is." Quickly, she turned to her son. "Erling, I want you to go upstairs to your room."

"But!"

"This is going to be a private discussion."

He looked around defiantly, his eyes coming to rest on Cordelia. "Why do you dress like that?"

"Erling!" shouted Maureen.

"No, it's all right," said Cordelia pleasantly. "Because I like to, Erling." She smiled. "Why do you like bugs?"

He shoved the water pistol into his belt. "Because my parents hate them. It's easy to gross them out."

"Enough," said Maureen. "Go to your room."

"I'll go outside," said Erling, walking by a bowl of Atomic Fire Balls and grabbing a fist full. He slid the balcony door closed behind him.

"You'll have to forgive the boy," said Maureen with a sigh. "Torald's death has hit him pretty hard."

Cordelia bared her teeth in what could have been construed as a sympathetic smile.

Even though Erling was obviously at a rather tedious

age, Jane's heart went out to him. She knew what he was feeling. "My mother died when I was thirteen," said Jane. "It takes some time."

Maureen nodded. "They weren't close, not like they should have been. Torald was a strange man. I loved him, don't get me wrong, but it was almost as if he wanted to prove to me he didn't deserve it. I never understood him and now . . . he's gone."

Jane let her have a moment before continuing. "Was he upset about anything the night he died?"

Her expression grew cold. "I saw him, you're right. I wish to God I hadn't. I'd come to talk to him about his father. I'd just come from Gaylord's suite—he lives a few blocks away at the Maxfield Plaza. Anyway, on Sundays I sometimes took him a pan of homemade brownies. Gaylord has a sweet tooth like you wouldn't believe. It had become almost a ritual with us. When I was there that afternoon, he told me about this Billy Brewster, Antonia's long lost son. He'd been to see him just that morning, at your home I believe." She glanced at Jane.

"Billy and his wife are staying with me right now. They're renting my third floor."

"Really?" She said the word with little interest. "Well, from Gaylord's excited tone, I gathered he was very impressed by the young man. The more we talked, the more concerned I became. I mean, this Billy is an heir . . . just like Torald. And as far as his other grandson is concerned, well, Erling's a lot like me. I could never act a part. I mean, acting is essentially lying, isn't it?"

Cordelia looked like she'd just swallowed ground glass. "I suppose you could view it that way."

"Well, I had to talk to Torald right away, didn't I? He had to know that his father might be considering leaving the rights to his plays to someone other than him."

"Did you specifically ask Gaylord what his plans were?" asked Jane.

"Oh, you don't know that old man. You'd never get a straight answer out of him."

"So what did Torald think?"

"I never told him."

"Why not?"

"Because I found him on stage with that whore."

"Anyone we know?" asked Cordelia.

"Of course you know her. You hired her. It was that Ida John person. They were standing close together, talking about as intimately as two people can get without actually exchanging body fluids. My God, I'm not an idiot. I know Torald had women. I'd just never seen him with one of his chippies before."

"Did they see you?" asked Jane.

"Yes. He tried to make excuses, but I wouldn't listen. He said something about a scene in the play. They weren't discussing any *bloody play*, I could see that much. He was lying. His whole life was a lie. God, to live with a man for twenty years and realize he was a total stranger." She started to cry.

"Perhaps we should be going," said Jane gently.

"Just leave his things," said Maureen. "You're right. I need to be alone."

Cordelia stood. "If there's anything we can do."

"Do?" sniffed Maureen. She made a mirthless sound deep in her throat. "Try explaining my life to me."

22

After dropping a sputtering Cordelia back at the theatre, Jane decided to drive to her father's office to see if he might have a few minutes to talk to her. Chances were, he was still in court, but perhaps it was late enough in the day that she might get lucky and find him in.

Pulling her Saab up in front of the old St. Paul row

house that had been his law office since the early Sixties, Jane noticed his car in the back parking lot. Score one for her. The first floor of the brownstone was a reception area. Sitting at the front desk, as usual, was her dad's law clerk, Norman Tescallia. His head was bent over a law book.

"Hi, Norm," she smiled, coming into the room. "Is my father receiving?"

Norm took the pencil out from between his teeth and looked up, nervously biting his lower lip. Jane had always found him a bit of a stress junkie, but otherwise pleasant. "He is. He's even in a good mood. We just won the Clifton case."

"Did you?" said Jane. She knew her father had been working on it for months. "Let me ask you something. Who was the officer in charge of that investigation?"

Norm flipped through a stack of notes on the desk. "Trevelyan, MPD. Why?"

"Just curious." She let her eyes rise to the ceiling. Her father's office was on the second floor. "Is anyone with him?"

"No. I'll buzz. Let him know you're on your way."

"Thanks." She crossed to the stairs and started up.

The row house was narrow yet handsome, with deep green wallpaper above rich oak wainscotting. The building was erected in the 1920s, shortly after her father's family had moved to Minnesota from Southern Illinois. One of her father's passions had always been the work of F. Scott Fitzgerald. Directly outside his office on a long wall across from a small reception area hung a series of framed photographs. The photos depicted the life and times of the Fitzgeralds. Jane's favorite was a shot taken of Scott and Zelda in St. Paul, shortly after the birth of their daughter, Frances, in 1922. Unlike the later photos, the young couple in this picture looked healthy and happy, the golden children of the twenties.

"Come on in," shouted her father.

Jane pushed open the heavy door. There, leaning back in his leather chair, his vest unbuttoned and his tie loose, sat Raymond Lawless. Behind him was a large, round, spoked window that looked out on the St. Paul Cathedral in the distance. Law books completely filled one entire wall of the airy, sunny room. Seeing him in this environment had always felt faintly curious to her, almost as if he was another person very different from the one she knew at home. The times she'd visited him here as a child still stood out vividly in her memory. It was the smell of leather and his spicy aftershave all mixed together with the scent of that special wood polish he insisted the cleaning staff use on his desk. It seemed to trigger so many feelings, so many sepia-toned photographs in her mind. She'd always been proud of his accomplishments. Yet, for some reason, in this office he seemed bigger, older, more certain. The room was like a large picture frame, allowing her a glimpse of her dad as others saw him. He was a striking man. Deep-set, intelligent eyes. A strong, square jaw. Thick silver hair worn just a touch too shaggy.

"What brings you all the way over here this afternoon?" he smiled, nodding to a chair.

"Cordelia and I just got back from Minnetonka. We took some of Torald Werness's things from the theatre over to his wife."

"A sad business," said Raymond, furrowing his brow. "That family has had more than its share of trouble."

Jane sat down. "You knew I was the one who found his body the other night at the theatre?"

Raymond nodded. "I tried calling, but you're a hard person to track down."

"Well, now it seems I'm a suspect in his demise."

He sat up straight. "That's preposterous. Who told you that?"

"I spent a good part of the morning in Orville Trevelyan's office. He thinks I know more about the case than I'm telling."

Raymond's expression grew even more serious. "You be careful of that man, honey. I mean it. He's very angry with me right now—I'd hate to think he'd take it out on you."

"Because of the case you just won?"

"Exactly. The thing is, he should be furious with himself,

not me. My God but it was sloppy police work. He's a better police officer than that."

"Right now I'd have to say that's a matter of opinion."

Raymond leaned back in his chair. "I'll see what I can do about it."

"I don't know, Dad. I think your involvement might just make things worse."

"Maybe. But at least I can check on what Trevelyan thinks he has on you."

"There is one other thing I could use your help on."

"Name it."

"Well, it seems to me I remember you represented Gaylord Werness once in a lawsuit. It was years ago. Something to do with the theatre, I think."

He shook his head. "Jane, you know I can't discuss my clients with you."

"But couldn't you at least give me a clue what it was about?"

"Not ethical. Besides, the whole matter was settled out of court."

"Great. That means it's not even a matter of public record."

"I'm afraid that's true."

Jane took a deep breath and decided to try another approach. "All right, let me ask you this. You know the Werness family. At least you used to. What did you think of them?"

Raymond put his hands above his head and stretched. "If I'm going to be cross-examined, I have a right to an attorney."

"Come on. I'm serious about this."

"Okay, honey. I'll play. But that's a rather broad question. Can't you be more specific?"

Jane tapped her nails on the wood. "What did you think of Gaylord?"

He scratched his chin. "These are just impressions, now, you understand. All right. My over-all impression of him was that he was a concerned father. His family has always been troubled. I think he often saw himself as the only person who could help, but he never quite figured out how."

"I know about Lucy's drug problems, and Torald's attempted suicide."

"Among other things. I'll grant you, Gaylord is kind of a crazy guy. Eccentric. Sometimes confusing. Lots of money and fame never helped him in his personal life. From what I'm told, his wife couldn't take the stress. She ended her days in an institution."

"Do you have any idea why Antonia and Lucy don't speak to Gaylord anymore?"

"None. I know it's hurt him a great deal. It would be nice if someday that family could work out its problems. Maybe now that this Billy Brewster's here, things will change for the better."

"Maybe," said Jane. She could see her father watching her. She knew what he was thinking.

"How's Beryl getting along?" he asked casually.

"Okay." She paused. "We had a long talk last night."

"Did you?"

Jane knew that if she started this conversation, she might not be happy with the way it ended. Yet she and her father had to talk. Their current rapport had been hard-won over the years, and she hated to put it in jeopardy. Still, if she was ever going to make any sense of things, she knew she needed his side of the story. At least he was in a good mood. There might never be a better time. "I asked Beryl to tell me why the two of you don't get along."

He raised one bushy eyebrow and crossed his hands over his stomach, hooking his thumbs in his belt. "I see. With the scorecard she's been keeping against me all these years, you must have been up all night."

Not a good opening. "I'd like to hear your side of it."

"Would you now? My daughter wants me to explain my life to her."

"It's not like that."

"Isn't it?" He stood and turned to the window, looking up at the cathedral on the hill. "Dammit all, I hate this. These things never end. How can I explain something so intricate, so many-sided as a life. I'm not even sure where the truth lies myself."

"Dad, I know. I'm not blaming you for anything. I just need to understand. Beryl isn't an evil person. Selfish, perhaps, but then we're all selfish."

He gave a small laugh. "From your mouth to God's ears." He turned around and looked at her. "I assume Beryl gave you the standard—*Ray came and took our lovely Helen away from us*—speech."

She smiled. "Something like that."

"Yes, well, from her perspective, I suppose that was true. Yet, no one else seemed so mortally wounded until Beryl went around convincing the entire clan that it was the biggest thing since the Battle of Britain. Maybe I'm wrong, but lots of people get married and move away. Last I heard, it wasn't considered *abduction*." He sat down on the edge of his desk. "When we got engaged, Helen knew I'd been studying for the bar here in Minnesota. She knew I had to return to take the tests. I mean, it wasn't a secret. I never hid it from her or her parents."

"And you did come back," said Jane.

"Yes, we did. For two years. You were born. That's when Beryl started applying the pressure for us to return to England for a visit. After all, everyone wanted to see the baby. Actually, at the time, I thought it was a great idea. I knew your mother was homesick, and it felt like the perfect solution. So we went. That's when Beryl came to me with her latest scheme. She mentioned that there was a firm in Southampton that was interested in talking to an American lawyer—a bit of consulting work, so to speak. I said sure, I'd go in and see if I could help. My father was a corporate lawyer, as you know, and I'd specialized in corporate law before I changed my mind and switched over to criminal. When I got there, I realized instantly that they weren't looking for a few hours of consultation, they wanted a fulltime employee. By the time I got home that night, I could tell Beryl had been working behind the scenes all day, preparing everyone for the news that I'd been offered a job and we could now stay in England. The thing is, I could see how excited Helen was. Everyone was pumped and primed and almost on the doorstep waiting for *the big news*. I felt like a total bastard. God, what was I supposed to do? I loved your mother very much. I could see it was what she wanted. So, after thinking about it for several days, I called this company back and told them I'd changed my mind and I would take the job after all. I think I secretly hoped that in the interim the position had been offered to someone else, but no such luck. So, I flew back here and settled our affairs—I was already involved in a partnership, and boy was *that* sticky—and then returned to England. I think at the time I was even a little optimistic. After all, we wouldn't be staying forever. A few years at most. It might be good experience. Even fun."

"Did Mother understand you viewed it as temporary."

Ray nodded. "Absolutely. We never hid things from each other. But then a couple years later Peter was born. And I was given a promotion. You were so happy with all your friends and cousins. You were in school by then. Helen was helping her brother Jimmy part-time at his restaurant in Poole. Our lives seemed settled. Somehow, it didn't seem fair for me to break that up simply because I despised corporate law and wanted to come back to Minnesota to practice here. So, we stayed."

"And then Grandma and Grandpa died."

Ray got up and sat down in the chair next to her. "They did. Your mother was close to her parents and it was a hard time for her, but we got through it. Several months later, I decided it was finally my chance to make the change. Helen knew I was unhappy. Unlike Beryl, she realized compromises had to be made. She knew I'd been making one for almost nine years. She was the one who finally made the decision. She announced at dinner one night that I was quitting my job in Southampton in the spring and we were returning to Minnesota. I know it hit Beryl like a ton of bricks, but dammit, she had no say in our lives. None. She came to me the next night and told me that if I took Helen away from her family, it would kill her. I couldn't believe she'd be so cruel. That was the first time I felt I got a true inkling of what she was really like. Before, I had merely seen her behavior as meddling, but now I saw the power struggle for what it really was." Sighing wearily, he closed his eyes for a moment. "The thing is, your mother did take the move very hard. The adjustment was difficult for all of us. And then . . ." His voice trailed off to a whisper. "She did die. I wondered for a long time if Beryl hadn't been right."

Jane reached for his hand. "You mustn't think that. Even the doctors said it was terribly unusual. You had no way of knowing."

He cleared his throat, struggling with some internal emotion. "And then you left. I felt like my world was crumbling. If it hadn't been for Peter . . ."

There it was, thought Jane. The betrayal. She'd gone back to England shortly after her mother had died. It was like a lighted stick of dynamite, all the past emotions set to explode all over again. "I had to go, don't you see? I had to walk along the water where we'd walked—she and I—so many times. I had to see the house. Sit in the garden."

"I know," he said softly. "I understood that. I never tried to stop you from going. But you didn't have to stay for two years! I felt like you blamed me for making you move back here. In some part of your heart, you blamed me for your mother's death."

Jane was aghast. "I never thought that!"

"No?" He looked away. "It was such a confused time." Taking a handkerchief out of his back pocket, he wiped his eyes. Then, turning back to her he said, "I know you think it was entirely your decision, staying those two years. But let me tell you, you're naive if you think Beryl didn't have any input. I know her. And I know you. You've never understood manipulative people. I'm sure Beryl was desperate to have you stay. It must have felt like having a little bit of Helen back with her. You're so very much like your mother. Quiet. Strong. Introspective. And don't kid yourself. Beryl was angry at me. She wanted to win. She knew how much I needed you to come home. We were engaged in this crazy, sick, transatlantic struggle over a thirteen-year-old child. All my adult life I'd felt like I'd been doing battle with Beryl Cornelius. I simply couldn't stand it anymore. Your mother was dead. And now the 'great continuing argument' had switched to you. She'd worn me down. I'm ashamed to admit that instead of slugging it out, I simply withdrew. I guess I withdrew so totally that even when you did come home, I didn't know how to reach you anymore. I wasn't even sure I wanted to. You seemed like such a stranger."

"But it was my decision to stay," said Jane, surprised by the weakness in her voice.

"You think about that one a bit longer, sweetheart. You were thirteen years old. A child. Thirteen-year-olds don't make life decisions like that all by themselves." Ray got up and took hold of her hands, lifting her to her feet. "Jane," he said gently, "I know this is hard for you. Just like your mother, you've become the battleground, and I don't know what to do about it. Whatever I decide, it ends up hurting you."

She hugged him tightly. "I have to think about this. But you have to believe me, I love you, Dad. I've always loved you. I never blamed you for Mom's death." She could feel him trembling.

"And I love you." He drew back. "But you've got to understand one thing. I don't like that woman. And I don't know how far I can ever go in putting the past behind me. Not when I see things happening all over again."

"I don't know that they are," said Jane. "But I promise you, no one's going to come between us. You and Peter mean the world to me."

"And Beryl?"

"I don't want to hurt you, but after Mom's death she was like a second mother to me. I can't turn my back on her."

He nodded. "I understand."

"I'm not sure you do." They started toward the door. "Just give it some time, okay? We'll sort this out."

"You're so much like your mother." His smile was deeply sad.

Jane realized she hadn't said anything about having Peter

and Sigrid's wedding at her house. About Beryl's promise to turn the backyard into a garden.

"Well," said Ray, opening the door, "be sure to tell that old goat *we* had a chat. See how happily she swallows that little tidbit."

"I'll call you." She gave him a kiss on the cheek and started for the stairs. As she got outside and crossed the empty street to her car, she glanced up at the second-floor window. There he stood, his hand resting against the glass, silently looking down at her. Realizing she was staring, she turned her head away, afraid that he might see the tears in her eyes.

23

Fleur sat waiting in her car across the street from the Allen Grimby. It was a lovely spring afternoon. Earlier in the day she'd promised that on her way home from the university, she'd swing by and pick up Antonia. Her meeting with the theatre board would be over by four-thirty. Fleur glanced at her watch. It was almost a quarter-to-five. Antonia should be out soon.

Inside the glass front of the building Fleur could see people milling about. A young man was running a large vacuum cleaner across the plush carpet. A woman behind the ticket counter appeared to be counting something, most likely money. Outside the theatre, a man on a ladder was replacing Torald's name on the marquee with that of his understudy. Such a sad business she thought to herself. Actors might be interchangeable. People weren't.

Her eyes traveled slowly to the top of the building, watching a pigeon perch precariously on one of the ornate cement moldings. The Allen Grimby was a three-story, brick structure. The third floor contained all the office space necessary to run the large theatre company. Second floor held the costume department, the small prop shop, storage and janitorial supplies. The main prop area was in the cavernous basement, along with the actors' dressing rooms. Fleur's hand fiddled nervously with a gold pin on her sweater as her attention was drawn back to the street. Lately, this constant need to examine her surroundings had become almost a reflex. She'd finally gotten up the nerve last night to tell Antonia about her suspicions.

For weeks, Fleur had felt like she was being watched. She even thought she'd seen a face in one of the parlor windows late one night. And several days later a stranger had been standing outside under the grape arbor. She hadn't gotten a good look. The person disappeared around the side of the house almost as soon as Fleur opened the curtains.

Antonia had listened, her politeness feeling like condescension. When Fleur insisted the police be called, Antonia had laughed! It was simple imagination, that was all. Who on earth would want to watch them?

Fleur had to admit that she didn't have an answer to that question. Yet the feelings wouldn't leave. She imagined strange eyes watching her all the time now—even in the shower, or alone in her bedroom. She knew her reactions were becoming almost paranoid. She should never have said anything. And anyway, Antonia simply couldn't handle any more worries right now. She had enough on her plate. Fleur had never meant to add to her problems. Everything she'd done—*everything*—was only meant to help. No matter what anyone said, she *had* helped. Still, for whatever reason, Fleur couldn't shake the sense that they were all being watched.

A bus whizzed past, sending a spray of puddle water over the windshield. Damn. She'd just gotten the car washed. And where the hell was Antonia? Fleur had envisioned a leisurely drive home. Perhaps stopping at their favorite café for coffee and a warm chocolate croissant. They hadn't done anything like that together in months.

Even though Fleur and Antonia lived in the same house, during rehearsals Antonia was never around. After all these years, Fleur was used to it—a hazard of the trade. Living with a successful playwright had never been easy. But then, when she compared her life to Antonia's, her own problems felt small. It was funny. Human pain had the strange ability to make a person bitter, sour on all of life's possibilities. Or, for those who could rise above it, pain could make a person terribly strong and resourceful. Even hopeful. Antonia was strong. Sometimes too strong for her own good. And yet the bitterness was also there. Fleur was powerfully drawn to both sides of this complex woman. For good or ill, after all these years, Fleur knew she was deeply in love.

The car door opened.

Fleur jumped. She realized she'd been lost in thought.

"God, am I glad that's over," said Antonia, easing into the seat. She leaned her head back and rubbed her neck. "I hate these rah rah meetings. I know the play will do well for them. Why do we have to talk about it endlessly?"

Fleur started the motor. "Are you up for some dinner?"

Antonia turned on the radio and found her favorite classical station. "Sure." She hesitated. "I suppose we should see what Victor's got on the agenda tonight. He might want to come along."

Fleur scrunched up her nose.

"Hey, I thought you two liked each other."

"Pavic is . . . Pavic. I consider him a friend. I was just sort of hoping we might get away from the madding crowd this evening. Stare into each other's eyes for an hour or two."

"Over a plate of pasta? With the entire world watching?"

"Why not?"

Antonia slipped her hand around Fleur's. "I could use a night off."

"I know."

"All right," she smiled. "I'm in your hands."

"Good choice." As Fleur pulled away from the curb, she noticed a figure standing in one of the theatre's third floor windows. She could feel the dark eyes following them.

Straightening her back, she headed quickly into the ano-
nymity of rush-hour traffic.

24

Beryl wiped her hands on her paisley apron and opened
the front door. Cordelia stood outside, a finger pressed to
her lips.

"Shhh," she said, slipping inside. She was dressed
completely in black. Black boots, black jeans, black sweatshirt, black silk scarf tossed rakishly over one shoulder, and
her auburn curls pulled back into a black tam. "Where's
Janey?"

"I'm right here," said Jane, coming down the stairs.

Cordelia shook her head disapprovingly. "Go back up
and change that shirt. It's much too light colored."

"Let's live dangerously."

Beryl touched the black gloves in Cordelia's back
pocket. "You look like you belong in a spy novel."

Cordelia crouched lower and whispered, "The game's
afoot." She sniffed the air. "I smell cookies."

"Chocolate chip," said Beryl, walking back into the
kitchen.

Cordelia followed. "By the way, is Billy here?"

"He and Erin are sitting by the fire in the living room,"
said Jane. "After dinner, Beryl invited them down for des-
sert."

Cordelia stuck her finger into the cookie dough for a
taste. "I've got good news. Billy! Erin!" she shouted,
"Front and center. You are wanted in the kitchen." She
walked over to the stove and peeked inside the oven.
"When will they be ready to eat?"

Beryl slapped her hand. "If you don't leave that door closed, they won't be ready at all. Now, go stand over there or you won't be allowed a single morsel. I mean it." She tapped her foot.

"Yes, ma'am," said Cordelia meekly.

Billy walked into the room, followed closely by Erin. "Did someone call us?"

"I did," said Cordelia, gazing longingly at the cookie dough now so far out of her reach. "I have some wonderful news. You will be receiving official word by mail, but the Allen Grimby has decided to offer you a permanent position in the repertory company. Congratulations." She extended her hand.

Billy shook it excitedly. "This is absolutely great!" He turned to Erin and gave her a squeeze. "We can stay!" he squealed. "We can look for that house now. We can start our new life."

For such good news, Erin seemed more than a little subdued.

"Is something wrong?" asked Jane, noticing her serious expression.

Erin shrugged. "No. Well, I mean, I was just thinking about Torald."

"Oh, honey," said Billy, putting his arm around her, "we get to be happy about this. A position at the Allen Grimby is like having lightning strike you. It doesn't happen to many people."

"That's true," said Cordelia, inching ever closer to the magic bowl.

Like a good soldier, Erin nodded. "Of course," she said, giving everyone a quick smile. "I just can't help but think about him."

"You're a kind person," said Beryl. "Nothing to be ashamed of."

"Yes she is," smiled Billy. "I don't know what I'd do without her." He gave her another hug. "You know, I can't wait to tell Gaylord. Grandfather, I mean. What do you think, sweetheart? Should we give him a call?"

Silently, Erin looked from face to face. "Sure, I suppose."

"Or we could drive over. Tell him the news in person. I have to be at the theatre by seven-thirty. We'd have plenty of time. He's just a few blocks away."

Erin played with the bow around her neck. "Well ... sure, I guess. It's just ... I don't think he likes me very much, Billy. Why don't you just go. I could stay here and help Beryl clean up."

"No!" he insisted. "What do you mean he doesn't like you?"

"You mustn't think that," said Beryl.

Cordelia was now mere inches from the bag of chocolate chips. Sensing the bag was in peril, Beryl snatched it away and put it back in the cupboard.

Cordelia glared.

"Come on, Erin," said Billy, taking her hand. "I'm getting your coat. And hey, maybe we should stop by Antonia's first. She wasn't planning on coming to the theatre tonight. She'll want to know, too."

Even though Erin's disinterest was all too apparent, she let Billy lead her out of the room.

Jane glanced at her watch. "Cordelia, we'd better get going. It's getting late."

"But the *cookies*?" said Cordelia, a look of desperation in her eyes.

"Where are you off to?" asked Beryl, putting on the oven mitts.

"Oh, you know," smiled Jane. "To the mall. Cordelia needs more black clothes."

"She does?" Beryl eyed her curiously.

Cordelia closed her eyes and thrust her chin in the air. "My true calling in life is to roam *Uptown*. One simply cannot exist there and express any *attitude* at all unless one is dressed in black. Preferably, with studs and spikes."

Jane grabbed Cordelia's arm and dragged her toward the front door.

"But I could do with a cookie before I go."

"I'll save you some," said Beryl. She waved goodbye.

* * *

"The light's still on," groused Cordelia, unwrapping another lump of bubble gum. "That secretary's still inside."

"He's Dad's law clerk."

"Whatever." She adjusted her sunglasses.

"It's pitch dark out," said Jane, turning down the heat in her car. "If you don't take those things off, you're going to kill yourself walking across the street."

"I was just wondering. Maybe some people might think I'm Roy Orbison."

"He's dead."

"Humph." She tossed the gum wrapper over her shoulder. "You always know just the right thing to say."

They sat in silence and watched the night wind blow dry leaves under the street lamps. The row house was dark except for the front, main-floor window.

"He'll be leaving soon."

"Always the optimist. I hope your father pays him overtime. By the way, I know you've got a key to your father's office, but what if the files are locked?"

"I know where the extra set is kept."

Cordelia blew a bubble. "Just checking. What do you think you're going to find, anyway? I mean, is it worth all this trouble?"

"Gaylord Werness retained my father many years ago. Dad can't tell me what it was about—client privilege. He said it would be unethical. But I remember him saying something about it, and believe me, it was no small matter. Now, I don't want to hear any moralizing. Since it was settled out of court, there are no public records. I have to know what it was about."

"Enough to be arrested for breaking and entering?"

"It's not breaking and entering if we have a key."

"Humph." Her second bubble lingered in the air and then burst all over her chin.

"Cordelia, do you realize how irritating that gum is?"

"You were the one who wouldn't wait so I could have a cookie. You're simply going to have to put up with it. After all, I have to have some fun, don't I?"

Jane groaned. "Look, he's leaving."

The light was switched off in the front room. A moment later a man came out and got into a car.

"That's our cue," said Jane. "Come on."

As he drove away, Cordelia unwedged herself from the seat and puffed across the street. "That automobile of yours is too much. Why don't you donate it to the government. NASA's having difficulty with the space shuttle. They might want to run some longevity studies on it."

"Quiet," said Jane. "Let's get this over with. I've got to get back to the restaurant."

"Deary me, a curdled sauce?"

"A dinner date with Dorrie Harris."

"Ah, trouble at City Hall."

"No, not really. She said she might be able to help me figure some of this out."

They walked quietly into the hall. As they entered the front room, Jane nodded to a series of files against the back wall. "I want you to check those while I run downstairs."

"Key?" said Cordelia, rubbing her fingers together.

Jane felt around inside the coat closet until she found the extra set. She tossed them to Cordelia. "See if these fit."

Cordelia moved down the row until she came to the W's. "Yup," she said, pulling the drawer out. "Let's see. No, I don't see any Werness. There's a *Wilber vs. Brinkmann. White vs. Adolphson.*"

"It's probably too old," said Jane. She turned around. "What was that?"

"What was what?"

"Cordelia, be still. I think he's coming back."

"Oh God."

"Close that drawer and get over here."

Cordelia shoved it shut and leaped over a chair as she bounded toward Jane and the waiting closet.

"Get in here!" Jane pulled her inside and shut the door.

"Why do I let you get me involved in these things?" whispered Cordelia.

"Shhh!"

"Your elbow is in my ear."

"Zip it!" Jane put her hand over Cordelia's mouth. Outside, the light went on. She could hear the muffled sound of someone dialing a phone.

"Hello, Carol?" said the voice. "I forgot. I promised I'd bring home dinner tonight." There was a pause. "Okay, no that sounds fine. What do you want besides the Moo Goo Gai Pan?" Silence. "No, I won't forget the chopsticks. Hey? What's this? I don't remember seeing this scarf before."

Cordelia's hand flew to her neck.

"That's funny. Huh? What did you say, Hon?" The floor creaked as he walked toward the closet door. "Jesus, can't we spend one night without your sister coming over? She eats enough for three people. I don't know why we put up with it." He put his hand on the doorknob and twisted it back and forth in a nervous gesture. "She's a total mooch, that's why. No, I won't accept that. I'm not cold and uncaring. I married you, not your tubby sibling. What? Now that's totally unfair." He opened the door a crack, the scarf dangling from his hand. "I am not! How can you say that? See what's she's doing to us? Is she worth it, Carol? Is she? I mean, screw this." With his eyes fixed on the phone, he drew the door open and slammed it for emphasis. "This isn't the first fight we've had about her. I'm not saying that, Carol." Again, silence. "Fine. You do that. Call her and tell *her* to bring you dinner. I'm going to a movie." He threw down the receiver and a second later burst out of the building.

Jane could feel something wet stick to her nose. She knew what it was. "Suck that thing in."

"Helps relieve the stress," said Cordelia. "By the way, you smell good. Is that the oil Christine liked so much? The stuff she bought for you?"

"Why Cordelia, I didn't know you cared. Come on. If that guy comes back again, we may not have much time."

"Okay by me. We can leave now if you'd like."

They climbed out of the closet.

"Not before we check the basement files." Jane slipped a flashlight out of her back pocket and together they started down the steep back steps. The deeper they went, the stronger the smell of mildew became. As they entered a long, narrow room, Jane shined her light on the filing cabinets. "Here we go."

Cordelia dumped herself into a folding chair and put her head in her hands. "I hate basements. They're always full of spiders and centipedes. Not to mention—"

"Good thing you didn't go into basement waterproofing."

"Very funny."

"I don't believe it," said Jane. "Here it is." She drew out a tattered manilla file with the names *Werness v. Millhauser* on it. She sat down next to Cordelia and took our her glasses. As she was reading, Cordelia fidgeted.

"Maybe I'll just run upstairs and get that *Wilber vs. Brinkmann* file. Might be interesting."

"Look at this," said Jane. "This case didn't involve Gaylord at all. It was Torald. Gaylord must have been the one who came to the office to retain my father."

"What did Torald do?"

Jane read quietly. "Jesus. Statutory rape. The girl, Karen Millhauser, was fifteen. Apparently she had a part in one of Gaylord's plays. So did Torald. It was at the Blackburn Playhouse, back in 1975. The parents accused Torald of taking advantage of their daughter. They were going to take him to court."

"But your dad helped settle it before it got that far."

"So it would seem. Looks like there was quite a large cash settlement—paid by Gaylord. And Torald was supposed to enter a counseling program."

"I wonder if he ever did?"

"And I wonder what happened to the girl," said Jane. She continued to read. "Dad's scribbled some notes at the bottom. *Gaylord terribly concerned about the kind of counseling Torald would receive. Suggested a minister. Specifically requests we give no information about the case to his daughters or to a man named Malcolm Coopersmith.*"

"I wonder if they even knew?" mused Cordelia aloud. "Some loving family."

Jane closed the file and got to her feet. "We better get going. We found what I was looking for."

"More dirt on the Werness family. What good is it? I mean, what does it tell you other than that Torald was a complete mess. You knew that already."

"I knew he was a womanizer. A fifteen-year-old girl is hardly a woman."

"Good point." Cordelia followed Jane up the steps to the main floor.

"I can't help but feel it's all part of some larger pattern. Eventually, I'm going to put it together."

"I wish you luck," said Cordelia, cracking open the front door. The cathedral on the hill was lit by the diffuse light of several tall street lamps. It looked like a Salvador Dali painting. The only thing missing was a melting pocket watch. "All clear. Now, instead of taking me home, I want you to drive me over to the theatre. I have some work I need to finish before tomorrow. I'll catch a ride with someone else. Not to worry."

"But Cordelia," said Jane. "I thought you wanted to hit the Uptown area. See what's shaking. In that outfit you might be able to find a super deal on some Grateful Dead albums."

Cordelia pulled her tam indignantly down over her eyes and, with a sweeping gesture, unwrapped another lump of bubble gum.

25

A little Thirties jazz, thought Cordelia, adjusting the volume on her stereo receiver. Woody Allen wasn't the only one who found it good mood music. She switched off the overhead light and sat down behind her desk. The flexible artist's lamp next to her was now the only source of light in the room. She absolutely adored her third-floor office at this time of night, loved the tacky glitz of the city lights against a cold indigo sky. It was like an aphrodisiac. Looking out her window at downtown St. Paul, she felt alive with possibilities. But now, down to business. Where was that proposal Gaylord had sent over? She'd made a firm commitment to the head of the board that she would study it before the meeting tomorrow.

As she paged through the typed document, she stopped at a page labeled, "Special Requests." Gaylord was asking that, when he was at the theatre for *any* reason, Evian water and orange juice be available to him at all times. That was request *one*. Reading down the rest of the list, she found herself snorting with laughter. Lord, this guy must think he's a rock star.

Outside the door, Cordelia could hear footsteps heading her direction. "Don't knock. Just enter," she called.

The footsteps stopped.

Her eyes fell back to the page. Vitamin shots? The Grimby was supposed to staff a nurse for Gaylord's vitamin shots?

"Come!" she shouted impatiently. "Contrary to popular opinion, I do not take the form of a vampire until much later in the evening." She looked up. "Is anyone there?"

No answer.

She stood and crossed to the door, yanking it open. The reception area was dark and quiet. Humph. She resumed her position behind her desk. Perhaps *she* was the one who should demand vitamin shots—and ear exams. She picked up the top page and continued to read.

This time, the phone interrupted her. "Speak," she snarled into the receiver. Evenings were usually the best time to work. Nobody bothered her with trivia.

"Hi, Ms. Thorn?"

"Get to the point."

"Ah, sure. This is Barbara down at the ticket counter. There's a guy here who says you were supposed to leave him some comps for tomorrow night's performance. I can't find them."

Cordelia could hear her snapping her gum. "I don't remember promising anyone comps—"

"He says you did. His name is Charlie Prather."

"I don't know a Charlie—"

"No, sorry. It's Charlie *L.* Prather."

Cordelia had always been suspicious of people who used their middle initial. They were probably all Young Republicans with *attitude.* "Oh, Charlie *L.* Prather. That makes all the difference."

"What should I do?"

Cordelia took a deep breath and attempted a cheerful smile. "Give the man his tickets—on my authority."

"I can't do that."

Cordelia felt herself beginning to erupt. With a brief overpowering sense of calm she said, "Why, Barbara?"

"It's SRO."

This was the last straw. She stood. "Tell him to wait for me. I'll be right down." She jammed the phone back on its hook and headed for the elevators. Incompetents. She was surrounded by incompetents!

On her way to the elevator, she noticed a light on in the stage manager's office. Strange. He should be backstage. She glanced at her watch. Nine-fifteen. Perhaps it was intermission.

Swinging off the elevator, she approached the ticket window. Instead of a woman, a young man sat reading a magazine behind the counter. He was biting his nails furiously.

"Excuse me?" she said, tapping on the glass.

"Yes? Oh, hi, Ms. Thorn. I didn't recognize you for a minute." He glanced at her clothes. "A death in the family?"

"Cute. Where's the man who wants the comps?"

"Excuse me?"

"I just got a call from Barbara. She said there was a man down here insisting that I—"

"Barbara who?"

"How should I know! Barbara Bush! Barbra Streisand! Barbara Billingsly!"

"Who's that last one?"

"Barbara Billingsly?" She closed her eyes. "Don't tell me you've never watched 'Leave It to Beaver?'"

He shrugged. "I was reading Neitzche when I was nine."

"Poor boy." She looked around. There didn't seem to be any irate Charlie L. Prather in the vicinity.

"I also liked Ernest Hemingway and—"

"Don't tell me. Jack London."

He cocked his head in surprise. "How did you know?"

"It figures." She turned on her heel and headed back to the elevators. Somebody was playing games with Cordelia *M*. Thorn.

After an eternity of pushing buttons, smiling at theatregoers and silently cursing, the elevator finally arrived. The mirrored elevator did nothing to restore her good mood. She really *must* take off the tam. It made her head look like a mushroom. Stepping into the darkened third-floor corridor, she noticed that the light in her office had been switched off. Wonderful. Another overly zealous night janitor. She approached the door. "Oh *great*," she said out loud as she realized it was also locked. Well, at least he or she was thorough. She fished in her pocket for her keys. Maybe she should just give up and take the papers home. Except, she wouldn't be able to catch a ride until tonight's performance was over. Damn that car of hers. The garage still hadn't been able to figure out why that little red light came on all the time. As she slipped the key into the lock and pushed it open, the door instantly slammed back into her body. The momentum sent her rocketing backward across the hall to the far wall. In her shock and surprise, she felt herself sliding to the floor, her legs splayed and her tam knocked down over her eyes. Well!

Dazed, she was aware of the sound of her door being locked from inside.

She took a moment to get her bearings. What the fuck? She gave herself another minute and then heaved herself up and raced to the phone on the reception desk. "Security!" she hissed into the receiver. "This is an emergency." She waited. After what seemed like days, a man's voice said, "This is Ed. What's the problem?"

"Cordelia Thorn here. My third floor office is being burgled." Somewhere in the distance, she could hear the sound of glass shattering. She didn't even want to think what it could mean.

"I'll be up in two shakes." The line clicked.

Good, thought Cordelia, still holding on to the buzzing phone for dear life. She wondered if she should head for the stairs and make a getaway. She listened for a moment. Everything was very still. The only sound was coming from the water cooler in the corner. All of a sudden, she simply *had* to have a glass of water. God, she was suggestable. She returned her gaze to the door. If there was burgling going on, they were damn well doing it quietly.

The elevator opened and two men stepped off.

"Which office?" whispered Ed.

Cordelia pointed.

"Is there another access?"

"No. That's the only way in or out."

The men positioned themselves on either side.

"This is Security," said Ed loudly. "You can't get away. Just unlock the door and come out."

They waited. Ed looked at his partner. They both shook their heads.

"Try once more," whispered Cordelia. "Maybe the guy has his head inside my coat closet or something."

Ed nodded. "This is Security," he said again, this time even louder. "You can't get away. Just unlock the door and come out."

The partner put his ear to the door. He listened for a long moment. Then, pulling a set a keys out of his pocket, he fumbled for the right one and unlocked it. The room was dark. Drawing a gun, Ed stepped in front of him and switched on the light. After a second he called, "It's empty."

"What?" Cordelia bristled. "It can't be."

The other man entered.

Coming from the open door, Cordelia could feel a cold gust of wind. Resolutely, she moved around the desk and approached the office herself. What she saw took her breath away. She gripped the door and swallowed hard as she took in the ravaged sight. The entire room had been trashed. Drawers opened, their contents scattered on the floor. All her books dumped from their shelves. Everything was askew. Paintings. Schedules. Tapes. Everything except— She stepped further into the mess. There on her now empty desk, totally untouched and still in its proper place, rested her FEMINIST HELLHOLE sign. Her mouth fell open.

"Looks like he got out through this window," said Ed. He motioned for Cordelia to come over. Bending down he pointed, "See? He tied these jump ropes together to make a long cord. Then he tied that to the base of the radiator. I'd say he used it to get down to that second-floor ledge. I'll bet we find he broke into one of the offices down there. That's how he got away."

Limply, Cordelia nodded.

The other security guard knelt down for a better look. "I wonder if he brought the jump ropes with him?"

"No," said Cordelia. "They were in my closet." As they exchanged confused looks she erupted. "Well, what are you staring at? I *exercise*! I didn't entirely miss the point of the Eighties!"

Ed motioned to his partner. "You get downstairs and see what you can shake loose. I doubt you'll find our guy. He's had too much time to get away."

"Probably right." He got to his feet and left.

Cordelia was beginning to regain her composure. As Ed started his examination of the room, Cordelia put her hand on his back and drew him close. "Listen, Eddy. I know you're going to have to file a report on this."

"Yup." He nodded.

"Well, I wonder if you could do me one rather teeny little favor?"

"Sure, Ms. Thorn. What?"

"Don't mention the jump ropes."

"But . . . I have to. They were used by this guy to escape. I couldn't leave that out."

"No," she said, putting a finger to her lips. "I see your point." She thought for a moment. "Well, how about this. Why don't you say the burglar found them in my closet—and that I told you they were props. You know? From the prop department. Get it?" She elbowed him in the ribs. "Come on Ed. My reputation is at stake here."

"Well?"

"Good man, Edward. I knew I could count on you."

26

Jane found Dorrie seated by the brick hearth in the darker, more intimate room of the downstairs pub. Since it was a busy Friday night, Jane had reserved the table. As she walked past the bar, she'd asked for a lager and lime, waiting while the young bartender lowered the brass beer pull and drew her drink. Then, picking up a basket of fresh popcorn, she approached the table in the back. "Have you ordered dinner yet?" she asked, setting the basket down between them.

"Are you kidding?" crowed Dorrie, "I ordered my favorite. Beef and kidney pie."

Jane grinned. "Would you like another beer?" She nodded to Dorrie's almost empty glass.

Dorrie shook her head. "One bottle is enough on an empty stomach." She stretched and then took a handful of popcorn.

They both listened for a moment to the Celtic harp music coming from the next room.

"Heard anything more about the murder investigation?" asked Jane.

"Just that Trevelyan had you in his office this morning."

Jane was surprised that Dorrie knew. News must travel fast. "Unfortunately, true. I think he's trying to push wherever he can. See what happens."

"I heard you were the one who found Torald's body."

Jane looked down into her drink. Every night since it had happened, she'd seen that gruesome image in her mind as she was trying to get to sleep. It was like a bad dream that wouldn't go away. "I was. And two nights before he'd broken into my garage. It's kind of a long story. Do you know about Billy Brewster?"

"I just found out."

"Well, Billy thought Torald was going through some of his papers. They're all stored out there. Billy and his wife, Erin, are renting my third floor right now. Anyway, Trevelyan thinks there might be more to it than that. He's trying to find someone who had both the motive and the opportunity to murder Torald. I had the second—he's trying to determine if I had the first."

Dorrie leaned back and studied Jane for a moment. "How much do you know about the Werness family?"

"I'm learning."

"Would it surprise you to know that Antonia and I had an affair many years ago?"

Startled, Jane looked up. "It sure would. I thought Harris was . . ."

"My married name? It is. I was married for six years to a man named Brad Harris. He died several years ago. But before Brad, I had my share of lovers, both male and female. During one of Antonia's separations from Fleur—and there have been several—we were an item for about ten months. Remember, I'm not talking about yesterday. This was a good fifteen years ago. I even lived in the Kenwood house for a time."

Jane whistled. "Do other people know?"

"You mean the people who voted me into office?" She shook her head. "I decided that if someone brought it up,

I'd talk about it. I figured I had the energy to either attempt to educate the public about bisexuality or win an election. I couldn't do both—not even in this town. At any rate, I took great care to make sure my positions were crystal clear. I've always supported gay and lesbian issues. I'm certainly not going to deny anything. But very little about my personal life ever came up. During the campaign I was dating a lovely man who works for the St. Paul Chamber Orchestra. I still see him now and then, but it never went anywhere. I hope I have another good relationship in my life somewhere down the line, but it doesn't make much difference to me whether it's a man or a woman." Dorrie adjusted her glasses. "But, let's get back to Antonia."

"All right." Jane was much too curious not to bite. "How did you meet?"

Dorrie smiled. "Actually, my mother introduced us." She took a sip of beer and sat back a bit more comfortably. "It became clear to me almost immediately that Antonia was interested in something beyond a friendship. She told me her lover had just moved out and then she invited me to dinner. One thing led to another."

"So you know the family pretty well."

"That would be overstating it, but I know them better than most."

"And how do you think you can help?"

"Well, I thought perhaps I could tell you a little about my experience with them. Who knows? You might just find something that could help."

Jane grabbed a handful of popcorn. "All right. Sure. I'd love to hear anything you have to say."

"Maybe I'll take that other beer."

"Why not?" Jane waved over a waiter and placed the order.

"Now," said Dorrie, making an arch of her hands and resting her chin on top. "I've been thinking about this. Let's start with Antonia. As you may have already gathered, she's an immensely powerful personality. She's also very controlling. Shortly after I moved to the Kenwood home—I was teaching tenth-grade American History in Bloomington at the time—I told her about a problem I was having with another one of the teachers. Two days later I found out she'd gone to the school and accosted the man in the hall, demanding to know why he'd taken a certain position. She even threatened to have him fired. As you might expect, this didn't help me or the situation one bit. When I finally got home that night, I demanded to know what she thought she was doing. She was absolutely aghast. Totally innocent. She was merely trying to help. She couldn't understand why I was so upset."

"That's unbelievable." As Jane listened she was trying to imagine Dorrie and Antonia together. There was at least a ten-year difference in their ages, not that it mattered. But Jane had never imagined Dorrie with a woman before. It changed things.

The waiter arrived with the fresh drink. He set it down in front of Dorrie and removed her empty glass.

She took a long sip before continuing. "It was like that almost from the beginning. Antonia is a great deal of fun, and highly seductive. She gets her way most of the time by simple force of personality. But, even though I found her periodically very loving and attentive, in my experience she's not someone who knows how to nurture. That's true of Torald, too. Lucy is probably the most nurturing, but she seems to confine it to animals and birds. Anyway, back to Antonia. After living at the house for several weeks, it became apparent that I was going to need a study in which I could work undisturbed for several hours each night. Antonia was only too happy to comply. The only problem was, she treated the closed door as if it didn't exist. Lucy was every bit as bad. Even after I went so far as to put up a sign, they simply ignored it and barged into the room whenever the spirit moved. I found it annoying at first. Later, I became positive enraged. It's one of the reasons we broke up. I had *no* privacy."

"What about Torald?" asked Jane. "Was he around much?"

Dorrie shook her head. "It was my impression that

Antonia and Torald didn't get along. I don't think he felt comfortable at the house when she was there."

"Do you know why?"

"No. And she never said. But he and Lucy were very close, that was clear. He'd come over sometimes when he knew Antonia was away."

"Did you like him?"

Dorrie looked into the fire. "I don't know. No, not really. I found him distant. He was never very interested in anything I had to say."

"What about Lucy?"

"Actually, I liked Lucy a great deal. But she was having some terrible drinking problems during my stay at the house. One night, I remember it vividly, I'd just come home from a late meeting. I came in through the kitchen instead of the front door so no one heard me. The house was quiet except for some Gershwin playing on the stereo in the living room. As I walked through the darkened kitchen on my way upstairs, I heard voices. It was Torald and Lucy. They were sitting at the dining room table, Lucy with a half-empty bottle of Jack Daniel's in front of her. I decided to listen for a moment to see what I was about to interrupt. Torald was crying—I mean *really* crying. Lucy just sat and stared at him. After a minute she took his hand and tried to get him to stop."

"Do you know what it was about?"

"Not really. It seemed Lucy had done something that afternoon, something that must have set him off. I hadn't seen her drink anything in weeks, so my impression was that it'd upset her, too, only she was just dealing with it in a different way. Torald was pounding the table and cursing a blue streak when Antonia and Malcolm Coopersmith walked in."

"Really? Was Malcolm there often?"

"He and Lucy were dating—for many years I think. It was obvious he cared about her a great deal." She laughed a bit self-consciously and shook her head. "You know, so many nights I came home to find him and Antonia sitting together on the couch in her study, you'd almost think she and Malcolm had the relationship. Anyway, getting back to that night, Malcolm put his arm around Torald and led him away into the living room. Antonia waited about thirty seconds and then grabbed the bottle of whiskey and threw it against the wall. I'll never forget the look in Lucy's eyes—she didn't say a word, she merely grabbed her car keys and left."

"Did she come home later? I mean, how much had she been drinking before she left?"

"Plenty," said Dorrie. "We found out about three in the morning that she'd totaled the car. The police called and told Antonia to pick her up at Hennepin County General. A hearing was set for the next day. Other than a few cuts and bruises, she was fine. But for Antonia, that was the last straw. She'd been insisting for months that Lucy enter a treatment program. Lucy wasn't buying any of it. Said she didn't have a drinking problem. At the time this all happened, she had a job as a veterinary assistant at a local pet clinic in the Uptown area. Antonia had been pressuring her to quit and attend the University of Minnesota. She was determined that Lucy get an education. It was easy enough to tell that it was a perennial argument between them. Lucy insisted she hated school—it was a waste of time. With her job she was making a little money, but certainly not enough to replace a car. I found out later it was the second car she'd totaled in less than a year. When Lucy got home that night, Antonia grabbed her purse, found her driver's license, and took it into the kitchen. Without even stopping to think, she dumped it into the blender and switched it on. We both rushed in after her, but it was too late. Antonia screamed that this was the last car Lucy was ever going to wreck. Unless she entered a treatment program, there weren't going to *be* any more cars! God, it was an awful scene."

"This all happened while you were staying there?"

"Unfortunately, yes."

"Did she ever get into treatment?"

"I understand she did, but it was many years later. Long after Fleur was back and I was gone. You know, Antonia put up with a lot from her sister, and yet, I don't know. It was like Antonia saw herself more as Lucy's mother."

"I suppose people assume roles that they feel are needed."

"Maybe."

"What about Gaylord?"

"Never saw the man. I think I heard Lucy talking to him once on the phone. They were going to meet or something."

"Interesting," said Jane. "Do you have any idea why he and his daughters are estranged?"

"Absolutely none."

"Did his name ever come up in general conversation?"

"Oh, sure. Usually it was a joke—especially if Torald was talking."

"Do you think Antonia's dislike of Torald might have grown into something more serious?"

"You mean do I think Antonia murdered him? Boy, that's a terrible thing to even contemplate. Let's just say that if she had a mind to murder, she'd be fully capable of it. Of that I have little doubt."

"I'm just curious about something. This Malcolm? What did you think of him?"

Dorrie's expression softened. "I really grew to love that man. He was so available and willing to talk about anything you had on your mind. The Wernesses need someone like him—someone to referee, someone to take the role of confessor. We've remained friends, by the way. And I know for a fact that he's still in great pain over them. You'd think he'd get tired of all their problems, but he never seems to. You don't find friends with that kind of commitment every day." She took another long sip of beer.

Jane sat back and mulled over what Dorrie had just told her. She couldn't help but think she held on to some very significant threads in solving Torald's murder. Still, for now, it was a mystery she was far from solving.

"Excuse me," said the waiter, arriving with the beef and kidney pie.

"Aren't you eating anything?" asked Dorrie.

"Just the popcorn."

After setting everything down in front of her, the waiter took out a piece of paper and turned to Jane. "You had an urgent phone call."

Jane cocked her head. "Who from?"

"Cordelia. I talked to her. She said to tell you she was nearly faint from fright. She just had one of the worst experiences of her entire life."

Jane glanced skeptically at Dorrie. "Continue."

"Well, she wants you to pick her up at the stage door in half an hour. Said she'd be waiting. But first, she has to lie down. Gather her strength for the drive home."

"Really. Did she say what frightened her?"

"Someone broke into her office. From what she said, she was nearly killed."

"Wow," said Dorrie. "That's terrible."

The waiter tried to stifle a smirk. "She wants you to drive her home and sit with her until she falls asleep. She said she's much too upset to be alone. Also, she wants you to run by that rib joint on Chicago Avenue and pick her up—" He checked his notes, "a double order of Kansas City back ribs, Texas toast, cole claw, and make sure they don't short you on the jo-jo potatoes."

Jane looked at him gravely. "I understand."

"I thought you would." He nodded to Dorrie and then left.

Jane held up her hands. "Sorry. Duty calls. Do you mind eating that alone? Maybe we could try this again sometime—without the crisis."

"It would be my pleasure." She smiled warmly as she took a bite. "This tastes wonderful—as usual. And don't worry, I'm used to eating alone—usually something out of the microwave while I watch the ten o'clock news." She took another bite. "Now, you'd better get going. We wouldn't want Cordelia to dissolve in a mist of anxiety out by the stage door."

27

The night had turned bitter as Jane drove up the long gravel drive next to her house. As she got out and leaned against the hood, she breathed a sigh of relief that she'd finally been able to get Cordelia into bed. After a long, hot tub and a glass of brandy, Cordelia was now snoring peacefully amidst her pillows and quilts, her fringe and feathers, and one particularly pathetic stuffed dragon.

Jane leaned into the backseat and began to empty it of assorted junk. She couldn't help but wonder if the person who broke into Cordelia's office wasn't the same one who trashed Torald's. If it was, then whatever they were searching for probably had some bearing on Torald's death. Jane had a gut feeling that this was the case.

Sidestepping a piece of treacherous-looking ice, she headed quickly for the front door. The light was off in Beryl's room, which meant she'd probably already gone to bed. As she moved inside, Bean and Gulliver bounded down the stairs and began sniffing their evening snack of meat scraps from the restaurant. "Just a bite," she said, leading them into the kitchen. "The rest in the morning." She lifted up their dog bowls and dropped in a few pieces. "Next time you talk to Cordelia, tell her I don't abuse you." She scratched their tummies before setting the bowls in front of them.

The house was pleasantly quiet. From the smell of wood smoke, she could tell Beryl had kept the fire going late into the evening. A plate of fresh chocolate chip cookies sat on the counter beckoning to her. She eyed them briefly and then reached inside the refrigerator for an apple. No use adding insult to injury. She'd eaten a couple of Cordelia's BBQ ribs about an hour ago, and they still sat in her stomach like a cement block.

From the minute she'd entered her restaurant this morning until now, the day had felt like a roller coaster. She knew she needed time to think. Grabbing her junk, she headed into the sun room. "What's this?" she said out loud, as a book mailer nearly slipped out of her hand. On the outside someone had written the word *Thron*. Funny, it sounded like a science-fiction thriller. She carefully tore it open. Inside was a video tape. Nothing was written on the outside. She wondered where it had come from. She pushed it into the VCR and switched on the TV set. Then, sitting down in her favorite chair, she reached for the remote.

The tape began to play. At first, everything was out of focus. Definitely a home movie, no cinematographic extravaganza. Suddenly, she recognized someone. It was Lucy Werness. She was standing in the backyard of the Werness house in Kenwood. It was early evening, the light nearly gone. Even though the filming was jerky and the illumination poor, there was no mistaking her. She was joined a moment later by Malcolm Coopersmith, who was tossing a snowball at a wood fence in the distance. As they came to an evergreen tree, he put his arm around her and they began to kiss. Jane couldn't help but wonder what kind of voyeur had taken this? Impatiently, she tapped her fingers on the arm of the chair. It was obvious the couple had no idea they were being taped. Jane felt more than a little uncomfortable, but was entirely too curious to turn it off. She fast-forwarded through the end of the scene.

Next came a shot of Torald Werness. He was being filmed from a distance—and from above. As the camera adjusted to the dim interior light, she realized it was the main stage at the Allen Grimby. The person doing the taping was no doubt in the balcony. Torald was standing near one of the back curtains and he was in the process of undressing a woman she'd never seen before. The theater was dark. She knew she wasn't watching a play, that is, unless the Grimby had recently revised its artistic standards rather dramatically. A bra was flung backward into the air.

Abruptly, the scene changed again. This time it was Torald's car. A dark Lincoln Continental. He and another, this time a different, woman, were in the backseat. Jane opted once more for the fast-forward. What Torald lacked in style, and he definitely *did* lack style, he seemed to make up for in sheer exuberance.

The next scene was a shot of the exterior of the Maxfield Plaza in St. Paul. Gaylord Werness had just come out of the building, and a bellman was holding open the rear door of a cab for him. After the car had gone, the camera panned over the scene. The snow was quite deep on the boulevards, and the roads looked full of slush. There hadn't been that much snow since early February. Interesting. This film had to be at least a month old. If not older. As the camera came back to the entrance, Jane thought she recognized someone. She rewound slightly and then went, frame by frame, until the woman reappeared. There, smoking a cigarette and watching Gaylord drive away, stood Gloria Lindy. There was no mistaking her. But, wait a minute. If she hadn't started working for Gaylord until the last week of February—Jane had checked with the secretarial service— why would she be standing outside his hotel several weeks before that, observing him from the shadows?

Her apple now abandoned, Jane continued with the tape. The camera appeared to be back inside the theatre. She found herself staring at one of the familiar rear stage doors. A little further down the hall, Antonia and Fleur had stopped next to a dolly and were engaged in a rather intense conversation. The sound was muffled so Jane wasn't able to hear what they were saying, but both looked furious. She knew from more than one source that Antonia and Fleur's relationship was often volatile. If she'd wanted proof, here it was. They didn't seem to care if anyone heard the argument. Arms were flailing. Antonia stomped off. Fleur followed.

Once again, the scene changed. Jane could see a floor somewhere. Black and white tiles. It looked like the person doing the filming was running, totally unaware that the camera was still on. Everything was out of focus. Now and then Jane could glimpse what looked like a woman's foot thrust into the center of the frame. A second later, the film went black. She sat a moment longer fast-forwarding, but that was it.

Where on earth had this tape come from? Who'd taken it? And even more curiously, how had she gotten hold of it? The whole thing seemed creepy. Why would someone follow the Werness family around, sneaking pictures of private moments? It was one of the weirdest documentaries she'd ever seen. It almost felt like someone had been stalking them. Jane wasn't generally paranoid, but she wondered if each of these poor people shouldn't be warned, especially since one of them was now dead. But warned of what? Feeling a little sick, she got up and switched off the TV.

28

Antonia grabbed her mug of morning coffee and hurried from her chair in the first-floor library to the front door. Fleur had spent a restless night and was still asleep upstairs. Antonia didn't want the bell to wake her.

"Yes?" she said, drawing back the heavy door.

"Hi," said a young woman standing outside. She held a small box under one arm.

Antonia thought she looked familiar but couldn't quite place the face. She glanced down at the woman's shoes. They were funny, pointed green slippers. They made her look like an elf.

"My name is Gloria. I wonder if I might come in for a moment?" She paused expectantly.

Antonia found herself staring at the box. "Well," she said, not at all sure she wanted visitors this early in the morning. "May I ask what it's about?"

"Of course," said Gloria, smiling easily. "It's this little bird." She held up the box. "It's not eating right, poor thing. I understand your sister takes care of small animals. Nurses them back to health. I thought I'd bring it over and see what she could do."

"My sister?"

"Sure. You're Antonia Werness, aren't you? I've seen your picture in the paper many times. I'm looking for Lucy. May I come in?"

The young woman was certainly knowledgeable. Unfortunately, at least from Antonia's standpoint, the house was often visited by strange people referred to her sister by the wildlife veterinary staff over at the university. They usually came bearing sick or injured animals of one kind or another. Hesitating only for a moment, she backed up a few steps and allowed the young woman to enter. "You say this thing is ill?"

"Yup. What a lovely home." Gloria's eyes skipped around the room, giving everything a bit too much attention. "How many bedrooms do you have here?"

For a moment Antonia wondered if this impish gnome wasn't really a real estate agent. It seemed an odd question for someone merely bringing over a sick bird.

"I suppose you've lived here a long time," chirped Gloria.

"Since the Crusades," said Antonia. No doubt about it, this Gloria was beginning to annoy her. "If you'll excuse me, I'll go find Lucy."

"Great. I'll just wait in here." She strolled uninvited into the living room and stood underneath an oil painting of an elderly woman—Antonia's grandmother.

Of course, thought Antonia. That was who the young woman looked so much like.

Gloria was still standing there when Lucy, clad in bib overalls and a plaid flannel shirt, and Antonia returned a few minutes later.

"Gloria Lindy," said the woman extending her hand. "I'm delighted to meet you."

Lucy looked up at the painting and then down at Gloria. "Thank you. My sister tells me you have a sick bird."

"Yeah. Right. It's not eating very well. I thought I'd bring it by."

"Have you spoken to someone over at the U?"

Gloria unglued her eyes from a grouping of family pictures on the piano long enough to say, "What? Oh, well, I was told you were better."

Lucy stared at her for a moment and then took the box, opening the lid just a crack. Gently she reached inside and drew out a gray cockatiel. "Where did you buy this?" she asked, looking it over briefly.

"It was at a pet store downtown. It seemed healthy enough, but the past couple of weeks it won't touch its food."

"Is that right? What are you feeding it?"

Gloria shrugged. "Oh, you know. Bird food."

"Like what?"

"Oh, well, let me think. Cabbage leaves. Flies. Sometimes a cracker. Yeah, it used to love crackers. And then, those pellets. The stuff you buy."

"Pellets," repeated Lucy, giving Antonia an amused look. "Is he all right?"

"It's a she, Gloria."

"Really? You can't believe anyone anymore." She tittered.

"No, I suspect not."

Without being asked, Gloria made herself comfortable on the green brocade love seat. She seemed to become instantly rooted to the spot, a clear statement that she did not intend to leave anytime soon.

Lucy stepped over to a small bird cage and placed the bird inside. Then, turning around, she put her hands on her hips and studied Gloria. "I doubt you've had her long enough to know what she eats and doesn't eat. Let's stop playing. I'd like to know why you're here."

This time, Gloria opted for a more serious expression.

"Curiosity, I guess you could say. I didn't figure you'd let me in if I just came calling. After all, we've never met."

Both sisters glanced at each other.

Antonia spoke first. "Who the hell are you?"

"I work for your father."

Her expression tightened. "How wonderful."

"He's told me a great deal about you both. I guess I just wanted to meet his two daughters. I've already met Torald. I'm very sorry about what happened to him. I liked him," she said flatly.

Lucy cleared her throat. "Ms. Lindy, I don't know why you're here, but—"

"You want me to leave. Please, call me Gloria. All right, I understand. It's just, I was hoping you'd tell me why you and your father are on the outs. He seems like a decent enough guy—kind of full of himself, sometimes, but then he's pretty famous. It would be strange if he wasn't."

Antonia was amazed at the young woman's gall. "He's an unpredictable sociopath with delusions of grandeur. Other than that, he's positively swell."

She waved away the remark. "His birthday party is on Sunday. I know he'd like both of you to come."

"Did he send you here?" demanded Antonia. An ugly flush darkened her cheeks.

Gloria held up an innocent hand. "No, you've got it wrong. He doesn't even know I'm here. You don't need to take my head off, you know. I just thought I'd bring it up." Her eyes shifted to Lucy. "You really like this animal business, huh?"

"Yeah," said Lucy, "I guess you could say I think animals beat humans hands down when it comes to honest companionship. Where are you from?" Lucy sat down opposite her, crossing her ankle over her knee.

"I've traveled a lot."

"Not an answer."

Again, Gloria shrugged. "Say, since we're getting a little more personal, I understand you've never married. Why?"

Lucy shot another amused glance at her sister.

Antonia could tell what was coming. She relaxed a bit and sat down by the window.

"Drugs, Gloria. And booze. I'm a sad case. Just a burned-out wreck of my former self. No ability to orgasm anymore."

Gloria face colored. "Really?"

"Sure. It happens. You don't drink, do you Gloria?"

"Of course I drink." She smoothed her hair. "But not that much."

"Do you orgasm easily?"

Her eyes widened.

"Ever had herpes?"

"I beg your pardon?"

"Gonorrhea? Syphilis?"

"I don't think that's any of your business."

"No? But you think my love life is open to *your* scrutiny? Say, since you're here, maybe you'd like to look at my Tibetan Sex manual. The pictures are great."

Gloria glanced at Antonia with eyes that demanded an explanation.

"You know what the Bible says," continued Lucy. "It's better to marry than to burn." She stretched. "I don't know. I've always thought the burning part was more fun myself."

The young woman stood.

"We'll take care of the bird, Gloria. We have lots of cabbage leaves. Flies. And pellets."

"Of course." Gloria had the slightly disoriented look of someone who didn't understand what had just happened to her. She began to inch toward the door. "I'll find my way out."

"Of course you will," said Lucy. "Stop by anytime. Give our regards to Daddy."

They waited until the door had closed and then both sisters burst out laughing.

"What did you make of that?" snorted Antonia, settling her large frame more comfortably in a chair. She took a sip of coffee.

"I'm not sure. She had an uncanny resemblance to Grandmother Lillian. Did you notice?"

"Lots of people in Minnesota look like they belong in our family. You shake a tree and two or three dozen Norwegians fall out."

"I suppose that's true. I'm just naturally suspicious."

Instantly, the amusement left Antonia's face. "You're changing the subject."

"I am?"

"You're talking about Billy now."

Lucy shrugged. "Maybe. Something tells me he's not telling the truth. Since that lawyer in New Orleans closed up shop, we have no way to verify anything anymore."

"You don't believe the story he told us about his sister?"

Lucy shook her head.

"No. It was too easy."

"What are we going to do?"

Antonia's eyes darted quickly to her sister and then away. "You know, that police detective seems to think someone in the family might be involved in Torald's death."

"That's preposterous."

"Is it?"

The light dawned. "You mean Billy?"

Antonia hesitated a moment and then got up and crossed to the window overlooking the barren grape arbor. "Let's change the subject. I can't handle this right now."

"All right." Lucy lifted her sock-clad feet up on the coffee table.

Antonia gave it a moment before asking, "You know, I was wondering something."

"What?"

"Well, Fleur mentioned the other evening that . . ." She shook her head and laughed. "You're going to think this is crazy. I did."

"Try me."

"Well, see, Fleur said she felt like we were all being watched."

"Watched? Why? Who?"

"She didn't know. She said she's felt it for at least a

month. I . . . ah, I don't suppose you've sensed anything like that?"

Lucy let her chin sink down on her chest. "No, I can't say that I have."

"No. I didn't think so. I suppose the answer is pretty clear. Fleur is just letting everything get to her."

"Probably." Lucy pinched the bridge of her nose. "That's easy enough. I can't say that I blame her." She looked away. "So. How long is Victor staying? He's beginning to get on my nerves—strutting around here like the doting papa. He took Billy and Erin out to lunch yesterday, did you know that? Then they drove over to the Walker. Some famous friend of his from New York is having his paintings exhibited."

Antonia turned to face her. "He'll be here until the end of next week. He wants to see the play several times."

"Do you intend to tell him the truth?" There was an edge in Lucy's voice that worried Antonia.

"No. Victor's presence does complicate things, I grant you, but I promise, I'll handle it. Speaking of . . ." Her voice trailed off.

"You want to know how Malcolm is?"

Antonia nodded.

"We haven't really talked since Billy laid his golden egg. So to speak." She smiled weakly.

"Sometimes I think it's harder on him than anyone."

"I know. If I'd only stayed in Minnesota twenty years ago instead of joining you in New Orleans, I probably would have married him. I would have ruined his life."

Antonia gave a self-conscious little laugh and then looked away. "Some might say it's never too late to start afresh."

Lucy glanced at the cockatiel inside the small cage. She'd always hated cages. Out in the annex she had an entire room for the birds. But then again, wasn't it just another, somewhat larger prison? She closed her eyes and listened to the tiny thing twittering away on its perch. "My dear sister. Always the optimist."

29

"You've got to see this," said Jane, bursting through Cordelia's back door.

"I can barely make out the crumbling form of my kitchen," said Cordelia, rubbing her sleepy eyes. She sat in the cluttered breakfast nook, her chin resting on her hand. She looked to Jane as if she were about to fall over sideways. Lucifer, an ancient striped tabby cat, sat in the sink, licking the remnants of a butter wrapper. He eyed them noncommittally.

"Is your VCR working?"

"God, not another episode of the Frugal Gourmet?" She stumbled into the living room behind Jane. "I don't suppose you thought to bring over any croissants, any Danish—a tiny, dry little muffin-morsel for my piteous breakfast?" She looked pathetic as she hunched next to the bentwood coat rack in the corner.

"Sorry." Jane lifted a stuffed puppet off the machine and slipped in the tape. "Now, you've got to watch this." She turned on the TV and pushed play on the VCR. A moment later the first shots of Lucy and Malcolm came into focus.

Cordelia backed up and fell onto the couch, narrowly missing Miss Blanche, the first of her cat colony. Silently, she sat biting her nails, her eyes glued to the screen. When it was over, she let out a low chuckle. "Serious voyeurism, dearheart. Not PBS quality at all. More like ABC."

"That's what I thought," said Jane.

"Where did you find it?"

"Somehow, it managed to get into the backseat of my car. It was in a book mailer."

Cordelia tapped a thoughtful finger against her cheek. "By any chance, did it have the word *Thron* on it?"

"That's right. How did you know?"

Cordelia patted away a yawn. "It's a long story. Come on. I've got some cold pizza in the fridge. I'll buy breakfast."

Jane glanced at Melville who had jumped up on the mantel and was now pretending to be fast asleep on top of a copy of *Moby Dick*. His favorite. "Just a cup of tea for me, thanks."

"I finished the last tea bag yesterday. But, not to worry. You can join me for a glass of black cherry soda." She rubbed her hands together in anticipation.

Jane could feel last night's undigested barbeque ribs still in her stomach. Fifteen minutes later, she sat over the dregs of her glass of water while Cordelia finished the last slice of goat cheese and pesto pizza. "You don't know what you're missing," she said between bites and gulps.

Jane smiled patiently.

"Well, anyway, so I got the tape yesterday afternoon and I guess I must have left it in your car last night. With those sunglasses on, how could I be expected to see anything. It was pitch dark out when you dropped me off at the theatre."

"Really? I didn't notice. And you say the only description you got of the person who rented the video camera was that he was in his twenties, light brown hair and beard, and basically average."

"That's it."

"Doesn't fit anyone I know."

"I can't think of anyone at the theatre who looks like that either."

Jane scratched her head and looked into the pantry where Cordelia had hung two rather grotesque papier-mâché masks. "Say, what if—?"

"What if what?"

"You're going to think this is crazy, but what if it's a disguise?"

Cordelia brushed several crumbs off her fake leopard skin robe. "You're right. Kind of far-fetched."

"Maybe. Maybe not. I'd say it depends."

"On what?"

"Well, if the person who took the video had something to do with Torald's death, then he may have been involved to some extent with the theatre. Disguise wouldn't be a foreign idea."

"True. That's interesting, Janey. You do have a fecund mind. Then, shall we take it a step further? Maybe it wasn't a man at all."

Jane thought for a moment. "Cordelia, I think you may be a genius."

"Tut tut."

"This bearded man might easily be the missing sister."

Cordelia hooted at the inanity.

"I'm serious," said Jane.

"I know. It's one of your more endearing qualities." She patted Jane's hand with a mixture of indulgence and condescension. "So, let's think this through logically, if that's possible. If we limit our exercise to those people who were at the theatre the night Torald died, who might possibly be able to disguise themselves as a nondescript, brown-haired, bearded young man?"

"Erin Brewster," said Jane without even a moment's hesitation. "I mean, she's sort of androgynous. Or, then I suppose it could be Ida John. Properly dressed, she could pull it off."

"Say, come to think of it, the night Torald died, I found Ida in his dressing room going through his desk. She made up some excuse, said she was looking for cigarettes. I didn't buy it then and I still don't. Oh, and something else. There was a note on his desk that simply said 'Sunday, five-fifteen.' I wondered if he wasn't planning to meet someone."

"You think it was Ida?"

"I have no way of knowing."

Jane stared into her glass. "Five-fifteen. He died right

around then. I wonder if the person he had the appointment with was also his killer."

"An appointment for murder," mused Cordelia. "Sounds like the Book-of-the-Month Club Alternate Selection." She smoothed her robe. "We haven't finished yet with the subject on the table. Who else at the theatre that night could disguise themselves as a young, bearded man?"

"Well, I suppose Gloria Lindy. No, that wouldn't work. She's too short. Too round. Not average enough."

"And besides, she was in the video. Doesn't work. What about Maureen Werness?"

"Why would she want to take videos of her family?"

"Home movies?"

Jane groaned.

"But, then again, she's middle-aged. And very distinctive. It would be hard to disguise those teeth unless you were impersonating a giraffe."

"True. I guess that leaves only one other person."

"Who's that?"

"Billy Brewster. It would have been easiest of all for him to put on a beard and a wig."

"But why take pictures of his own family?"

"To get to know them better before he comes clean about his real relationship."

"No, it doesn't wash. Why not just watch them? You don't need a camera for that."

Lucifer leaped up on the table and began to nose through the empty pizza box.

"Good point. There's something not right here. Something we don't understand."

"Maybe you ought to show it to Malcolm Coopersmith. He knows that family better than anyone. He might be able to help you come up with a theory."

Jane leaned her head on her hand. "I don't know. He fits somewhere, too, I just don't know where. I suppose you've been invited to Gaylord Werness's birthday party tomorrow?"

"Of course. As part of the Twin Cities *glitteratti*, I am in constant demand."

"Well, for some reason, I was invited, too. Since Billy and Erin are staying at my house, I suppose I received an invitation right along with them."

"Lucky you. Better bring a suitable present."

"Like what?"

"Oh, I don't know. How about the complete works of Tennessee Williams."

Jane grinned. "You're evil."

"Excuse me?" said a young, bearded man, walking up to the bellman on duty at the Maxfield Plaza. It was nearly noon. "I have a gift for Mr. Gaylord Werness. It's his birthday tomorrow, and I'd like this delivered to his suite."

"Of course." The bellman took the large square box and set it on a rack behind the counter. It was wrapped all in black with a shiny black bow nearly covering the top. "Would you like a receipt?"

"No." The bearded man held out a fifty dollar bill. "He's in room 2325. It should be delivered at three tomorrow afternoon. No earlier, no later."

"I'll see to it."

"Thank you." The young man turned on his heel and walked quickly across the lobby.

"And thank *you*," said the bellman, stuffing the money into his vest pocket and giving it a small pat.

Jane needed to stop home for a minute on her way to the restaurant. When she'd left for Cordelia's house earlier in the day, she'd forgotten some important papers on the dining room table. As she entered, she noticed Erin sitting alone in the living room, her eyes closed, listening to an old Carly Simon album.

"Where's Billy?" she asked, scooping the papers into a file.

Erin jumped. "Oh . . . Jane. Hi. I didn't hear you come in."

"Lost in thought, huh?"

Her smile was faint. "I guess."

Jane dumped everything into her briefcase and then

joined Erin in the living room. "I suppose he's over at the theatre."

"No, actually he's upstairs meditating. He does that every afternoon. I hope you don't mind that I'm down here. He likes to be alone."

Jane held up her hand. "Absolutely not. Where's Beryl?"

"She and your neighbor went downtown to do some shopping?"

"Uhm. Quite a developing friendship there. Have you had lunch?"

"Yeah. Just a sandwich. I'm waiting for Billy to get done. We've got an appointment with a real estate agent."

"Of course," said Jane. "I suppose it's time you two look for a house."

"I'd be happy with an apartment, but Billy says the interest rates are so low right now, we'd be dumb not to look around. See what's available."

Jane nodded. There was an uncomfortable silence. "Well, so, I haven't really had a chance to congratulate you and Billy on his new job offer at the Grimby."

Erin shifted in her chair, brushing her thin blond hair behind her ears. "Thanks."

Jane could tell something was wrong. "You don't seem like you're very happy about it. Don't you like the Twin Cities?"

"Oh, no. It's not that."

"Then what?"

"Oh, I'm just being silly. Billy always says I worry too much."

"I don't know. You seem pretty level-headed to me."

Erin attempted a smile. "Well, see, I just wonder. What if Torald hadn't died? Billy might never have been offered this position."

"But Billy had nothing to do with Torald's murder. And he's got as much right to it as anyone else."

Erin hesitated. "Sure. Of course . . . you're right. But I guess, for some reason, it still feels wrong." She crossed and uncrossed her legs until she found a more comfortable position. "You see, things have always come so easily to him. He's not used to waiting, to deferring in any way. This is just one more example. Someday you have to pay the piper. Oh, I'm not saying his parents spoiled him, but he grew up surrounded by love. I never had any of that. I see the world very differently. It's caused more than one problem between us. The thing is, I've seen the other side of that love."

Jane sat quietly, taking in her words.

"Oh, just listen to me, will you? Waxing morbid again. It's getting to be a habit. I understand completely if you're not interested in listening to another one of Erin Brewster's anxiety attacks."

"No," said Jane. "Don't sell yourself so short. I am interested. I guess I thought we were becoming friends."

Erin looked into the cold hearth. "Thank you, Jane. Right now, that means a lot."

Jane checked her watch. Erin needed some serious cheering up. "What time is your appointment?"

"Ah . . . two-thirty."

"Well, that's a good hour and a half from now. While Billy's reciting his mantra for the seven thousandth time, why don't you come over to the restaurant with me. We're trying out some new vinaigrettes. You must have room for a little fresh salad?" She got up and pulled Erin to her feet.

"Well, maybe I could. . . ."

"Of course you could. Now." She put her hand on Erin's shoulder and began walking her toward the door. "Instead of red wine vinegar, my favorite new dressing has fresh orange and lime juice as a base. We serve it over chilled escarole. You like escarole, don't you?"

"I think so."

"Well, we have romaine, too, and Boston Bibb for the less adventurous. And then we have fresh baked breads. We serve those with flavored butters. My current favorite is . . ."

The door closed softly behind them.

30

Jane spent the rest of the day at the restaurant. She had plenty of paperwork to catch up on, as well as a short meeting with the banquet chef about an upcoming wedding reception that was going to be held at the Lyme House in early April. Around four, she made a last round of the kitchen. Everything seemed to be running smoothly. The night manager had already arrived and would be taking over the evening shift. As she climbed into her Saab, she thought again of what Cordelia had said about Ida John. On an impulse, she swung onto I-94 and headed for St. Paul. Thankfully, she'd asked Cordelia yesterday for her address. There might never be a better time to talk to her than right now.

En route, her car phone started to beep. Still a bit self-conscious about this perceived luxury, she picked up the receiver. "Yes?"

"Jane?"

"Speaking."

"This is Dorrie."

"Oh . . . hi."

"Where are you?"

"Well, actually, I'm in my car."

"You have a car phone? Wait, don't answer that. It was a dumb question. Obviously you do. *Why* do you?"

Jane changed lanes. She could hear the amusement in Dorrie's voice. "Well, see, there *is* a legitimate reason. The restaurant has been doing a lot more catering this past year. I'm often out of the office all afternoon talking to different clients. It's just easier for me to be reached this way. I mean, it's already paid for itself." She stopped. "What are you laughing at?"

"I'm not laughing."

"Then you must be crying."

"No. Just ... reacting."

"Well, stop it."

"It's just ... I can't help but think that this phone is worth more than your car."

So that was it. The car again. "Look, Dorrie ..."

"No, I'm sorry. Cordelia told me how sensitive you are about your car."

"Is that right?"

"Calm down. This is a social call."

Jane tugged indignantly on her scarf.

"Are you still with me?"

"As long as you don't insult my wheels."

"All right. Deal. Now ... are you seated?"

Jane had to laugh. "Yes, Dorrie, I'm seated."

"Good. I'm inviting you to dinner. What's more, I'm even going to cook. No take-out Chinese. I know you're a woman with standards."

Jane had never been invited to Dorrie's home before. For some very obvious reasons, the idea appealed. "Sure. I'd like that."

"Good. Next week. Thursday night."

"What can I bring?"

Dorrie paused. "An open mind."

So, that was it. It wasn't an unwelcome prospect. "I'll be there."

"Seven o'clock. And Jane?"

"Yes?"

The line was silent for a moment. "Not to belabor the point, but ... I ... well, I mean ... I was hoping ..."

"Me, too," said Jane. "See you then."

She set the receiver back in its holder. So. *Dorrie Harris.* How very interesting. What was that quote Cordelia liked so much? "Strange invitations were often dancing lessons from the goddess." She couldn't turn down something like that, now could she?

* * *

Grinning a bit stupidly, Jane pulled her car into the far right lane and took the first off ramp. She knew Ida lived in a small town house on the east side of the city. It was just another couple of blocks. Unfortunately, she had to drag her mind back to the business at hand. As she pulled up to the curb in the nouveau yuppie neighborhood, she could see a light on in what was probably one of the upstairs bedrooms. It was a wood-frame structure, made to look old and Victorian but missing the point entirely. Looking closely, Jane could see the construction was shoddy. Some of the outside moldings didn't even match. The brass knocker on the front door was peeling, revealing a cheap aluminum base underneath. Everything about the building was calculated to express an image. The fact that the substance was totally lacking probably upset no one, least of all the inhabitants. It was a depressing sight.

Jane knocked on the door. As she stood waiting, she noticed a head peek out through a drawn curtain in the next apartment. She nodded pleasantly. A moment later, Ida appeared in the open door wearing a green and gray sweatshirt and matching sweat pants, a towel wrapped around her head. In her hand she held a can of diet soda.

"Hi," said Jane, not waiting for Ida to invite her in. "I'd like to talk to you."

Ida looked her up and down.

Jane assumed her jeans, peacoat, and boots didn't pass the fashion muster any better than what she'd worn the other night at Torald's reviewal. "I left my leather gloves and matching Givenchy briefcase in the car."

"In your dreams," said Ida, with an amused sneer. "What do you want to talk about?"

There was no use lying. Jane knew she might be able to get into the house on a pretext, but she'd be thrown out as soon as Ida didn't like the turn of the conversation. "It's about Torald Werness."

"Torald? What about him?"

"Can I come in?" asked Jane. "It's kind of chilly out here."

"I don't know." Ida took a sip of pop. "Well, I suppose. But I can't talk long. I've got to get to the theatre. We're doing *Bride Doll* again tonight. Actually, it's kind of a special evening. I found out through the grapevine that Gaylord Werness has tickets. The whole thing's making me nervous as a cat." She folded her long, sleek frame into a cheap imitation of a Barcelona chair. "So, what do you want?"

Jane sat down next to a plastic palm, opting for the direct approach. "I was told you were in Torald's dressing room the night he died. It was before the meeting called by the stage manager. As I understand it, you were going through his desk."

"You've been talking to Cordelia," she said with another sneer.

"I have. She didn't buy your story about the cigarettes."

Ida shrugged. "So what? Why should I care?"

"Well, if you've really got nothing to hide—"

"Of course I've got nothing to hide! What are you insinuating?"

"Well, then I'd say you haven't got anything to lose by telling me the truth."

She thought it over, playing absently with a rip in her cuff. "I suppose you do have a point. Okay, what could it hurt? The truth is, Torald had promised me an invitation to his father's birthday party tomorrow. Lots of big names will be there, and I'm not one bit ashamed to say that I wanted to be included. So what if I'm ambitious? I want to succeed at my career. I knew Torald had some extra invitations in his desk, so, just in case he decided to get cute on me, I thought I'd help myself. And that's what I was doing when Cordelia butted her way into the room." She reached over and held up a cream-colored card. "See?"

Jane recognized it as looking just like the one she'd been sent. "I understand from Torald's wife that she caught you on stage that same night with Torald. It was after the meeting. She seemed to think you two weren't just chatting."

Ida snorted. "That woman has a nasty mind. No wonder

Torald slept around. He was probably being accused of it hourly. What a way to live."

"Are you speaking from experience?"

Ida crushed the empty pop can in her hand. "No. And I don't care what Maureen thought she saw, Torald and I *were* just talking."

"About what?"

"None of your business."

"Look," said Jane, struggling to hide her growing impatience, "everyone who was at the theatre that night is now a suspect in a murder investigation. I'm sure you've already talked to Detective Trevelyan."

"Several times. Funny thing about that. Seems we both adore schnauzers. I found him quite delightful."

"You did?"

Again, Ida shrugged.

"Does he know you and Torald were alone together after the meeting?"

"I don't know why I'm even talking to you. You're just trying to make trouble."

"I'm trying to find some answers," said Jane. "If you're innocent, I repeat, you've got nothing to lose by telling me the truth."

Ida lowered her chin and seemed to be thinking. "Okay. I mean, it's not a deep, dark secret. Torald had some crazy idea that I might be Billy Brewster's sister—ergo his niece. He'd been poking around in my private life for weeks. I didn't get the real point until that night."

"And are you Billy's sister?"

Ida considered her fingernail. "No. Believe me, if I was related to that family, I'd hire a skywriter. Do you realize how lucky Billy is? He's part of a theatrical dynasty! Doors are going to fly open for him. The rest of us peasants have to work for our breaks—that is, if they ever come."

Jane couldn't help but notice the edge in her voice. Was it anger or jealousy? "Do you have any idea what time it was when you were talking to Torald?"

"Well, I think the meeting got over around four forty-five. By the time everyone cleared out it was probably close to five. We hadn't been talking long when Maureen showed up."

"Did you leave when she got there?"

"Not right away. She and Torald exchanged a few withering comments about life and love in general, and then she took off. I left to go down to my dressing room a few minutes later."

"You didn't see anyone else around?"

"No one."

"Torald may have been meeting someone at five-fifteen. Did he mention anything about that?"

"Nothing." She glanced at her watch. "Look, this has been terrific fun, but I'm going to have to get ready if I'm going to make it to the theatre."

Jane rose and took one last look around the room. "Thanks. I appreciate your help."

Ida accompanied her to the door. "If you ask me, I'd just as soon forget that whole evening." She wrapped her arms around herself.

"Good luck tonight," said Jane. "Or do I say, break a leg?"

"I hate that expression. I don't believe in all those stupid, theatrical superstitions. Besides, I make my own luck. I always have."

"I'll remember that," said Jane. "See you tomorrow."

Ida cocked her head. "Tomorrow?"

"Sure. At Gaylord's birthday party."

"You're invited to that?" She looked totally disgusted.

Jane grinned. "There goes the neighborhood? I promise, I'll even shine my boots—just for you."

31

"Filthy weather," muttered Antonia as she watched the ice pellets beat against the side of the house. March in Minnesota was often the worst month of the year. Tomorrow was supposed to be warm and sunny, but tonight the forecast called for sleet. She rested against the deep, mullioned window in her study, lifting her hand to the cold glass. It was nearly dark out now. Tonight, Victor would attend her new play for the first time. As she reached for her glass of wine, there was a knock on the door. "Come in," she called.

Victor poked his head inside. She could see that he was already decked out in his evening clothes. "You're not dressed?" he frowned. "I thought we had a date. Dinner first and then the theatre."

She took a sip of wine to fortify herself. "That was your idea. Never mine."

He gave a low chuckle. "Playing hard to get? Aren't we a little past that?"

"Come on, Victor. That's hardly funny."

He entered the room and patiently unbuttoned his suit coat. As he draped himself over a chair he said, "What's wrong?"

She rubbed her neck for a moment and then sat down. "I don't have the energy for this conversation right now."

"Is it me? Have I done something to upset you?"

She put her hand to her mouth to stop herself from laughing out loud. He had *such* a talent for being obtuse—for saying the exact wrong thing. It was almost getting to be a joke. "Of course it's you."

"Why? What?"

A small giggle leaked out. "Everything." She emptied the wineglass and then poured herself another.

"Would you care to explain?"

"Well, for one thing, all this talk about taking the play to Broadway."

"But Antonia—"

"Victor, we've been arguing about this for decades. You know how I feel. I've always thought that there shouldn't be this intellectual chasm between working-class people and the social elite. High art and great ideas belong to everyone. I absolutely abhor the economic elitism of Broadway. It's pure garbage. The whole system encourages that chasm. Why should I do handsprings to have my play produced in a place where the going ticket prices are fifty dollars a seat—and more? It's insanity."

"Still a socialist at heart."

"God," she shrieked, burying her head in her arms. "I'm talking to a wall."

"You may not like New York, but from what I've gathered recently, you don't care much for the social climbing of several of our more well-respected regional theatres either—all of which shall remain nameless, of course."

She waved her hand above her head. "Of course."

"So, does anything please you these days?"

Wearily, she shook her head. "Am I no longer allowed opinions?"

"Ah, is that it? I'm stifling your individuality by offering you the opportunity to finance less commercial projects by shepherding your new play to capitalist land."

Again, she began to laugh. "I've had entirely too much wine to engage in this debate."

"Good, then the sides are equal for once." He stroked his chin. "Your father had great success on Broadway. You could, too."

She bristled. "Of course I could, if that's what I wanted! But I can't help but think I'm not as easily understood. Gaylord made his reputation as a playwright by telling the American public they were loathsome, morally repulsive warmongers. It was the Sixties. Self-flagellation was becoming a national pastime. The Nineties are a much different era. My works are more tentative, more psychologically probing. His were blatant diatribes. People are always drawn to certainty, and Gaylord Werness was there with the certainty of a tent preacher. I've never known a man who saw the world more simply. I'm positive that's what gave his writing its primitive strength. You remember what Sartre said? Modern audiences will believe anything dark you have to say about them—as long as you never suggest they can do something about it. Gaylord never made that mistake. Having the guts to sit through one of his plays must have felt like an atonement. It bought you one big fat indulgence. For some unfathomable reason, his work became part of the canon of the Sixties. Don't you find that rather telling?"

"You really hate him," said Victor.

"Is that what I said?"

"That's what came through the loudest."

Antonia downed half the glass of wine.

"Come on, you have to go easy on yourself. This has been a bad couple of weeks, what with Torald's death, and the reappearance of your son."

She grunted, refilling her glass once again from the decanter on the desk. "You want some?" She held it up.

"Have you eaten anything recently?" he asked.

"Later."

Victor shook his head. "You know, Billy's a fine young man. Anyone would be proud to be his father."

"You're not his father, Victor."

He scowled. "I don't believe you. I can tell when you're lying. I mean, who the hell ever heard of this Eric Hatch anyway?"

"He existed, trust me."

Victor turned away. "I can't. I won't! When you left New York that spring to return to Minnesota for Torald's high school graduation, we were planning on being married. I'd even given you a ring. Two days after you got back you took it off. Why, Antonia? And why wouldn't you ever talk about it?"

"It's not what you think."

"Goddamn you, you have no idea what I think."

She was surprised by the sudden anger in his voice. "All right, why do you suppose I did that? You wouldn't believe that I'd had some time to think while I was away. I realized things weren't right. I didn't love you the way I should."

"Bullshit! What about those letters?"

"What letters?"

"You never knew I saw them. I never told you. But one night, about a month after you got back, you appeared on my doorstep drunk out of your mind. It seems to be a family curse, Antonia, and not a very attractive one. I poured you into my car and took you back to your apartment. After getting you into bed, I went in search of an extra blanket. That's when I saw them in your closet. Jesus Antonia, there were at least *thirty* of them. All from the same guy. All in less than a month." He hesitated, trying to regain his composure. "Even after all these years, I still can't stand the sound of his name. Malcolm Coopersmith. What happened Antonia? Did he get you pregnant? Were you in love? How many letters did you write *him*?"

Slowly, Antonia got to her feet. "Get out."

"Why won't you talk about it? Is he the father? Does he know? My God, woman, did *Lucy* know?"

She picked up the decanter. "I want you to leave, Victor. *Now.* This conversation is over."

"It won't work. Your threats are meaningless now. It's all coming apart."

The phone on the desk cut them off. Antonia picked it up and said curtly, "What do you want? What? Who? No, Fleur can't come to the phone right now." She paused, her eyes still holding Victor's. "All right. What's the message? You're what?" She listened, her eyes dropping to the floor. "Yes. I understand. Of course. Now, if you will kindly mail Fleur the bill, you'll be paid immediately. That's right, Mr. Barlow. You're being *canned*." Her eyes were almost wild as she hung up the phone.

"Antonia, we can't leave it like this. You've got to calm down. You're going to have a stroke."

"No more, Victor. Go to the play. Go to a restaurant. Go to hell for all I care!"

"Fleur is concerned, Antonia, just like the rest of us."

"I don't need her concern. I can take care of everything."

Slowly, he got to his feet. "No you can't. That's always been your problem. And, as far as I can tell my dear, it's going to kill you one day. Now, when you feel like talking again, I'm here for you. I know Lucy wants me to leave, but I'm not going to go until all this is settled."

"It's *settled*, Victor."

"Are you done with your bath?" Antonia rapped loudly on the bathroom door. "Fleur?"

"Just a minute!"

She waited, her anger growing by the second.

With a leisurely nod of her head, Fleur opened the door and stepped into the hall. She was wearing a white terry cloth robe, her black hair completely covered by a shower cap. "What's the big rush? I thought you were going off to the theatre tonight with Victor." She walked into their bedroom. "Wretched weather. I prefer a good book and a hot cup of cocoa. You're still welcome to join me." She wiggled an eyebrow seductively.

Antonia followed her into the room. "I know about the lawyer."

Fleur sat down behind the dressing table and carefully removed the cap.

"Well? No explanations?"

"Would it matter? You followed me in here to pick a fight, right? Well, go ahead. Get it out of your system. Scream. Rave. Drool for all I care. When you're done, then maybe you'll sit quietly and listen for a moment."

Antonia stood rigidly by the bed.

"I'm waiting," said Fleur, combing out her hair.

It was no use. Antonia felt like the weight of the world was crushing the life out of her. She crumpled into a chair.

"Now maybe you'll listen to me for a minute. Even

though I think you need legal help—you obviously have grounds for a lawsuit—that's not why I hired this lawyer. This guy happens to work with a very good private investigator. Among other things, I wanted to have Billy checked out."

"But I tried calling that lawyer in New Orleans. He's evaporated. No forwarding address. You know I have people working on it, but so far . . . nothing."

"Okay. But what about his family in Boston? You'll be pleased to know I've already gotten the report."

Gravely, Antonia said, "And?"

"Well, so far so good. He's Billy Brewster, all right. Only son of Margaret and Emery Brewster. And he was adopted as a baby."

"Alone?"

"Yes. There was no mention of a twin sister." Fleur laid down her brush and turned around. "That much is true. But there's still a problem."

"Come on, Fleur. Cut to the chase."

"All right. Gladly. The private investigator checked out Erin at the same time. I asked her the other night what her maiden name was—where she was from." She paused. "The P.I. found no trace of her. It was all a lie, Antonia. Billy may be on the level—at least as far as we know—but Erin is a complete phoney."

"But—I don't get it. Why would she lie?"

"Good question."

"You think she's Billy's sister?"

Fleur shrugged. "Gloria Lindy also doesn't seem to have a legitimate past. If you hadn't fired Mr. Barlow, we might have found out. I was also having Ida John investigated. Who knows? Maybe Torald was right about one of them."

"But . . . I don't understand." The despair in her voice carried into every corner of the room.

Fleur rose and went to her, standing behind the chair and giving her neck a rub. "I know one thing. If you don't stop acting like you're King Kong around here—"

Antonia let her chin sink to her chest. After a long moment, she began to giggle at the image. "Fleur, I would prefer you to use the term *God* when referring to me."

Fleur threw up her hands. "Exactly. That's your problem." She sat down on one arm of the chair. "You're *not* God. You can't control everything. You can't fix it all up and make everybody happy."

For the first time since Billy had come, Antonia felt herself on the verge of tears. She put a hand over her eyes.

"Go ahead," said Fleur. "I'm here for you. We'll get through this."

"I'm not so sure," said Antonia, putting her arms around Fleur's waist and burying her head in the softness.

"Trust me. After all these years, you must know how much I love you." She could feel Antonia's body convulsing with tears. "That's good, sweetheart. Let some of it out. For once, don't try to be so strong. Let me be here for you." She held on tightly, stroking her back and whispering words of tenderness.

32

Juggling several packages, Jane entered the festively decorated living room of Gaylord Werness's hotel suite. The birthday party was in full progress.

Acting as hostess, Maureen Werness swept over and gave her a little peck on the cheek. "So good to see you again. If you want to follow me, I'll show you where we're putting the gifts."

Jane hesitated, looking over her shoulder.

"Oh, you've come with someone," smiled Maureen. She waited while a large gentleman in a black tuxedo and silk top hat turned around. "I don't believe it!" Maureen stepped back a pace. "Cordelia!"

"Lovely to see you again." She lifted Maureen's hand to her lips. "If I may say so, you look wonderful this afternoon." Taking off her hat, she tossed in her gloves and handed it to her. "Thanks ever so much." Then, adjusting her black tie and smoothing an errant wisp of hair back into its tight bun, she said to Jane, "Well. Party time. I'm off to mingle. Save me a dance."

Jane waited until she was gone and then caught Maureen's eye. "Where do I put these presents?"

Maureen seemed still to be transfixed by Cordelia's transformed presence. "What do you people call it when you dress like that?"

"Drag," said Jane.

"Yes, that's it. Drag." She nodded very slowly.

Jane waited. She saw Maureen's eyes shift to Gaylord who was holding court at the far end of the room. Jane cleared her throat. "Maureen?"

"Yes?"

"The gifts?"

"Oh yes, I am sorry. Why don't you follow me?" She led the way into the formal dining room where the entire table was covered with gorgeously wrapped presents. "There you go," she said, helping her find an empty spot. "Now, be sure you check out the dim sum brunch. Gaylord had it catered. Shrimp stuffed mushrooms, steamed pot stickers, spare ribs with black beans and pepper sauce, and cream cheese–filled wontons. Those last ones are the killers." She patted her stomach. "I'm already stuffed. Oh, and by the way, we're going to start opening presents in just a few minutes."

"Thanks," said Jane. She saw Maureen look at the door. More guests had just arrived. "You go ahead. I'll be fine."

"See you later then." She steamed off through the throng.

Jane took a moment to get her bearings. Balloons and streamers hung everywhere in the large, airy rooms. As she glanced into the hallway, she could see at least three bedrooms, their doors partially open. Off the kitchen was a spacious study filled from floor to ceiling with books. A well-worn leather chair sat in front of the desk. She would have loved to go in and check it out, but the room was deserted. She figured Gaylord would probably take her interest as intrusive. Under other circumstances, she might have chanced it, but there were too many people milling around today.

"Quite a display," said a familiar voice behind her. Jane turned to find Erin Brewster standing next to the dining room table. "Some people have all the luck."

"I've never been big on birthdays myself," said Jane.

"I've never had the opportunity to be. It just seems like the people who *have* get more. The people who don't . . ." Her voice drifted off.

"Where's Billy?"

"Oh, haven't you seen? Gaylord has him chained to his wrist like a trained monkey. He's dragging him from person to person, making introductions."

"Weren't you invited along for the ride?"

Erin's smile was sour. "Sure. But Gaylord already has an entourage. Ida John and Gloria Lindy are acting as bookends."

Jane tried not to laugh. In this instance, the sarcasm was dead on. She looked down at the gifts. "Did you bring him something suitably wonderful?"

"Billy wanted to get him a Steuben glass angel." She swept her hand toward a grouping of religious art on the far wall. "I suggested a chrome-plated walker." She took a sip from her glass. "He wasn't amused. That's when I suggested the gilded jockstrap."

Only then did Jane realize Erin was slightly high. She'd never heard her be so snide before. "And?"

"And what?"

"Who won?"

Erin winked. "You'll have to wait and see." She turned her head partially away, listening to the string quartet in the next room. "It's funny. You'd think all this art and music would mean something."

"I don't understand."

"Oh, you know. That it would be ... *ennobling* in some way. Billy always says that going to the theatre is like going to church."

"You don't agree?"

Erin shook her head, stifling a hiccup. "Nope," she mugged. Then, realizing she was making a small scene, she stopped. "Just listen to me. I'm rambling. I'm not used to this stuff." She held up her glass and stared at it with intense curiosity.

Jane knew there was more to it than that. Erin, in her own way, was attempting to make an important point.

Out in the living room the music had stopped. Gaylord was talking.

"Must be time for the presents to be opened," said Jane.

Erin looked at her watch. "Nearly three. I'd better go liberate Billy." She winked.

"See you later." As she watched Erin disappear into the next room, it struck her how little this young woman ever talked about herself—or her past—in any specific way.

"Try this pot sticker," said Cordelia, moving up next to her. The room was filling quickly with guests.

"Thanks," said Jane.

"And stop thinking so hard about life in general and *enjoy the damn party!*"

Jane smiled. "Yes ma'am." She popped the pot sticker into her mouth.

Gaylord sat on a stool in front of the long dining room table. The rest of the guests had gathered around the sides. Once again, Cordelia had captured it perfectly when she'd called him a "degenerate Santa Claus." The only things missing were his little helpers. However, Jane was pretty sure his reddish cheeks and nose didn't come from riding through cold winter nights on a sleigh. By the looks of his liquor cabinet, he was a man who liked to imbibe. It had taken its toll not only on his face, but no doubt on his liver.

Jane and Cordelia watched from the rear of the room as, one by one, he ripped open the gifts. Paper was flying at a furious pace. Maureen was standing on one side of him. Ida stood guard on the other, snuggled as close as she dared get without sitting in his lap. Every so often Maureen would shoot her a withering look which Ida ignored. Instead, she glowed under Gaylord's periodic gaze. Billy and Erin stood behind him, helping tidy up the ribbons and wrapping paper as he tossed it in the air. Gloria Lindy flitted around the edges of the room, taking photos with a very professional-looking Nikon.

Apparently, the word had gotten around that Gaylord loved toys. Interspersed between the occasional wool scarf and pair of gloves was a variety of hand puppets, a picture puzzle, and an expensive wooden replica of some famous clipper ship. As she watched, Gaylord unwrapped a lovely piece of Steuben glass. Billy had obviously won.

With all the clapping and laughter, no one seemed to notice the knock on the door. Jane backed out of the room and went to answer it.

"Hi," said the bellman who stood quietly outside. He held a present wrapped entirely in black. "I was asked to deliver this to Mr. Gaylord Werness this afternoon." He handed it to Jane.

She felt around in the pocket of her slacks for some cash.

"Thanks," he said quickly, "but I've already been well taken care of." He tipped his hat and started for the elevator.

Jane closed the door and carried the present into the dining room.

"Ah," said Gaylord, spying it at once. "One final gift. What could it be?"

It was passed carefully from hand to hand until it reached him.

"No card?" he asked curiously.

"It's under the bow," said Gloria, pointing to a small black envelope. It blended in almost perfectly with the wrapping paper making it difficult to see.

"Of course," said Gaylord, slipping it out. He adjusted his bifocals and read out loud. "The Bloodstone." He looked up delightedly. "That's my birthstone!" Then continuing,

Who in this world of ours
there eyes,
In March first open, shall
be despised.

"Ha," he chuckled. "Must be from a theatre critic." Everyone laughed.

In days of peril, foul
unsaved,
And wear a bloodstone
to their grave.

He looked up, still smiling. But this time the smile was a little more uncertain. "Agh," he said, attacking the wrapping paper. "No one ever said Gaylord Werness didn't have strange friends."

There were a few amused snickers, but the crowd seemed to be waiting to see what was inside.

"A jack-in-the-box," he cried, lifting it out with a delighted grin. "How absolutely wonderful." The outside was painted with strange, colorful masks.

"Play it," said Billy, leaning over his shoulder. "Let's hear the song."

Gaylord grabbed the crank. A moment later the familiar strains of "Pop Goes the Weasel" were plunked out as he turned the lever, grinning expectantly at the trap door in the top of the metal box. As he got to the end of the tune, the room had become deathly silent. The crank made its preparatory clicking sound but the top remained closed.

"Maybe it's stuck," said Maureen, moving in a bit closer.

"No," said Gaylord, holding up one finger. "I'll take care of this. Sometimes you have to play the song through more than once." He bent over the box, pulling it nearer. As he turned the crank, the song began to play once again. Several times the melody played through, all with the same result. On the fourth try, Gaylord was becoming visibly frustrated. He banged the box on the table and rapped his knuckles on the top. As the song came to its conclusion, the top suddenly clicked and then flew open, propelling a disgusting slurry of sticky, reddish liquid into his face and beard. "Ugh," he said, falling backward off his stool. Billy managed to catch him before his head hit the side of the buffet.

"What is it?" Almost in unison, the guests backed away.

Gaylord lifted his hand to his beard. Tiny, blood soaked rocks were embedded in the white strands. "Good Lord," he said, clutching his heart.

"Give him some air," shouted Maureen, bending down to loosen his tie. "Call someone. His doctor. Someone! For God's sake, he has a *heart* condition."

"Get me my pills," he whispered. "They're on the table next to my bed."

"I'll get them," said Gloria. Jane noticed that she'd managed to snap several pictures of the scene as it was unfolding. A rather prurient reaction to something so revolting.

Billy carefully stood back from his grandfather and announced, "I'll make the call to the doctor."

Erin followed him into the kitchen, swiftly blocking his access to the phone. "Let's get out of here," she pleaded.

He pushed her aside. "We can't."

"Why not?"

"Are you crazy? I have to be here when the doctor comes. I need to know what he says." He dialed the number written on a card next to the phone.

"I'm leaving then."

"Fine. Do what you have to."

She didn't move.

He spoke calmly into the receiver. "Yes, Dr. Highsmith?" He briefly explained the situation. "That's right. He's taken his heart medication." He paused. "I see. What? The police?" He hesitated. "All right . . . sure, I'll call them if you think that's necessary." He waited. "Fine. I'll tell him you'll be right over. I'm sure he'll appreciate that." He hung up.

Erin's eyes were full of tears when he turned around.

"Come on, this was just a joke, honey. A bad one, I'll grant you, but everything's going to be fine."

"Coming here was the bad joke, Billy. This wasn't how we planned it."

"How can you say that?"

"Because it's the truth." Her eyes implored.

"You know, Erin, sometimes . . ." His voice trailed off.

"What?"

"Well, I mean, sometimes I wonder what you're thinking. You don't tell me . . . things."

She turned her head away. "I'm afraid, Billy."

"Of what?" He waited. When she didn't answer, he said, "Of me? Is that what you're saying? You're afraid of me!"

"Of course not!"

He put his arm around her and began walking her to the door. "We have to stick together, Erin. And anyway, you're just tired. You haven't slept well in several weeks. Maybe you're the one who should see a doctor."

"I don't need a doctor, Billy. We have to stop! Think things through better."

"I know what I'm doing. Everything will work out fine."

She leaned her head against his shoulder.

"Come on, why don't you lie down in one of the bedrooms? There's plenty of room. That doctor will be here any minute. I'll have him come in and take a look at you before he leaves."

"Billy?" she whispered. "I *do* want to talk to you."

"We will."

"No, I mean *really* talk."

"Of course," he said soothingly. "But not right now." He gave her a little push toward the hall. "Go on now. Rest a bit. I promise, we'll make some time soon. Okay?"

"Right," she said. There was no conviction in her voice.

33

Gaylord was resting comfortably when Billy entered the bedroom a few minutes later. "Dr. Highsmith will be here any minute. He suggested I call the police."

"Good idea," said Maureen. She was sitting on the other side of the bed, picking pieces of rock out of Gaylord's beard. "Whoever did this was sick. Trying to scare an old man into his grave. Bloodstones? Whoever heard of such a thing."

Gaylord motioned for Billy to sit next to him. "Let's just hope the police can get to the bottom of it. I'll have someone's hide if they don't." He dabbed at his eye with a tissue. "I've been thinking, son. I'd like you and Erin to move in with me here. There's plenty of room. You'd be much closer to the theatre. And it would be a good thing for the family. We need to get to know each other better."

Billy scratched his head. "I don't know. I'd have to ask Erin what she thought."

Gaylord glanced at Maureen. "Will you leave us for a few minutes?"

She stiffened. "Why? Aren't I part of the family anymore?"

"Of course," said Gaylord impassively, "you and Erling are very important to me."

"Important enough so that you're going to keep your word? You're going to leave the rights to your plays, if not to Torald, then to our son?"

"Now Maureen, I don't believe I ever made that promise. It was wishful thinking on Torald's part, that's all."

Her eyes grew wide with fury. "Wishful thinking? How

190

can you say that? After all these years? After everything I put up with?"

"Calm down. I tell you, you'll be taken care of."

"That's not the point. I don't want charity. I want what's mine. What was promised me and my son."

Gaylord glanced at Billy, putting his hand over his heart. "Will you get her out of here? I can't take this right now."

Billy stood. "Maureen? This isn't the time."

"No? Then when? This was the appointed day. What's the decision, Gaylord? I demand to know."

"Please," said Gaylord, looking helplessly up at Billy.

"Maureen, I'm going to have to insist." Billy's arms rested calmly at his side.

"You're both *bastards*, do you know that? You'll both pay. This is fraud! You're not going to get away with it." She moved angrily to the door. "Go ahead," she roared at Billy. "Take your blood money. See where it gets you. Torald was right. This family is disgusting. Welcome to the brood." With her eyes flashing, she slammed the door. A tiny figurine rocked on the shelf above Gaylord's head.

He motioned for Billy to sit back down. "When you have something people want," he sighed, "things can get complicated. Billy, I'll say it again. I want you and Erin to come live with me. And yes, one of the reasons is that I've decided to leave the rights to my plays to you."

Billy could feel a bolt of adrenaline shoot through his body. Here it was. More than a dream come true.

"But I don't know you very well. Even so, I can tell you're a fine man. We need to learn about each other and that takes time. I'm not sure how much I've got left. Say you'll move in? No matter what Erin says, put me first *just this once*." He gripped Billy's hand.

Billy's mind was spinning. "I'll talk to her. I promise, we'll do it. It may take a little time."

"Not too much," said Gaylord. His smile had become serene.

"If you're going to be all right, I'll go out and talk to her now. The doctor will be in to see you any minute."

"That's fine, son. You go find her. I'm sure she'll see the

wisdom in what I suggest. It will feel so good to have my family around me again." He sighed and pulled the quilt up over his chest.

"It's not real blood," said the sergeant glancing at Trevelyan. "It's that stuff—what do you call it? Theatrical blood. My son used it in a play he was in last winter."

Trevelyan leaned over the box, scrutinizing it closely. "Have this checked immediately. I want to know everything there is to know about it. Fibers, fingerprints—everything."

"Will do," said the sergeant.

Noticing Jane near the side door, he scowled. "I might have known you'd be here."

"It's nice to see you, too."

He crossed to where she was standing and pushed her back into the empty hallway. Most of the other guests had been allowed to leave. "You think you're pretty clever, don't you?"

"Pardon me?"

"I'm getting some heat, Ms. Lawless. At least in St. Paul I know where it's coming from. Your father's touch is about as delicate as a prize fighter's. But, Jesus, lady, who do you know on the Minneapolis City Council?"

Jane smiled as she thought of Dorrie. That was quick.

"All right, if that's the way you want to play it, it makes no difference. No one is going to tell me how to do my job."

"I'm not playing," said Jane. "Any more than you are."

The sergeant poked his head around the corner. "That bellman's here. The one who brought the present up."

"Bring him in," said Trevelyan, taking out a cigarette and lighting up. He inhaled deeply and then blew the smoke directly at Jane.

The same middle-aged man who'd handed her the box entered, taking off his cap.

"Name?" said Trevelyan, opening his notebook.

"Earl Smith."

"You delivered the package to this suite?"

"Yes sir."

"Where did you get it?"

"Well, see this guy came into the Maxfield yesterday around noon. He gave me a fifty dollar bill and told me to deliver it to Mr. Werness's suite exactly at three."

"What did the man look like?"

The bellman shrugged. "I don't know. Average. Light brown hair and beard. Young."

"How was he dressed?"

"Suit and tie."

"There was nothing about him that struck you as unusual?"

"No." He glanced at Jane. "Not that I remember."

"Okay, that's all. For now."

As the man disappeared out the door, Billy came out of Gaylord's room. He looked so excited, Jane thought he was about to burst.

"He's feeling much better," said Billy, taking a deep breath.

"That's great." Jane wondered what was going on.

Erin came out of one of the vacant bedrooms rubbing her eyes. They looked sore. Like she'd been crying.

Billy rushed to her and gave her a big hug. "Gaylord's leaving the rights to his plays to me! Isn't that fabulous?"

As if in a trance, she nodded.

"Honey, listen to me. He wants us to move in here with him. It won't be forever, but he wants to get to know us better."

Jane watched a look of shock grow on Erin's face. Nervously, Erin began to step in and out, and then in and out again of her right shoe. Something was wrong.

"Move here?" whispered Erin.

"It's just for a short time."

"He said that? Just for a short time?"

"Well, not in so many words, but don't worry. We'll find that house we want. Erin, you've got to trust me. And besides, this will be great. There's lots of room here. I'll be closer to the theatre. It'll be perfect."

Tentatively, Erin touched her forehead as if she were trying to get her bearings.

Trevelyan cleared his throat. "I need to talk to you for a few minutes, Mr. Brewster. Your wife, too."

"Of course," said Billy.

"Let's use one of the empty bedrooms." He nodded to a partially open door. Turning around he glared at Jane. "I'll get to you later. Don't feel you need to stay."

"Thanks." She waited while they made their exit and then walked to the dining room doorway. Cordelia was sitting alone at the table, looking pensively out the window.

"Time to hit the bricks," said Jane. "You'd better go find your top hat."

"I have it right here," said Cordelia, pulling it out from under the table. "You never know when Ginger Rogers might show up and want to dance."

Jane smiled.

"What an awful afternoon," groaned Cordelia, getting up. "And now I get to continue the merriment by heading over to the hospital. I promised Celeste I'd come by. Her mother is driving her nuts."

"Feeling better, huh?"

"It's a matter of opinion. And what are you up to for the rest of the day?"

Jane knew she had to tell the police about the video tape. Trevelyan would string her up by her thumbs if he knew she'd held out on him. "I want to watch that video one last time. Then I've got to give it to the police."

"And hope they don't still use firing squads." Cordelia popped the hat on her head. "I assume this would come under the heading of 'withholding evidence.' "

Jane swallowed hard. "Maybe I missed something. After Trevelyan gets his hands on it, I'll never see it again."

"Such a shame. I know how much you've enjoyed it."

Jane shook her head.

"Say, I've got it. I could have someone take a video of me. You know? Cordelia coming out of the bathroom. Cordelia eating a chocolate eclair. Cordelia sneezing. Why, you'd never miss that other tape."

"Thanks. I think I'll pass."

"No. This could be great! I can see it all now." She

threw back her head and began to slink toward Jane until they were almost nose to nose. Her eyes were wild. "Mr. DeMille," she crooned, "I'm ready for my close-up now!"

34

Antonia bent over the flower patch she'd just raked out in her backyard and examined the dirt for signs of life. She'd planted a bunch of tulip bulbs here last fall, her fingers freezing as she'd tried to get them into the cold soil before the first snow. Behind her she heard the side gate open and then close. As she looked around, she saw Erin Brewster making her way grimly up the path. This did not bode well for the beginning of a new week. "Good morning," she said, scrambling to her feet and leaning on her rake.

"You've got to *do* something," said Erin. The intensity in her eyes made her face look distorted.

"I'm sorry?"

"Cut the crap, I know everything. I'm not here to discuss that now. You've got to get the Allen Grimby to rescind that offer they made Billy about becoming a permanent member of the repertory company. We have to get out of here as soon as he's done with the run of your play. Are you listening? *You're* the only one that can do anything about it."

Antonia could see Erin was on the verge of a breakdown. Could it be possible she did know the truth?

"I haven't time to waste explaining this to you. I would think you could see what's happening. Yesterday your father invited Billy and me to come live with him at his apartment."

"You're not serious?"

"Billy accepted. Do you understand *now*? I won't be responsible for what happens if you don't do something and do it quickly."

"Erin! I—"

"Do something, goddammit! Do it today. Or what happens will be on your head." She turned and marched out through the gate.

Antonia felt like she'd been hit over the head by her own gardening shovel. As she stood immobilized by Erin's words, she glanced up and saw Lucy standing near the garden shed. Had she heard? By the look on her face, she could tell she had. "Lucy," she called, but it was no use. Lucy had disappeared into the annex and slammed the door.

"Here it is," smiled the balding man behind the counter. "Everything's checked out and the waiting period's up. You're all set." He pushed the pearl-handled gun across the glass.

"Is it loaded?"

"Of course not." He reached behind the counter for a small box. "I'll include this in the price. Would you like the name of a good shooting school? You'll want to learn how to use this properly."

"No. Thanks anyway."

"You're sure, now?"

"Perfectly. I've got everything I need right here."

"All right, then. Anything else we can help you with, you come on down. You'll feel safer tonight just knowing you have it."

"I feel safer already."

35

Jane walked into her rear screened porch and settled herself in a wicker rocker overlooking the backyard. Bean, the tennis ball held firmly in his jaws, hopped up on her lap and quickly went to sleep. She could see that her aunt was busily engaged in finishing the brick raku kiln she'd started several days before. Beryl was wearing her favorite sweatshirt, the one her son, Anthony, had sent her from London. A red bandana was tied around her hair.

This was a balmy evening by late March standards. The sun sat just above the steeple on the Lutheran church in the distance. She knew it wouldn't be long before she saw her first robin, smelled that first scent of flowering crab apple. As she stroked her little dog's fur, enjoying this, the golden time of the evening, her mind turned once again to the conversation she'd had with her father. She hadn't yet mentioned anything about it to Beryl. The time just never seemed right. And anyway, she'd needed a few days to mull over what'd been said. It was no simple matter trying to find one's way through a bog of family opinion. In the end, perhaps it wasn't important who was right—who, if anyone, was to blame. What was important was that she find a context in which to frame the past. A way to understand each side.

Jane noticed the sun begin to slide slowly behind the delicately rendered wooden steeple. Her aunt rose from her crouching position and brushed the dirt and brick dust from her clothes. "Looks beautiful," shouted Jane.

Beryl waved and then picked up her tool box, heading for the porch door. "It's going to be, when it's done. I'm building a rounded arch above it—just like the one I have at home. It's certainly not going to detract from the garden, which, by the way, I intend to start next week." She sat down heavily on a wood bench and set the box on the floor next to her. "Did I tell you Peter rang us this morning? It was just after you left for the restaurant."

Jane shook her head, letting her eyes wander about the dingy, dusty porch. It needed a good cleaning after the long winter. "And what did my charming brother have to say for himself?"

"He and Sigrid will be flying back next Sunday. He'd like you to pick him up at the airport. I wrote down the time and flight number."

"Did he say how the visit was going?"

Beryl gave an amused smile as she removed the bandana from her hair. "He's being looked over very carefully, poor boy. Sigrid's family is somewhat more orthodox than ours."

Jane decided not to pursue that. Peter would fill her in soon enough. Still, there was something she knew she had to say. Now was as good a time as any. "Speaking of our family," she smiled, "I thought I should tell you that I had a long talk with Dad the other day."

Beryl fixed her eyes on the bandana in her lap. She began to fold it into a tight square.

"I guess you could say he told me his side of the story."

"Well then, you understand a bit better why Raymond and I never cared for one another."

"I think you had rather conflicting agendas."

Beryl straightened her back.

"Oh, Beryl, can't you see that you've both made mistakes? You've been such a loving aunt to me, always there when I needed you. Couldn't you find it in your heart to forgive Dad for what you think he's done wrong?"

Beryl looked off in the distance, her face retreating into shadow. "I'm no longer young, Jane dear. I don't know if you can understand this, but I have given a great deal of thought to my life. From my vantage point now, I'm afraid there are many things I would go back and change if I could. Still, I absolutely refuse to live my life in profound regret. The truth is, given the same set of circumstances, I doubt I would have done anything differently. That's the crux of the problem for me. I never set out to hurt anyone. My motives weren't always pure or unselfish, but I did what I thought was best. I don't think I should have to apologize."

"I understand that," said Jane. "But don't you think perhaps my father feels the same way?" Her voice grew gentle. "Can't you grant him that much?"

The phone in the kitchen began to ring.

"I'll get it," said Beryl, rising quickly.

Jane could tell she was eager to get out of the room and put an end to the discussion.

"Hello," said Beryl, tossing an empty soda can into the recycling bin.

Jane could see her aunt pour herself a cup of coffee.

"Of course," said Beryl, her voice becoming tight and formal. "Did you want to speak with your daughter? She's right here." There was a pause. "Oh. I see." Another pause, this time a longer one. "No, that . . . I suppose that would be fine. Seven o'clock. What?"

Jane got up and walked to the door.

"I agree." She hesitated. "No, don't worry. I shan't back out. I'll see you then." She hung up and then leaned her full weight against the counter, her back to the doorway.

"I take it that was Dad." As Beryl turned around, Jane could see her determined expression lighten into a shrug. "You're getting together?"

"Tomorrow night."

Jane grinned her approval.

"Don't expect anything positive to come from this. I mean it, Jane. We're just going to talk."

Jane gave her a playful hug. "Of course I'm going to expect something positive! I wouldn't be human if I didn't."

"I've got to get ready. Evelyn Bratrude and I are having dinner out this evening."

"You and that next door neighbor of mine are becoming pretty tight."

"What? Oh, you mean friends. Well, I enjoy her company." She said the words a bit too primly.

Jane could tell she was still smarting from their earlier conversation.

"She has a great deal of common sense. That's a quality that is hard to find these days." Beryl took several gulps of coffee and then dumped the rest into the sink. "Are you staying in tonight?"

Jane nodded. "I'll be fine. You go on. You don't want to be late."

Beryl patted Jane's hand. "Thank you, dear. Don't expect me early. We may take in a movie." She headed for the stairs giving a little wave over her shoulder.

Jane was delighted her aunt was getting acquainted so quickly. Even some of the shakiness was disappearing. There was no doubt in her mind that it had been the right decision to invite Beryl here to Minneapolis. Being all alone in that drafty cottage in England, who knew how long it might have taken her to recover? Now, if only she and her father could reach some sort of understanding.

Jane looked out the dining room window at the growing dusk. Her mind turned almost immediately to thoughts of Billy and Erin. To Torald's death. And to the video.

What if Billy and Erin really were brother and sister? The fact was, Jane had been presented with a fait accompli and had never really questioned it. Clearly, there *was* love between them. Yet, sometimes they did seem a bit stiff and awkward with each other. What if their relationship was all part of some elaborate charade? But why would they do that?

She moved about aimlessly, trying to think the situation through. Had Torald suspected? Had Erin been on stage with him the night he died? Did she know what happened to him? Or worse, had she caused it? Or was it Gloria Lindy? Or Ida John? Spying the video tape next to the VCR, Jane decided it was now or never. If there was something incriminating to be found, she'd better figure it out fast. Even though she dreaded sitting through each tedious scene, it was possible she'd missed something before.

Slipping the tape into the machine, she dumped herself in a chair. Resolutely, she resisted the urge to fast-forward. Her eyes felt like gravel as the scenes progressed in an endless, boring stream. She knew she was learning nothing, yet she had to give it this final shot. As the last blurry image appeared, she realized her mind had nearly shut off. Yet something on the screen caught her eye. She slowed the footage down and watched very carefully. There! My God, that was it. She froze the frame on an indistinct foot thrust into the center of the picture. What she recognized this time was the same shoe Erin had been wearing yesterday at Gaylord's birthday party. That had to be it. Same color. Same little gold bow. Erin was the secret photographer. If she only could put it together with the other information she had, she knew it would all make perfect sense.

Quickly, she turned off the TV set and set the VCR to rewind. Her mind was racing over the events of the last few weeks. Why did this tape exist in the first place? Why was Torald dead? Realizing the significance of what she was thinking, her eyes were drawn like a magnet to the stairway. Of course. She switched off the table lamp and headed into the hallway. Erin was probably still upstairs. As far as Jane was concerned, she had some pretty important explaining to do.

36

As Jane reached the door to the third-floor bedroom, she saw that it stood ajar. Quietly, she looked inside, "Erin," she called softly. "Are you there?" Giving her eyes a moment to adjust to the darkness, she became aware of a figure seated on the bed, gazing up through the skylight at the moon. It had risen just to the east of the house. The young woman's attention seemed so completely fixed on the nearly full orb, she barely registered Jane's presence.

"I'm sorry to bother you," said Jane, "but I think we need to talk." She realized it was useless to simply stand and wait to be invited in. The invitation was not going to be forthcoming. "I saw **Billy** leave several hours ago. When do you expect him back?"

Erin drew her knees up to her chest, continuing to look up. "I don't know. He may stay at Gaylord's tonight. We had . . . sort of a fight."

"I'm sorry," said Jane. She crossed silently to the sofa and perched on the arm. She could see now that Erin had been crying. There was no use prolonging this. "I know about the videos you took of the Werness family."

Erin lowered her head.

"I have the tape. I'm not sure why you did it, but it's my guess you were doing it for Billy. To prove something to him. Is that right?"

She was silent for a long time. Finally she said, "I wanted to show him that not everything was as rosy as he thought. You don't know him very well, Jane, but he's a kind man. He believes people are basically good. Unfortunately, I think that leaves him terribly vulnerable. That tape was going to be my way of showing him what the Werness family was really like. They aren't noble and grand. But he's so starry-eyed about all of this. How could I be the one to destroy his illusions? I felt . . . like a thief."

"But you left that tape in the video camera."

Erin's shoulders sank. "I was in such a hurry to return the thing, I forgot to take it out. And then, when I called to get it back, the man said he'd sent it over to the theatre. To Cordelia. I guess I panicked. I wasn't sure I hadn't left something incriminating on it, so I went to her office. You know the rest."

"When you rented the camera, you dressed up like a man. You disguised yourself so that no one would know it was you. And you were the one who sent that jack-in-the-box to Gaylord."

She lifted her chin, still not looking at Jane. "Can you possibly understand? I felt so thwarted. I . . . I don't know what I wanted. I simply had to do *something*."

"You're not Billy's wife are you?"

She shook her head.

"You're his sister."

She sat very still, watching the moonlight fill the space between them. "After he talked to that lawyer in New Orleans, he found out about my existence. It was a relatively simple matter to find me. By the time we'd gotten together, he'd conceived this grand scheme. We'd return to Minneapolis together. He wanted us to meet our family, but initially he felt it was best to hide our true identities. That part I agreed with. The thing was, I wasn't sure I ever wanted to make myself known. We argued a lot. How could he know what kind of a situation we were getting ourselves into? He countered by saying that the Werness family was well known. Well respected. He listed the plays Gaylord and Antonia had written. Talked about their ideas, their lives."

"He'd done his homework."

"I suppose he felt he had. He was confident these were people he wanted to know, people he'd be proud to be related to. You know Billy. He's so eager, so enthusiastic. He even had me believing it . . . at least at first. But I got cold feet. When we arrived, I told him it wouldn't work. That's when he suggested we approach them as husband and wife. I could be as careful and cautious as I wanted, but we could still get to know them *together*. Even so, several times I nearly got on a plane and left. What I never counted on was that all the while, I was getting to know Billy better— coming to care about him. After the two drooling cretins I grew up with, well, I couldn't simply walk away from Billy. He's been the one good thing that's ever happened in my life, Jane. Besides, as I saw it, he needed someone to look out for him. Someone less impressed by that famous Werness charisma."

"And the pendant," said Jane. "The one Billy wears around his neck. You have one, too."

Erin's hand flew to the heart-shaped locket Billy had given her. It was inside.

"I thought so," said Jane. "The night I found Torald, I saw it on the floor next to the bleachers. You must have picked it up sometime later. Before the police started taking pictures."

Erin gave a guilty nod but said nothing.

"That means you were on stage with him that night. Did he suspect you of being Billy's sister?"

"Yes," she said softly. "Somehow, he seemed to know."

"Did you see how he died?"

Her mouth twitched. "What's the use? I can't go on like this anymore. I can't sleep. I can't eat. It was bound to come out sooner or later." She tipped her head back and spoke as if to the moon. "It was an accident. A hideous, horrible accident. He'd been drinking. While we were talking, he kept backing up and before I knew what was happening . . . he'd fallen. I tried to reach out to him, but it was too late. That's when I ran. I'm not sure exactly what happened after that."

"Did you go downstairs to his dressing room?"

Erin didn't move. "Yes, I think I did. I was . . . upset."

"But why did you make such a mess? All the posters were torn to bits. His makeup mirror was shattered. What were you so upset about? It looks more like anger."

Slowly, she began to rub the back of her neck. "It's all so confused. It was like . . . a blackout. I don't remember much. At some point I guess I realized my locket had sprung open and the pendant had fallen out. Billy gave me the locket the night Antonia's play opened. It was so that I could still wear the pendant, but nobody would see it and ask questions. I had to get it back, don't you see? Someone might find it and draw the wrong conclusion. So I went back to the stage. That's when I found you there."

Jane didn't buy it. There were too many holes. "Where were you standing when you lost the pendant?"

"What?"

"When you were talking to Torald, where were you? Where was he?"

"Well, uhm, I was sitting. Sort of in the center of the bleachers. He was standing close to the edge."

"And when he fell, what did you do exactly? Did you go to him?"

"Well, I reached out my hand, but I could see it was useless. The tines of that fork had already . . ." She looked away. "I was in a daze, Jane. When you came in I'd just slipped behind the curtain. When I saw my chance, I left through the back."

"But the necklace? I found it at the edge of the bleachers on the floor. That's where you must have picked it up. How did it get there if you never came toward him?"

Erin crossed her arms over her chest. "I . . . you're confusing me."

"I'm just trying to understand," said Jane. She was positive now Erin was lying. "What were you and Torald talking about?"

"He wanted to know if I was Billy's sister."

"Did you tell him the truth?"

"At first I lied, but I could see it was useless. It was like he already knew."

"Was he happy about it?"

"He was . . ." She hesitated. "Neither. I think he was simply triumphant that he'd figured it out."

"And then what?"

"Well, then he sort of slipped. Fell backward. He was drunk, Jane. I couldn't do anything to help him. Don't look at me like that, *it was an accident*! You've got to believe me!"

"Does Billy know?"

"No!"

The strain of keeping something like that a secret must have taken quite a toll. No wonder she'd seemed so tightly strung lately. "He never suspected?"

"Absolutely not."

"But why wouldn't you tell him? After all, if you're innocent of any wrongdoing—"

Erin erupted. "If? See? See what's happening? Just like you, Billy might not have believed me. He might have jumped to the wrong conclusion, like you're doing. You think I murdered him, don't you? Admit it!"

Jane knew Erin wasn't telling the whole truth. Beyond that rather useless generality, she hadn't a clue. "I don't know what to say, Erin. Are you sure that's everything that happened?"

"Of course I'm sure."

"And you ran away because—"

"I was in shock. It was a natural reaction to something so terrible. You saw how he died. And then I suppose I thought the police might feel I had something to do with it."

"It's a logical conclusion, Erin. They may."

"What do you mean?"

"Erin, we have to call them."

"No!" Her expression turned desperate. "This is just between us, okay? You can keep a secret, can't you? It will only hurt Billy if all this comes out. You don't want that, do you?"

"Erin—"

"Please!"

"Look," said Jane, knowing she needed to be firm. "Trevelyan has made it very clear that everyone in the theatre that night is a suspect in a murder investigation. I can't, with a clear conscience, withhold information that might harm others. It would make me your accomplice."

"Accomplice?"

"You know what I'm saying. We have to call him. But I have an idea. We'll call my father first. He'd be glad to represent you, I'm sure of it. Maybe we can get him to come over here tonight. You could talk to him until you felt confident enough to face the police. He'd be able to advise you better than anyone I know."

"You mean now?"

Sadly, Jane nodded. "I'm afraid so."

Erin pulled limply on her sweatshirt. "I suppose. If that's the only way. But, I mean ... what if he can't come?"

"We'll never know unless we try. Do you want to phone Billy first?"

Her voice faltered. "No."

"Why don't you come downstairs, then? After I've made the call, we can sit in the living room and wait together. You probably shouldn't be alone."

Taking several deep breaths, Erin got up. "Thanks," she said ineffectually. She looked up through the skylight at the moon one last time. "I guess it's time to pay the piper."

this same   He said everything was fine with me two

PART THREE

The Children's Game

Or what man is there of you, whom if his son
ask bread, will he give him a stone?
Or if he ask a fish, will he give him a serpent?

Matthew 7:9–10

37

Trevelyan sat on the front of his desk, chewing resentfully on a toothpick. He'd been interrupted in the middle of his dinner, and his mood reflected it. He glanced over at the tape recorder to make sure it was on. "I have a statement here that you gave a few minutes ago."

Erin fidgeted with the buttons on her coat. "Yes."

He looked down, reading for a moment. "You say you were on stage with Torald Werness the night he died."

"That's correct."

"Ms. Brewster," he frowned, "are you trying to tell me this was an accident?"

Erin twisted a lock of hair behind her ear. She knew Jane was probably furious with her. She hadn't waited for her father to arrive. Giving some lame excuse about needing a sweater, she'd gone back up to her room, grabbed her coat and left by the outside stairs. It had been a simple matter to call a cab from the nearest 7-Eleven. Erin knew Jane would never understand why she didn't *want* her father's help. The less questions the better. Still, the jig was indeed up. She knew she had to go to the police, if for nothing else than to put an end to the nightmare she had been living through for the last several months. And at all costs, she had to protect Billy.

"Ms. Brewster?"

"Yes?"

"Will you answer the question?"

"Ah . . . sure. Yes, it was an accident."

Yanking the toothpick out of his mouth, Trevelyan tossed it in the wastebasket. "All right. Let's start at the beginning.

The night Torald died, you had a five-fifteen appointment with him at his request."

"That's right. He'd called me earlier in the day, and I agreed to meet him."

"Did he say what it was about?"

She shook her head.

"Please, Ms. Brewster, answer the question audibly."

Erin's eyes fixed angrily on the recorder. "No."

"Did you ask?"

"I figured I already knew. I thought, given his general nosiness, that the meeting was probably inevitable."

Trevelyan studied her for a moment. "When you got there, was he alone?"

"Yes."

"You stated that he'd been drinking."

"I could smell it on his breath."

"You got that close, did you?"

She bristled. "I didn't need to. He was an actor. He *projected*."

Trevelyan didn't smile. "Where were you standing during this conversation?"

"I was sitting in the center of bleachers . . . well, not quite the center. Sort of more to one side."

"And Mr. Werness?"

"He was standing near the edge."

"How did the conversation begin?"

"He asked me flat out if I was Billy's sister. I felt it was useless to try to hide the truth from him, so I said I was."

"You'd gone to rather elaborate extremes to hide your identity, Ms. Brewster. I don't understand why you would admit it so easily."

Erin touched the bridge of her nose. "It wasn't easy, Detective Trevelyan. I don't mean to give you the wrong impression. Nothing about any of this has been easy."

"All right. After you told him the truth, what was his reaction?"

"Well, I suppose, smugness. He'd guessed. I just confirmed it for him."

"You didn't like him very much, did you?"

"No."

"But what were his actual words?"

"I don't remember."

"Did he say, for instance, 'Welcome to the family'? "

"He wasn't that generous."

"Well, didn't he wonder why you and Billy had kept your identity a secret for so long? Wasn't he curious why *your* relationship with Antonia was still being kept a secret?"

"I suppose. He never asked."

"I find that hard to believe."

Erin shrugged.

"Perhaps you'd take a moment to think a bit harder, Ms. Brewster. I'd like you to characterize his response for me—even if you can't remember the exact words."

She paused, reaching for the locket hanging around her neck. "Well, just like I told Jane, he seemed terribly satisfied with himself that he'd figured it out." That was true. The closer she stuck to the truth, the harder it would be for him to trip her up.

"And was he going to keep your little secret?"

She looked away.

"No?" He sat forward, realizing he'd struck a nerve. "Is that when the argument started?"

"What argument?" She tried to keep her voice calm.

"Did you struggle with him?"

"Certainly not."

"And during that struggle, did he fall backward off the the bleachers?"

"No!"

"Or, Ms. Brewster, did you perhaps push him? You couldn't have him revealing any secrets now, could you?"

"What do you mean by that?" Her voice rose higher with each word. She was completely losing her grip. This was what she'd feared most.

"There was some compelling reason you didn't want your identity known. Something you were willing to commit a murder for."

"That's not true!"

"Isn't it? Are you going to sit there and continue to feed me this crap about a staid little conversation ending with Torald accidentally falling off the bleachers?" His voice was filled with malicious indignation. "You're the crazy one if you think I'm going to buy that! Now, either you tell me the truth, or I'm booking you for murder."

Desperately, she knew she had to hold on. There was still so much at stake. "I've told you the truth. I have nothing more to add."

Trevelyan was about to hit the intercom button on the telephone when Billy burst through the door.

Erin watched helplessly as he knelt beside her. He was the last person she wanted to see.

"Mr. Brewster," said Trevelyan, rising from the desk. "What an unexpected surprise." His voice was calm, and yet it held a clear threat.

Billy glared at him as he touched Erin's arm. "You're not saying another word without a lawyer present. Jane called me when you . . . left. She thought I might know where you were. We've been calling all over. She finally had the idea to call here. Her father's right outside."

"What a stroke of luck," said Trevelyan, making a fist and thrusting it into his suit pocket. "She can talk to him after she's been processed."

"Processed?" Billy struggled to control the muscles in his face.

"Murder, Mr. Brewster. I shouldn't think this would come as a complete surprise." His eyes shifted to the door where a uniformed policeman had just entered. "Bonner, take her outside and read her her rights. Then book her for the murder of Torald Werness."

38

"I'm not an expert, but I'd say she's on the verge of total nervous collapse." Raymond Lawless lifted his leather briefcase over a wooden barrier and led his daughter to a lounge area in the rear.

"She's holding something back," said Jane. "I could tell that as soon as we started talking earlier this evening."

Raymond loosened his tie and rubbed his forehead in frustration. "Trevelyan probably caught that, too. With his experience, he can smell something rotten. Unless she tells me the whole truth, he's going to hang her with that silence. Her one hope is that she was the only one on stage that night. If she says it was an accident, who's to say it wasn't? Except . . ."

"What?"

"Well, if what you told me is true, the fact that she tore Torald's dressing room apart . . . see, it doesn't fit. I mean, if it was an accident, then why was she so angry? And it *was* an act of anger."

"It almost feels like she's protecting someone."

Raymond shook his head. "Minds are a fragile thing. Mark my words, she's going to snap. She'd better tell someone what she knows, and fast—it's the only way to relieve some of the pressure." He looked up as Lucy and Antonia Werness entered through the front doors of the police station. "Billy must have called them."

Jane watched them give their names at the desk. A few moments later, a uniformed policeman appeared and ushered them behind the locked door. "Interesting."

"Very." He pulled out a roll of peppermint LifeSavers and offered her one.

"No thanks. Have you talked to Billy yet?"

"Yes, but he seems to be every bit as much in the dark as we are."

"You believe him?"

Raymond sucked on the candy. "It's hard to tell. He'd be great on the witness stand. I think he could take just about any emotional stance he wanted and pull it off. As for telling the truth, I don't know."

"I think I might know someone who could help."

"Who?"

"His name is Malcolm Coopersmith."

"The minister? We've never met, but I know who he is. Pastor of Lakeview Unitarian."

"And a close friend of the Werness family."

"Is that right? Well, at this point, I'll try anything. Okay, here's the plan. You call him. Set up an appointment ASAP."

Jane glanced at her watch. "It's kind of late tonight. How about if I try first thing in the morning?"

"Fine." Raymond seemed to hesitate.

"What is it?"

He shook his head. "Just considering the possibilities. Some of them I don't like."

Jane slipped her hand over his. "What did I get you into?"

"Just the usual," he shrugged. "We do what we can. Unfortunately, the age of miracles is past. If that young woman doesn't try to help herself, there's not much I can do."

Next morning, Jane knocked on Malcolm's office door. When there was no answer, she opened it a crack and called his name. She'd decided a personal visit was better than a phone call. Since the room appeared to be empty, she returned to the main vestibule and climbed the polished granite steps to the second-floor landing. The library was on the far end of a long hallway. The woman at the front desk had said he often spent his mornings reading up there. As she approached, she could hear someone laughing.

Malcolm looked up from the book in his lap as she entered. "Good morning," he smiled, still terribly amused. He turned over a corner of the page to mark his spot.

Jane glanced down at the title. *God Bless You Mr. Rosewater.*

"Kurt Vonnegut," said Malcolm. "Ever read it?"

"At least three times."

He grinned. "I've worn out several copies myself."

Jane sat down on the other side of a narrow wooden table. She noticed another book resting on the top.

"*Palm Sunday*," he said, opening it to a chapter near the end. "I'm using one of his essays as a text for my sermon on Sunday. He's truly an American saint."

"He'd be flattered. That's how he refers to Mark Twain."

"You *do* know his works well." He closed the book and folded his hands on the table. "To what do I owe this unexpected visit? Perhaps I'm wrong, but you seem ... upset."

Jane traced a scratch in the oak with her index finger. She hated being the bearer of bad tidings. "I'm afraid it's Erin Brewster. She's been arrested for the murder of Torald Werness."

He nearly jumped out of his seat. "I don't believe it!"

"It all came out last night. It seems she's not really Billy's wife after all. She's his sister."

He didn't move.

"What's going on, Malcolm? You know that family better than just about anyone. Erin's holding something back, I know it. If she doesn't tell the truth, I'm afraid she'll go to jail. You're one of the only people who can help."

"Tell me everything you know. Don't leave anything out." Closing his eyes, he leaned back and listened as Jane recounted the events of last night. She ended by telling him that her father was going to represent Erin, but his hands were tied if she didn't tell him the truth.

"That's everything?"

"Well, actually, I did find out one other thing. Something

I'm not supposed to know so I'd appreciate it if you wouldn't mention it to my father when you talk to him. I'm not sure this has any bearing on the murder, but Torald was accused of statutory rape back in 1975. It was a fifteen-year-old girl in a production of one of his father's plays. My father represented him in the matter. It was settled out of court."

"Yes," answered Malcolm. "If *settled* is ever the right word in a case like that." He considered something for a long moment before asking, "Do you believe in evil, Jane?"

The question took her by surprise. "I don't know. I suppose," she said. "Why would you ask that?"

He seemed to hesitate. "I'm not talking about evil in the abstract. You see, years ago I had a terribly hard time believing a human being could be evil. Sinful perhaps. Selfish. Psychologically damaged. I knew we humans were all capable of *performing* evil acts. But I'm talking about something quite different. I'm not speaking of an *act*, but of a *personality*."

"You mean like a serial killer?"

He pushed the books away from him and leaned into the table. "When I was a young man, I found that I desperately wanted to understand what motivated people. Part of my dilemma came from the fact that I was never able to put my finger on just why my mother—who happened to be a pastor of a small Christian ministry in Minneapolis—made me feel so insignificant and always in the way. Don't get me wrong, I'm not suggesting she was evil, but she was a lousy parent. My father died when I was very young. I never knew him. It takes a long time for a child to come to any mature understanding of his parents. My mother never made much time for me, and I didn't understand why. Of course, when I got to college I blamed her religion for everything. I became a very vocal atheist. I think human beings invariably think going to the opposite extreme will provide them with a solution. Since Mom's answer to my probing was always the same—man was sinful and fell short of the glory of God—I decided I needed to look elsewhere. Sin, as a concept, had long ago ceased to have any meaning for my life. I decided science would provide the answers theology couldn't. So I began to pursue a degree in psychology."

"But you're a minister now," said Jane.

"Yes. But one with a Ph.D in Jungian psychology. My dissertation was on a specific personality disorder, which, though I couched it in the going psychological terms of the day, I always referred to in my mind as 'the evil person.' The thing was, I found that psychology had its limitations, too, just like religion. The psychologist, of necessity, shies away from a more metaphysical word like evil. That seemed strange to me. I began to think that I'd been too hasty in my assessment of God and the Bible. So, I entered the seminary."

"But why were you so interested in this one aspect of human nature?"

"I'll get to that. Soon after I began my studies, I found I was still meeting resistance. Among clerics, I discovered a similar reticence to really deal with the concept of the evil personality. Again, the *act* may be evil—usually termed wicked or sinful—but not the *person*."

"There *is* quite a chasm between the two."

"Indeed." He lowered his voice. "But I've seen it, Jane. Face-to-face. I've seen evil. The problem is, how do I describe it? It's so confusing. That's the one characteristic about it that never changes. It's couched in lies and illusion."

Almost instinctively, she drew back from the table.

"Look, I'm not trying to frighten you. Most of the evil people I've known—and I've met very few—look just like you or me. They're not criminals. They're certainly not insane. In fact, they have a very highly developed sense of right and wrong."

"What's the point, Malcolm? Who are you accusing?"

Malcolm took off his glasses and drew out a handkerchief from his back pocket. "Did you know Torald tried to commit suicide when he was nineteen?"

"I'd heard that, yes."

"Let me explain the situation to you. When Torald graduated from high school, he desperately wanted to go out West to college. He wanted to assert his independence, make a name for himself apart from his father. Lucy had left a few months before to go live with Antonia in New Orleans. That devastated him. They were very close and I know he missed her terribly. But Gaylord insisted that he stay and go to the University of Minnesota. Family had always been this big ideal with Gaylord. He proclaimed it as something everyone needed to be willing to sacrifice for, to hold above petty personal concerns. It sounded good, but I could see how easily he used it as a club. Then again, my own mother talked about the sacredness of the family in lots of her sermons. I was used to tuning it out. Anyway, he convinced Torald to stay. As his freshman year went on, he became more and more depressed. For his birthday in November, Gaylord gave him a hunting rifle. Never to my knowledge had Torald ever expressed an interest in hunting. To the contrary, I'd heard him hold forth quite loudly about how stupid he thought it was. Gaylord must have decided it was a good gift for a virile young man. Assuming he used it for its intended purpose, it would get him out of the house, away from his studies, and into some fresh country air. Two weeks later, Torald attempted to take his life with that gun. He tried to shoot himself in the heart and ended up with a terrible wound in his stomach." He paused, watching Jane's reaction.

"I suppose I can see how Gaylord could have thought it was a good gift."

"For a highly depressed young man? Perhaps. For one who had stated his antipathy to hunting? Maybe. It's confusing, isn't it? But still explainable."

"What are you suggesting?"

"Let me tell you about the statutory rape situation in 1975. Everyone in that theatre company could see Torald was attracted to this young girl. Whether or not she understood his intentions, I don't know. But one afternoon the director came to Gaylord and insisted the girl be replaced by another young actress. Her understudy. He explained the potential problem in no uncertain—legal—terms. Gaylord, however, saw it differently. He pleaded with the director to keep the girl on. He said a situation like this could ruin her future career. She'd been working in the theatre since she was nine years old, steadily building up an excellent reputation. He also mentioned that he'd witnessed her and Torald together and there *was* a certain electricity, no doubt about it, but that energy was what made them so great together on stage. After all, the director didn't want the ruin of a budding career on his conscience, did he? Things were probably being exaggerated. The director countered by saying the girl was having difficulty learning her lines.

"This Gaylord knew was true. Still, he insisted he saw great potential in her. And then do you know what he did? He arranged for Torald to tutor her—in Gaylord's own house, at night. He suggested they use his patio. One evening, after they'd gotten started, he got a phone call and left. This happened several times. Perhaps the calls were a coincidence. We'll never know. But they got Gaylord out of the house, leaving Torald and the girl all alone. It wasn't two weeks later that her parents had a lawyer contact the director. The production company was being sued. Torald was being sued." Malcolm stopped to see what effect the story had had on Jane.

"I don't know what you want me to say?"

"No, but I believe I know what you're thinking. Torald was responsible for his own actions. To an extent, I'd agree. And curiously, Gaylord never did anything without an altruistic reason. He did everything he could to get the charges dropped, including hiring your father. When he saw it was futile, he ended up paying a sizeable amount of money to the girl's family to keep it out of court. Again, it's confusing. The stated motives are all reasonable. But don't you see? Something in both those situations was very wrong."

"You think Gaylord is evil?"

Malcolm put his glasses back on. "As much as it makes no sense to a great many people, yes. That's what I think. He destroyed Torald as surely as if he'd put a gun to his head. He destroyed his own wife." He shook his head.

"Now that was a study in terror. Before that woman was committed, he had her convinced she couldn't leave the house without him. He'd reduced her to something subhuman. She was afraid of everything."

"I don't see how——"

"No, I grant you. It's subtle."

"What about Antonia?"

"She was the lucky one. She's eight years older than Lucy, six years older than Torald. When she was growing up Gaylord was locked away in a room, writing. By the time his first plays began to hit it big, she was in her last years of high school. She got away from him before he could do very much damage. But she still feels terribly guilty. She thinks she could have done something to help her mother. To help Lucy and Torald get away from that house, from his influence."

"But she did let Lucy come stay with her in New Orleans when she was barely sixteen."

"From Antonia's point of view, it wasn't enough. Gaylord had become intensely blocked as a writer when Lucy and Torald were eight and ten years old. After that time, he did very little new writing. Instead, he began to pay more attention to his family. He's said many times that Antonia never felt part of it. They've never gotten along."

"But what does this have to do with Erin and Billy? So Gaylord is a rotten human being. I'm terribly sorry for his family, but right now I guess I'm more interested in what you think Torald and Erin might have talked about the night he died. What's going on?"

Malcolm leaned back in his chair and looked thoughtful. "Do Lucy and Antonia know about Erin's arrest?"

"They were at the station last night. They talked to her as soon as my father was finished—I suppose Billy must have called."

"I see." He drummed his fingers on the table. "No one thought to call me."

The woman who had been seated behind the reception desk appeared in the doorway. "Malcolm, there's someone on the phone who needs to talk to you. It sounded urgent."

Immediately, he stood and excused himself.

After he was gone, Jane rose and stepped to the window, leaning her head against the frame. This conversation had been interesting, but whatever Malcolm was trying to say, why didn't he just come right out and *say* it! She knew he was holding something back. Something that might be able to help Erin. If Gaylord really was an evil man, he'd probably hurt his children in many ways. Did Erin know something about Gaylord she was trying to keep from Billy? Or was it something about Antonia or Torald, or even Lucy? Was that information causing Erin's silence? It wasn't fair—all this philosophizing. Not when Erin's whole future was at stake!

Jane turned as she heard Malcolm return to the room. He was out of breath.

"I'm sorry, Jane. I have to leave. It's an emergency. Perhaps we can finish our conversation later."

Jane could see he'd gone quite pale. "My father wants to talk to you."

"I assumed that. I'll call him later today, okay? Do you want me to call you, too?"

"Yes, I do. I've got a few more questions myself."

"I understand. I promise, I'll call. I've got to run now." He turned abruptly and dashed to the stairway, disappearing down the steps.

39

"Excuse me," said Lucy, standing in front of the main desk at the Maxfield Plaza. She waited while the man behind the desk finished writing out a reservation request.

"Yes?" he answered, looking up.

"I'm Lucy Werness. Gaylord Werness's daughter."

"Of course, Ms. Werness. How may I help you?"

Lucy smiled easily. "My father was involved in a small . . . incident . . . several days ago."

The man's expression turned serious. "Yes. The birthday party. I was so sorry to hear about that."

"Thank you. The thing is, I'm supposed to drop off some medication for him." She held up a brown paper sack. "But I seem to have forgotten my key. I doubt anyone's with him right now." Lucy knew for certain no one was there. Half an hour ago she'd called Gloria Lindy and told her she wanted to meet her for a late brunch. For whatever reason, she knew Gloria was inordinately interested in the family. True to form, she'd jumped at the chance for a private conversation. Lucy named a restaurant in downtown Minneapolis and told her not to worry if she was a little late. She'd be there as soon as possible. "I wouldn't want to make my father get out of bed to answer the door," she continued in a confidential tone. "He's still somewhat weakened. Do you have an extra key?"

"Of course," answered the desk clerk.

Lucy could see him hesitate. She carefully slipped her driver's license out of the back pocket of her jeans.

"Thank you," he said, relieved. "I hated to say anything to someone like you, but we're supposed to ask."

"No problem," said Lucy, taking the key from his hand. "I'll be sure to tell Gay—, my father, how helpful you've been."

"That's kind of you."

Lucy fixed him with a broad grin and turned, heading quickly for the elevators.

Gaylord was fast asleep in his favorite easy chair as Lucy moved silently into the suite. She could see him nodding and snoring. Discarding the brown paper sack, she held the gun firmly in her left hand. So this was what it had come to. Perhaps she'd always known it would. In her adolescent fantasies, she'd often dreamed of murdering her father and never getting caught. But that was child's play.

And besides, that familiar sense of guilt would always return with such force that she'd be miserable for days. Back then, there was no way to win. Things were different now. Those adolescent torments had finally subsided into whispers. At least, most of the time they had.

She strode confidently across the thick carpeting and pushed the gun into the soft part of his neck.

Gaylord jerked awake. "What—?" He pulled his head away, his eyes locking on the gun. "Lucy!" A look of surprise mixed with horror spread over his face.

"Hadn't you better clutch your heart?" she asked coldly. "Even in this potentially fatal family crisis, one must never drop the act."

He shook his head trying to comprehend what was happening. "I'm not acting," he said indignantly. Then, realizing the imbalance of power, his voice grew fragile. "I do have a heart condition."

"Impossible," she said, moving around in front of him. "You don't have a heart."

He fumbled with the controls of what looked like a small transistor radio in his pocket.

"Ah, something new's been added since we last met." She pointed the barrel at his hearing aid. "I can't help but think you heard what I said. However, if you didn't I'd be glad to repeat it."

He shot her an angry look.

Lucy was intrigued. He was having difficulty finding her range. That was rare. Gaylord had always been a quick study when it came to people. Right now, he didn't know how to gauge his response because he didn't know what she wanted, or, more importantly, why she'd brought the gun. Clearly, it frightened him.

"Why are you here? What are you going to do?"

"Well, *Dad*, this gun's only got one bullet in it. Who knows how many times I can fire it before we actually see some blood. It may even be the first shot."

He stiffened and drew away from her.

"Shall we try?" She pointed it directly at his head and yanked the hammer back.

"You're crazy!"

"Me? Maybe. Or perhaps you've finally driven me over the edge. Either way, you lose." She pulled the trigger.

Gaylord jerked his head to the side, shutting his eyes at the sound of the click. When nothing happened, he opened them wide. "Lucy, we can talk . . . you know us? We could always talk."

"Could we? Seems to me I remember coming to you fifteen years ago. You didn't have much to say."

He pinched his mouth into a pout. "You've never cared about me."

"You? Oh no you don't." She felt her stomach begin to churn with the old acid. "I'm not letting you control this conversation. Besides, give me one good reason why I *should* care about you."

"I'm your father, honey. I love you."

He said the words with such a sudden tenderness that the hand holding the gun began to shake. *Breathe*, she ordered herself. "All those years ago I was insane enough to think you might apologize for what you'd done. Oh, pardon me. I forgot. That word's not in your vocabulary. Perhaps I should say, repent. That's a term you at least recognize. You are, after all, a righteous man."

He shifted uneasily in his chair. "I've made my share of mistakes. I told you that. All parents do."

"Ah yes, humility. You've always been big on stating the obvious. It's just, it has no meaning. For instance, can you name one mistake you've made? I'd be curious to know what you think some of them were." Again she leaned close to him and held the gun to his forehead.

With a great show of bravado, he glared at her and then turned away.

She cocked the hammer. "I didn't come here to listen to any more of your crap."

"What do you want then?" His voice was a desperate whine.

"To play a game," she smiled. "You always liked games so much." She squeezed the trigger. "Russian roulette. This time it's with *your* life."

"Stop this!" he yelled. He started to get up.

Quickly, she pulled back the hammer. "I guess you could say I want some peace. That's a simple enough request, isn't it? And not only for me, but for my children."

"What do you mean? Are we speaking of Billy now?"

She felt a surge of anger as he said his name. "I had twins, father dear. Billy and Erin are brother and sister." She could see by his sharp intake of breath that he didn't know.

"You accuse me of being a bad parent, and yet you won't even tell them the truth about you!"

"The truth?"

"Yes! You and that Coopersmith. Don't deny it. I've known from the very beginning. If you'll think back, I tried to protect you from him when you first met. My God, you were just a baby. I could see what he wanted. And he got his way, didn't he!"

Her legs began to tremble. Nothing ever changed. She was fourteen years old again and he was lecturing her on proper, Christian sexuality. "My therapist said you might never admit what you'd done. I couldn't accept that. I couldn't believe you'd be so cruel!"

"Me? I merely tried to save you from yourself. Who bailed you out when you were arrested for stealing that car? Who got you the best lawyer money could buy? Who tried to get you into drug counseling—"

"Who messed me up in the first place?" she screamed, surprised by her own intensity. "I wasn't Torald. I could see trying to please you was an endless, bottomless pit. If he could have just understood that, if he could have gotten away from you—"

"You make me sound like the black plague! You blame a son for loving his father, for sticking by him? Who's the cruel one now?"

"That love brought him nothing but pain. Everyone around you suffers—you see to that. I'm not going to fight this battle all over again. I'm not going to let you hurt my children! The things you set in motion years ago have already taken their toll on them. I couldn't stop you when I was a child, but I'm not a child any longer." With a sweaty hand, she waved the gun under his nose and squeezed the trigger. *Click.*

Gaylord ducked out of the way and then wiped the sweat from his forehead. "I don't know what you're talking about."

"No? You've forgotten 'The Children's Game?'"

"We played lots of games."

"This one was special. I was about four and Torald had just turned six. At first, you'd hide things in your pockets. Candy. Later it was coins, even dollar bills. You'd take us out for ice cream and we'd give the man the money all by ourselves. We felt so important. Torald and I would wait for you to come home and then we'd scramble all over you. Sometimes there would be a Tootsie Roll in your hand, a lemon drop behind your ear. But then suddenly, things changed. I don't remember when exactly, but it wasn't fun anymore. You wanted us to take off your clothes. You said we'd find special things in special places. First the tie. Then the suit coat. Then the pants. Do you remember now? You said the first game was getting too easy. We had to try harder."

"What are you insinuating?"

"Your favorite hiding place was under your penis."

"This never happened!"

"Goddamn you, it happened for years!" She grasped the gun in both hands. "Then, when Torald and I got a little older, you made us play the game with each other while you watched. God how we hated it. We never knew when you'd be in the mood. For years, we performed for you like trained monkeys. Do you know how much I wanted to kill you? *Do you?*"

"You're exaggerating! You always did blow things out of proportion. You've always used your past to justify the fact that you've never done anything with your life! You call taking care of sick animals a job? You couldn't even *support* yourself if it wasn't for the charity of your sister."

"Liar!" She stepped backward.

"Am I? Why didn't Torald ever accuse me of these

things? He never said a word. Not a word! No, he loved me, like you should have. Forgiveness is everything, and I forgive you Lucy. You deserted me in my time of need, but still, I love you. You have a responsibility to me now."

"To you? What about your responsibility to me?"

"When a child reaches adulthood, all that changes. You say I wasn't a good parent, but I always took your needs seriously. I worked hard to provide for you. I suppose next you're going to tell me you went hungry! You can scoff at things like that, but when I was a kid, life wasn't so easy. I've had to fight for everything I got. I never thought I'd have to fight for my children's love!"

She could feel herself beginning to crumble. Everything she said he turned around and used against her. No wonder silence had become her response to things. She distrusted language. How could she not? Her father was a master at twists and turns. No conversation ever satisfied, it merely confused her more. It had always been like that. *He* was the injured party. *He* was the one who was misunderstood. *He* loved, all everyone else could do was blame. God, his voice was in her ears so loud she thought her head would explode into a million pieces.

Tentatively, Gaylord touched his chest. "Will you get me my medication? I need it. It's in the nightstand next to my bed."

Lucy steadied herself against the window ledge, taking a deep breath. "You won't need it."

A look of abject horror crossed his face. "Lucy, look, I've told you, I know I've made mistakes."

"Except, you can never remember any. And besides, I'm not listening anymore."

"What are you going to do?" His voice had resumed a careful timidity.

She spread her feet wide apart and centered the barrel on his chest.

"We can talk, Lucy." His voice was full of panic. "Families need to talk. That's why this has been so damaging, all these years of staying away. I can still help you. I have plenty of money. I could set you up in a business of your own. Sure! That's it . . . a pet shop! How does that sound? Come on, Lucy, put the gun down."

"Only a few cylinders left. One of them is going to stun you, Dad. Even though you know it's coming, it will still be a shock. You'll know instantly that you're going to die. I can't imagine knowing my life will cease any second. My guess is that it will be horribly painful."

He squeezed the arms of the chair so hard his hands turned white. "Maybe you're right, Lucy. Maybe I did do some things I shouldn't have."

"Maybe!"

"If I hurt you . . . I'm sorry."

"If! Come on, you can do better than that. This is *your life* we're talking about now, not mine. Not Torald's. For the sake of your own life can't you force out a little truth?"

He grabbed his head with both hands and began to cry. "I'm sorry! I never meant to hurt you. It's hard for me to admit these things. I don't even . . . remember them very well."

"You don't remember raping me?" She stepped closer and stuck the gun barrel into the soft part of his cheek.

He closed his eyes and began to groan.

"What about Torald?"

"I'm sorry!" he shrieked. "I mean it. If I could go back and makes things right, I would."

"God," she whispered, "if only he could be here to hear this. To think it took a gun to get you to admit the truth."

He began to whimper, pulling his legs up to his chest.

She fired the gun. The only sound in the room was the faint click.

"Stop," he wailed, covering his head.

"One chamber left." Looking down she realized he'd wet his pants. "Say goodbye."

"Lucy," called a soft voice from the doorway.

She looked up.

"This time he's right. Put it down."

"Get out of here, Malcolm! I have to do this. Nothing is going to stop me!" She eyed her father to make sure he was still groveling sufficiently.

Malcolm walked further into the room.

"Tell her to stop," pleaded Gaylord. He reached up and grabbed Malcolm's arm. "You're a minister now. You can talk some *sense* into her."

Shaking off his hand, Malcolm was shocked at the ruin before his eyes. Gaylord looked nothing like the vigorous man he'd once known.

Lucy centered the gun again. "You know this has to be done."

Malcolm sensed something odd in her voice. It almost sounded as if she was reading lines from a script. "No I don't know that. What I do know is that if you go through with this, your father will have succeeded in destroying you completely. He's not worth it."

"But my children are!"

"Exactly. You have to be free to help them! If you're in prison, your chances of doing that are nil." He put his hand over the barrel. "And Lucy, I agree your children are important, but they're no more important than you."

Lucy could feel herself beginning to cry. At the same time she felt a great surge of triumphant release. She knew it was over. She'd gotten what she came for. "Here," she said, handing it to him.

"She's crazy!" said Gaylord leaping to his feet.

"Shut up," said Malcolm. The coldness in his voice must have frightened the old man because he sat back down. "We're not done just yet." He turned to Lucy. "Antonia is waiting with her car. Why don't you leave your own car here and let her drive you home. I'll be along in a few minutes." He took hold of her hand. "Promise me—you'll do as I ask?"

"I promise," she said softly. She touched his beautiful face, the familiarity of a lifetime overwhelming her. "I love you."

"I know," he smiled. "Something's different, isn't it? I can see it in your eyes."

She didn't answer, but simply walked out through the open door.

God, but his heart went out to her. It always had. She

was the real reason he'd tried so hard to understand human behavior. Everyone thought he was the strong one, but it wasn't true. Lucy had lived through things that would have shriveled him into a lifeless ball. And yet, she'd survived. He'd tried so often to tell her how much he respected her courage. The words never seemed enough.

"I should call the police," said Gaylord angrily, rising and bumping past Malcolm into his study.

Malcolm followed. "I can see you've had a rough morning." His eyes fell to the stain on Gaylord's crotch. Quickly, Malcolm sat down behind the desk.

"She's a lunatic," said the old man, striding aimlessly to the bookshelf. He didn't seem to know what to do with himself now that Malcolm had appropriated the only throne in the room.

"Have a seat," said Malcolm.

"If I didn't love her so much, I would call the police. Maybe it would show more love if I did call. She might get some help before she really hurts someone. Yes. Good idea." He made a move for the phone.

Malcolm reached down and with an angry snap, pulled the wires out of the wall.

"What are you doing?" asked Gaylord, his mouth falling open.

"I want to talk to you undisturbed."

"You have no right—"

"I have *every* right!" He could feel his own anger rising. He almost envied Lucy the gun she'd brought with her. Glancing down at his hand, he realized he was still holding it. It felt ugly and yet strangely powerful.

"Oh, I get it. Now it's your turn to trash me. Well, save it. You're the last person who should be talking about morals, you licentious little worm! You got my fifteen-year-old daughter pregnant. It nearly destroyed my entire family!"

Malcolm found himself staring in utter disbelief. Lucy had said her father wouldn't admit to the truth, but he still didn't expect *this*. "Do you really believe what you're saying?"

"What do you mean?"

"That I'm the father of her children."

"Of course you are. She was sleeping with the entire football team back in high school just to upset me, but you were her steady. If anyone is the father, you are."

"Do you realize how little you know your daughter? She wouldn't date anyone back then, not even me. We were friends, that's all. She was terrified of sex. I didn't understand why until years later."

"This is a conspiracy!"

"You committed incest with both Torald and Lucy from the time they first entered their teens. It went on for years. My God, man, why didn't you just take a gun and shoot them both in the head!"

"It's a lie! I loved them."

"You *owned* them. As head of the family, you considered it one of your rights. Torald broke down one night and told me everything. You had *needs*. You'd turned your wife into a vegetable and your children were supposed to take over. Can't you even admit the truth now?"

"He made it up, don't you see? Lucy came here today to force me into saying things that weren't true. I had to do it to save my bloody life!"

"Goddamn you!"

Gaylord began to repeat the words from a Psalm. " 'In thee, O Lord, do I put my trust; let me never be ashamed. Deliver me speedily; be thou my strong rock, pull me out of the net that they have laid privily for me.' "

"I've spent my entire life trying to understand people like you. Do you know what you are? Do you understand what you've done? You've been playing hide and seek with your soul so long you don't even know what it looks like anymore."

" 'I have hated them that regard lying vanities: but I trust in the Lord . . . I am like a broken vessel. For I have heard the slander of many.' "

"Gaylord, listen to me. Any conflict between your guilt and this righteous image you have of yourself—the guilt lost. And that action, fleeing from your own sense of right and wrong, that's where your sickness lies. You've got to admit what you did. Your self-deception is monumental."

He began to sing. "Mary had a little lamb, little lamb, little lamb. Mary had a—"

"*Listen*, damn you!" He felt the gun jerk in his hand. "When confronted by evil in a parent, a child usually decides it's in *them*. Lucy acted that out. The drugs. The stealing. But she got away from you, and she finally got some help. But Torald, all his life he wanted nothing more than to please you. I remember him as a young man. He was golden. He could have been anything. But later, in his early thirties, he didn't even know who he was anymore."

"Row Row Row your boat! Gently down the stream! Merrily Merrily Merrily Merrily life is but a dream. Row Row—"

"Gaylord? You haven't got much time left, man! Do you want to die never having admitted the truth?"

"Die?" His eyes fell anxiously to the gun. "I never said I wasn't a sinful man!" He touched his fingertips lightly to his head. "Can you get me my heart medication? It's on the nightstand next to my bed."

Malcolm shook his head in disgust. "Even the Jews in the Nazi concentration camps had a luxury your children never had. They could hate their persecutors. Do you know how hard it is for children to hate their parents? Lucy was so proud of you. She used to brag about you all the time. Can you imagine the conflict? You taught your children that your love came only when they denied their own selves, their needs, their sense of right and wrong. In order to live with that, Lucy did drugs. When I first asked her about you, she said, 'My dad loves me very much.' She always said it just that way. Almost like she'd been programmed."

"Why do you make everything *good* sound horrible?"

"Because it was! You want to condemn Lucy for coming here with a gun, but you're the real murderer."

Gaylord gave him a derisive little smile. "I see everything now. Of course! You're a humanist. You're no minister of God." He seemed to regain his composure so quickly, Malcolm wasn't sure he'd ever lost it. "My children may blame me for every rotten thing that's ever happened to them since they started to teethe, but with Billy I have another chance. He's going to be my heir."

The pride in his voice almost took Malcolm's breath away. "Heir? Your heir?"

"Before I die, I'm going to teach him everything I know. He'll inherit the rights to all my plays. Billy is going to be a rich man, Coopersmith. In more ways than one."

"Do you really think after he knows the truth he's going to want to have anything to do with you? Erin is willing to go to jail to keep it from him. You can't hide things like that forever. In case you're curious, Torald filled her in on everything the night he died."

That seemed to stop him. His expression turned strangely flat. "I won't accept that. He didn't believe this nonsense."

Again, Malcolm found himself staring. "It's not a matter of belief. He lived it! He was there."

Gaylord seemed to be thinking. "No, Billy will understand. He'll see. You all hate me because of what I've accomplished. You wanted perfection. When I fell short, you were merciless. Billy will see all that. He'll understand. He wants to be my heir. He won't turn an opportunity like that down just to pay lip service to some family squabble."

Malcolm felt himself begin to shiver. Never had he imagined Gaylord's denial was this powerful. "There's a play I've been reading for several nights. I think there's a couple of lines in it that would make a perfect epitaph for your gravestone."

He snorted. "Don't count me out yet."

"Oh no, I'd never do that." As he stood, he started to put the gun in his pocket. On an impulse, he clicked open the chamber. It was completely empty. So, Lucy had never intended to shoot him. For some reason, that realization depressed him more than he could say. The smell of sour sweat mixed with urine was beginning to make him nauseous. He had to get out of the room and find some breathable air.

"Go ahead," said Gaylord, puffing out his chest. "Name the play. I bet I can tell you the quote."

"Why am I even trying?" said Malcolm. "You haven't heard a word I've said."

"Oh, I heard it. I just have to remember the source." He smirked.

Malcolm stood a moment longer before walking to the door.

"Aren't you going to tell me the name of that play?"

Arrogant to the end, thought Malcolm.

"I'll even make you a bet. If I can't give you the quote after three tries, you have my permission to have it carved into my gravestone. I'll even put it in writing."

Malcolm felt numb. "*Mary Queen of Scots.*"

"Mmm," said Gaylord, pulling on his beard. "You would pick Maxwell Anderson. I've always hated his stuff. Too muddy. All right . . . give me a clue."

This was too much. "You lose. Think about this as you're brushing your teeth tomorrow morning. One day people will stand over your grave and read, 'He had no heirs. The devil has no children.' "

40

Erin sat holding Billy's hand as Antonia got up to answer the door. "Are you all right?" she whispered, putting her arm around his shoulder. The look on his face told her he was still in shock.

"I forgot my key," said Lucy, nodding formally to her sister as she stepped into the front hall. "Are they here yet?" She glanced into the living room.

"What did the police say?" asked Antonia in a hushed tone.

"I told them everything. Erin's going to have to fill in

the details, but at least she has a chance now. They know she was only trying to protect her brother, to keep the identity of his father from him. The whole thing was hopeless. I tried to get her to see that last night."

Antonia's face was ashen. "What if Billy and Erin don't—" She looked away.

"We've gone over this a hundred times, and the answer is always the same. We've tried to do what's best. That's all we've ever done. Come on. Are you ready?"

"No." Antonia took a deep breath.

Billy stood as the two women entered. Lucy knew that if things were different, she'd rush to both of them and take them in her arms, promising to make everything right. Unfortunately, it wasn't that simple. They weren't children anymore, and as much as she wanted to sweep the past away and start fresh, it would take years to sort through all the pain. Quietly, she sat down across from them.

Antonia moved a bit further away to the mantel and rested her arm on it for support. They had agreed, Lucy would talk first.

Billy started to say something, but Lucy held up her hand. "Please, let me explain a few things. When I'm finished, you can say anything you want." She turned her gaze to Erin. "Somehow I knew this day would come. No matter what I've done to prevent it, secrets don't stay secrets forever. When I talked to you last night, Erin, it was like this great house of cards I'd constructed years ago out of my love and my terrible sense of shame had finally toppled and was about to bury all of us alive. I had the crazy notion that by giving you two up for adoption, none of this would ever come out. But when you told me what Torald had said to you, how he . . ." Her voice faltered.

"What?" erupted Billy. He steadied himself on the edge of his seat. "Come on, Erin. You said you'd explained everything. What did Torald say? I *have* to know."

Erin played with the lace on her blouse. "He . . ." She looked up at Lucy.

"Go ahead. This is too important. Billy has a right to know what happened, why you did what you did."

"Well," murmured Erin, "that night at the theatre, Torald and I were talking. At first it was about the play. Just general things. Then, he moved closer to me and asked me point-blank if I was your sister. I didn't see any reason to keep it from him. I mean, I felt he'd already guessed, he was just going to make trouble. But before I could say anything, he began to explain what really happened. How Gaylord had raped Lucy. He talked on and on, detail after detail. It was like this speech he'd given so many times he knew it by heart, yet he said it with so little emotion it almost seemed like it was somebody else's story. I finally had to put my hands over my ears to stop the sound of his voice. And the worst thing was, when he got to the end, he started to laugh, like it was a big joke. He was drunk and he was sloppy and what he was saying was so incredibly *disgusting*. That's when he . . ." She hesitated, looking at Billy and then away. "He pulled me over to the side of the bleachers and said, 'I want to know what it feels like to kiss my sister.' "

Billy nearly jumped out of his skin.

Erin laid her hand on his arm. "That's when it happened. We struggled. I tried to get away from him, but before I realized what was happening, he'd fallen backward off the bleachers and had landed on the fork in the bride doll's hand. God, I didn't know what to do! I jumped off the side and went to him, but I could see it was no use. One of the tines had gone right through his heart. So I ran. I was still so mixed up by what he'd said. I went down to your dressing room to find you, but before I got there I saw that Torald's dressing room door was ajar. I was horrified by what had just happened, but I'm ashamed to admit I was more horrified by what he'd done, by everything he'd told me. In a rage, I went into his room and tore it apart. All I could think was that I was glad he was dead. I wanted to *erase* him . . . and Gaylord. That's why I destroyed those posters. Standing in that room I realized that I could never tell you about it. In an instant it all became clear. Antonia and Lucy were trying to protect us from that knowledge, that's why we were given up for adoption. I had to do everything in my power to see that you never found out. It was the only really important thing I could ever give apart from my love. I was going to keep that secret to my grave. But then, when I realized the locket you'd given me had broken open and the pendant was gone, I panicked. I knew when it must have happened. I had to get it back. So I went back up to the stage. Jane was already there, but I don't think she saw me pick it up. I got lucky . . . or so I thought."

Billy put his head in his hands, fighting back a wave of tears. "God, what I put you through. I should never have talked you into coming with me."

"All this guilt," said Lucy, her voice gentle. "We could drown in it. The real blame belongs to one man. We can't ever forget that. For years my own guilt was enormous. I became an expert at it. But no more."

Antonia moved away from the mantel and sat down next to her sister. "Billy, Erin, you've got to understand something. The night you made the announcement that you were—at least you thought you were—my son, I didn't know what to say. I was so overwhelmed, all I could do was react. But Lucy and I sat up all night talking. You see, many years ago when we contacted that lawyer in New Orleans, we insisted that the two of you be adopted *together*. That was absolute. About a week after I first talked to him, I was given the name of a couple in North Carolina who had expressed an interest in adopting you. We asked for a background check—which this lawyer was more than happy to provide—and when we were convinced the family was decent and loving, I signed the papers. My name had gone on the birth certificate so I was the one legally responsible. Even then I had my doubts about him, but with the strain of the time, I overlooked the red flags that should have warned me he wasn't legitimate. As you may well appreciate, I wanted to protect my sister as much as possible and handle the entire matter properly, but quickly. She was only sixteen and was in no shape to deal with it all alone.

"Then, many years after—it was about the time the two of you would have turned eight—we received a photo from this same lawyer. He said everything was fine with the two of you, and that the family was relocating somewhere out West. He didn't know where. We were both so delighted with the picture, we never questioned anything. But, you see, when you showed up here several weeks ago with the story that you were adopted by a couple in Boston, and no mention of any sister, well, we couldn't help but wonder. Still, you did have the necklace and the letter, and the family resemblance was uncanny. That's when Lucy and I decided to do some checking. Unfortunately, by the time we called New Orleans, the lawyer was gone. No forwarding address or phone number. We thought about contacting your parents, but then Torald died and neither Lucy nor I knew *what* to think! Fleur finally hired a private detective. I found out several days ago that Erin was an imposter. It just muddied the waters all the more. So, we waited. In our hearts, we both believed your story, Billy. We wondered if your sister was also here, but we had no way of knowing."

"Lord, I was so glad to find out it was you, Erin." Lucy gave her a tentative smile. "I was afraid my daughter might turn out to be that *god-awful* Gloria Lindy."

They all laughed, breaking the tension for a brief moment.

"Who the hell is she anyway?" asked Antonia.

"An investigative reporter," answered Billy. "Her real name is Gale Lind. She was standing outside the courthouse this morning when Erin and I came out. Seems she wants to make a name for herself by doing exposés of famous people. She wanted to interview us, even offered us money. I guess Gaylord is her present target. She knows she really hit pay dirt this time." He looked at his sister. "We tried to convince her to leave us out of it, but I doubt she'll listen."

Lucy's throat tightened with emotion. "I'm so sorry," she whispered.

"No," said Billy, sitting forward in his seat. "Please, you've got to understand. I've had some time to think about this now. I will admit it's been a lot to assimilate, but you've got to see, what I said the first night is still true. I don't blame either of you for anything. Neither does Erin. And I'm proud to think that you're my mother, Lucy, and that I have such an eminent aunt. I mean, look. We took a chance coming here. Erin was right. We didn't know what we were getting ourselves into. But speaking only for myself, I'm glad we came. It's a hard thing to say, but I'd rather know the truth."

"And now we know," said Erin softly.

Billy put his arm around her. "Jane's father is the best. He already said this new information was going to be highly mitigating. I don't know exactly what that translates into, but he was hopeful he could get the charges dropped."

"Time will tell," said Erin. Her tone told everyone she wasn't quite as hopeful.

"We're here for you," said Lucy, her voice firm and strong. "Anything you need. Anything you want."

"Thanks," said Billy.

Erin rubbed the back of her neck. "I'd just like this nightmare to be over. Most of all, I'd like that old man to get what's coming to him."

Antonia shook her head. "That's a tall order. Don't expect justice in this world. I don't know, maybe one day that God he says he believes in will show him the light."

"Or the *dark*," said Lucy.

Antonia glanced at the oil painting above the mantel. "I have a suspicion he's spent most of his life in the dark."

41

"What do you have there?" asked Jane as Cordelia swept into her house, wearing her bright red cape, a paisley turban wound around her head.

"What else? A crystal ball."

Jane watched as Cordelia whipped off her coat and set the heavy object on a table in front of the fireplace. "We could really have used that a couple weeks ago."

Cordelia ignored the remark, sitting down on the couch and rubbing her hands together eagerly. "I've been studying this for days. It's very interesting."

"Where did you get it?" Jane tossed her copy of the *Utne Reader* on the piano bench and picked up the poker, giving the fire a good stoke.

"Remember that woman I used to date? The one who was selling exercise equipment several years ago?"

"Andromeda?"

"The very same. Well, now she's selling New Age stuff to retail stores. You know, crystals, scented oils, Tarot cards. She brought this by last week. Sort of a belated birthday present."

"That was all she wanted?"

"Prurient to the very core, aren't we?"

"Get to the point." Jane sat down.

"Well, sure, maybe she wanted something. Her cousin wrote a play. She wants me to read it."

"And of course you agreed."

"She suggested I look into the crystal ball first. I might see something about the play's future."

"And what have you seen so far?"

Cordelia's shoulders sank. "Bubbles?"

"Bubbles?"

"Yup. See, look at the thing. It's full of them."

"A cheap crystal ball, Cordelia."

"Do you think so? I keep hoping I'll see something in-credible. The fall of nations. The birth of ideas. The amount of my next raise." She gazed intently into the murky orb.

Jane found herself staring at it, too, as if the bubbles might magically rearrange themselves into a shape.

"Where's Beryl?"

"Upstairs dressing. She and Dad are going out for coffee tonight."

Cordelia leaned back and sighed. "If this thing only

worked, just think how useful it would be." Her eyes flicked to the ceiling. "What do you make of their little date?"

"Hard to say." Jane lifted her feet up on the coffee table. "I'm just going to go with the flow. I don't expect miracles, but even a slight thaw would be welcome."

"I suggested to Beryl that every four weeks the two of them play a game of poker. Whoever wins gets to control the world that month."

"Cordelia, you're such a help."

"Think nothing of it."

Bean hopped into Jane's lap.

"Where are Erin and Billy tonight?"

"They went over to the Werness house. I imagine they've got lots to talk about. We spent several hours together before they left. They filled me in on everything. Lucy talked with Erin last night at the police station. I guess it was pretty emotional."

"Boy, I'll bet."

"Billy just found out this afternoon. Lucy came here to see him shortly after she left her father's hotel suite. After she was gone, he took off. He didn't say much of anything. Erin was a basket case. I guess he just drove around for several hours. Anyway, when he got back, he really needed to talk. Erin and I were already sitting in the living room. Mostly, I just listened. Oh, I did tell them what Malcolm explained to me this morning. They were both very interested."

"I'll wait for the book."

"What?"

"Didn't you know? Gloria Lindy was working for Gaylord so she could write an exposé. From what I heard today, and you might say I got this almost from the horse's mouth, she's now planning a full-length book. I'm sure Malcolm will be consulted on deep background."

"He'll never talk to her."

"I didn't think he would."

Jane was silent for a moment. "You know, it's all finally making sense to me. Do you realize what Erin did? She took the entire weight of that family's problems on her shoulders—simply out of love for her brother. She's a very courageous woman."

"Don't look for *that* in the book."

"And I think Malcolm Coopersmith is going to be a key person in helping them through all this."

"They'll need all the help they can get." Cordelia pointed at the crystal ball. "Maybe I'll give that to them."

"It's funny. I feel like I've known them longer than just a couple months. I've really grown to care about them."

Cordelia ran a hand over her eyes. "Jesus, I'm just like you. I can't get that image of Torald's body hanging on that fork out of my mind."

"I know. And you know, the awful thing is, he was a victim just like everyone else." She rose and started for the kitchen. "Come on, Cordelia. I think we should eat our soup."

"You're changing the subject."

"You wouldn't want it to burn, would you?"

Cordelia followed and leaned against the doorway as Jane got down two blue and white china soup bowls. "What kind is it?"

"Campbell's tomato."

"Get serious."

"Potato leek. Your favorite. I made it this afternoon."

Cordelia closed her eyes. "And the bread?"

"Fresh dill and cheddar scones from the restaurant."

She sighed. "I'm in heaven."

"I didn't know you thought so highly of Minnesota." Carefully, Jane ladled the soup into the bowls and carried them into the dining room where she'd already set two places. "Have a seat."

As Cordelia slathered some butter on a split scone, Jane poured two cups of tea.

"Cordelia?"

"Uhm?" Her mouth was already full of bread.

"Do you believe in evil?"

"Evil? Sure." She slurped her soup.

"No, I don't mean in the abstract. I mean evil as embodied in a person."

"I don't know." She stuffed another crumbly morsel into her mouth. "That's quite a leap. I'd have to think about it a while. Off hand I guess I'd say there's good and evil in all of us."

Jane nodded. "That's what I would have answered."

"Then we each get an *A* in Philosophy 101."

She studied her cup of tea before taking a sip. "I wonder."

From the author of *Stage Fright*...
an all-new mystery series,
starring food critic Sophie Greenway
and her husband Bram Baldric,
a radio talk-show personality.

THIS LITTLE PIGGY
WENT TO MURDER
by ELLEN HART

---

*"Strong characters and a rich
Lake Superior setting make this solidly
constructed mystery hard to put down.
Another winner for Ellen Hart!"*
—M. D. Lake

**Debuts in Fall 1994
Published by Ballantine Books.
Look for it in bookstores everywhere!**

Also by
ELLEN
HART

Published by Ballantine Books.
Available in your local bookstore.